If anything, Skadi was more beautiful now.

She'd become a mother since Agnar had last seen her, but she still trained regularly by the confident way she held her sword and shield. She had grown from a confused princess into a formidable queen.

He allowed his hungry eyes a moment to devour the sight of her. To reassure himself that he was finally here, ready to claim her. But then his eyes had locked on to the splash of blood across her thigh.

He needed her alive! That was the reason for his anger, surely?

But he knew in his heart it was more than that. He was possessive of her, despite only seeing her twice in his life.

Skadi rolled the sword with her wrist, and Agnar straightened his spine, trying his best to calm the fire in his heart.

"You know who I am," he said.

"Agnar Bjornsson," she replied coldly. "I remember you..." A bittersweet smile twisted her lips. "You've grown into a man... What do you hope to gain from this?"

"A queen."

Author Note

Thrudheim is the home of the God Thor, but I have used it as the name for my fictional Kingdom. I imagine Thrudheim might sit between the English and Danish coasts just south of Norway. The Kings mentioned are also fictional, but it is true that there were many petty Kings in the early Viking age.

RECLAIMING HIS VIKING QUEEN

LUCY MORRIS

Recycling programs for this product may not exist in your area.

ISBN-13: 978-1-335-83167-5

Reclaiming His Viking Queen

For questions and comments about the quality of this book, please contact us at CustomerService@Harlequin.com.

Harlequin Enterprises ULC
22 Adelaide St. West, 41st Floor
Toronto, Ontario M5H 4E3, Canada
www.Harlequin.com

HarperCollins Publishers
Macken House, 39/40 Mayor Street Upper,
Dublin 1, D01 C9W8, Ireland
www.HarperCollins.com

Printed in U.S.A.

Lucy Morris has always been obsessed with myths, legends, and petticoats. Her books whisk you away to another time and place filled with passion, drama, and vibrant characters. Lucy lives in Essex, UK, with her husband, two children, and two cats.

Books by Lucy Morris

Harlequin Historical

The Viking She Loves to Hate
Snowed In with the Viking
How the Wallflower Wins a Duke

The Eriksson Brothers

"Her Bought Viking Husband"
in *Convenient Vows with a Viking*
Wedding Night with Her Viking Enemy
A Viking Too Wild to Wed

A Season to Wed

The Lord's Maddening Miss

Shieldmaiden Sisters

The Viking She Would Have Married
Tempted by Her Outcast Viking
Beguiling Her Enemy Warrior

Visit the Author Profile page
at Harlequin.com for more titles.

For my talented makeup artist friend, Natalie Hunt,
who never doubted us going professional
in our dream jobs. "We did it!"

Chapter One

Thrudheim—late autumn, AD 879

Trust my absent husband to be more of a nuisance dead than alive!

Skadi strode purposefully along the defences in full armour. She was still Queen of Thrudheim—despite the loss of Heimdall—and she was prepared to defend her kingdom to the death. She needed her warriors to see her unbroken, to know they still had a leader.

After all, she was the true royal of this island, born from an unbroken line of Thrudheim Kings and Queens. While Heimdall… Well, he'd married her simply to wear a crown, not to rule.

The line of her family *could not* end with her.

Skadi squinted into the horizon, the sun low in the sky, making it difficult to distinguish between where the grey sea ended and the gloomy sky began. No oncoming ships darkened her view. The wind whipped across her face, pulling back her white-blonde braids. She paid it no heed; her silver crown was securely held in place by several interwoven braids at her temple.

There was no way it would fall.

Unless it is ripped from my head...

Skadi took a deep breath, welcoming the sharpness of the cold wind to clear her mind. Storms were common in Thrudheim, the wind battering the deadly Northern seas against the island's rocky shores. Her port offered the only safe haven between the land of the Saxons and the homeland of the Vikings.

Her kingdom wasn't particularly large: a rocky island in the shape of a horseshoe that was mostly a sprawling mountain covered in thick swathes of forest, which levelled out to some fields around the small harbour of her town.

But it was what lay within the mountain that mattered. Rivers of precious metals ran deep within.

Despite its small size, her kingdom was considered a fine jewel, placed at a strategic point between all the kingdoms of the Danes, Norse and Saxons. They had always negotiated well with their neighbours in the past, but all that had changed with Heimdall's death and suddenly covetous eyes had turned to Thrudheim's rocky shores.

Skadi would welcome a storm.

Oddmund, her second in command, moved to stand beside her and, as if reading her mind, he said quietly, 'The wind is picking up. But I doubt Thor will aid us tonight.'

She nodded, her gaze sweeping across the horizon like a hawk's, missing nothing. 'Then we shall have to be prepared. The Usurper must not breach our walls.' Finally, satisfied that her enemy wasn't sailing towards them at this very moment, she turned her attention to the battlements.

The huge wooden palisade encircled Thrudheim's bustling town and golden hall which stood at the top of the hill at the far back of the town. The substantial wooden wall was the height of at least four men and the walkway could take two men abreast. There were archery slots at regular points throughout. It would be impossible to climb without ladders or ropes. The turrets along the port side were filled with warriors and weapons.

The sight of it reassured her. 'Is everything ready?' she asked.

Oddmund nodded. 'Yes. Two hundred fresh arrows have been added to the turret stores. The wall and town roofs have all been doused in water to prevent fire. As you ordered, the ships have been pulled in from the harbour—they won't be able to use them for firewood or battering rams. Cauldrons of tar and water have been filled ready for heating and we have gathered in the livestock. The harvest is already securely in the barns and will last us all winter if the Usurper wants a siege, which he won't. *Opportunistic bastard!*' Oddmund spat on the ground as if even the mention of the usurper caused his stomach to revolt.

'Tell me again…' asked Skadi quietly. 'How did King Heimdall die?'

She couldn't remember Oddmund's words from two weeks ago, only the sound of Astra's weeping as she buried her face in her mother's skirts. Skadi had felt an odd mixture of relief and horror at the news of her husband's death. Followed quickly by guilt when her daughter's tears finally cut through the shock.

I should be more upset... But she wasn't.

Her love and passion for Heimdall had faded long ago—not long after she realised how little she meant to him.

Oddmund looked away from her, his gaze narrowed and his jaw tight. 'The raids were a success. King Sven spoke true of the Saxon King's wealth and lack of defences. Some of their men wet themselves at the mere sight of us!' He snorted in amusement, before continuing. 'But the *Usurper* was also there with his Rus men—no better than beasts, never following orders and causing havoc. And he still had his foolish claims on your kingdom, even daring to speak of them in front of King Heimdall and King Sven. Swearing openly that he would take back what was rightfully his… *The arrogance!*'

Skadi nodded—all of this sounded plausible.

The *Usurper*, as he was known, was a man named Agnar Wolf Slayer, who had always coveted the crown Heimdall wore. Half-brother to King Sven, he had been betrothed to Skadi as a babe by their respective fathers, so he believed Heimdall to have stolen his birthright, despite the fact that he'd been no more than a child when Skadi's father had died and had been too young to marry her. King Sven had also preferred that Skadi choose Heimdall over Agnar, so the betrothal had been dissolved in favour of his friend. A match agreed on both sides, herself included.

But Agnar and his mother had raged against the decision, had even come to Thrudheim to challenge it. Heimdall had been merciful enough to let them both live. Anyone else would have been grateful for his kindness, but not Agnar. He had travelled to the Rus in the east—his mother's people—and steadily risen in power until he had an army of his own. He'd returned to go raiding with King Sven, but had betrayed him openly with the unlawful slaying of Heimdall.

'Was it an open challenge?' she asked again, a strange, old sympathy for Agnar returning when she thought of the boy she had cast aside. She did not regret abandoning their betrothal. If she'd continued down that path, she feared things could have been much worse.

Oddmund frowned, and she realised he must have told her this before. 'No, my Queen. On the last raid, Agnar turned against him. No challenge was given, it was murder. I tried to get to the King, but he received the first cut before any of us had even unsheathed our swords. One of his men struck me from behind. When I awoke, King Heimdall was dead and Agnar was gone. It is only by the mercy of Rán that I arrived home before his army to warn you of it.'

Skadi nodded. 'It is fortunate, indeed, and good that you returned so quickly. We have had time to prepare our defences, and perform Heimdall's funeral rites. I am grateful you were so swift to return to us.'

She frowned at the lack of warriors on the battlements—she would have to concentrate all of her forces at the harbour gates, as that's where the enemy would sail in to attack. But it meant she would have fewer men around the back sections of the wall, which were higher up and a key position to spot oncoming ships. When the attack eventually arrived, she would have little warning of it. 'I only wish the rest of the ships had returned with you.'

Oddmund shrugged, as if dismissing her concern. 'We have enough men to keep them out. King Sven will follow shortly with our other ships. He thought it best to warn you first and, as the Saxon Kings were forming an army to retaliate, he needed all men at his disposal.'

Skadi didn't like that answer.

What *right* did King Sven have to dictate where and when her ships sailed?

She had to hope they would arrive soon. She did not want a long siege, as it would put her people in danger from disease and famine. The grain stores needed replenishing and, because of Sven's raiding, they had already been delayed. 'But they are returning, yes? King Sven will be here soon?'

'Of course, Queen Skadi. King Sven would never betray you.'

She gave a low grunt of acknowledgement, not entirely convinced, as King Sven cared more about himself than anyone else. However, she had no reason to doubt Oddmund, he had always been a loyal man. But it did strike her as odd that after such a heinous crime, Agnar would still not arrive before Oddmund's returning ship.

'I do not like all of this waiting,' she said, speaking more to herself than Oddmund. 'If Agnar wants Thrudheim's crown, why has he not come? Why the delay?'

'Perhaps King Sven has already captured and punished him for killing Heimdall? Or, the Usurper is seeking reinforcements before attacking? King Sven was worried that Agnar might seek aid from his enemies. If he has a large enough army, and he manages to conquer Thrudheim, it will be difficult for King Sven to help us.' Oddmund scratched and tugged at his blond beard thoughtfully. 'Your Highness, it might be wise to consider King Sven's offer.'

Marriage.

Skadi's stomach twisted, but it was not for herself that she worried, but her daughter. Astra was the bride he wanted and it sickened her. 'Childbirth is a battlefield for women, *not* children.'

'I am sure he does not expect—'

'She will not leave me until she is a grown woman,' snapped Skadi. This wasn't the first time Oddmund, or even Heimdall, had tried to change her mind about an alliance between Sven and her daughter. She could understand their logic. Promising Astra to King Sven would ensure an alliance between their two kingdoms that went above the trade of grain and silver. It would safeguard Thrudheim from further attacks, not only from Agnar, but from any other petty king or powerful man who sought to steal her kingdom from her.

However, Sven wanted Astra to *immediately* join his court and that disturbed her, for many reasons. Sven was older than

Skadi and already had two wives. Could she condemn her child to marry an old man?

A further alliance with him would also weaken Thrudheim's sovereignty and force it to become a vassal to Sven's kingdom. What guarantee did Skadi have that Astra would return to rule Thrudheim after her death? *None.* Thrudheim needed a ruler on its throne, not a queen held hostage in another kingdom as a third wife!

Not only that, but King Sven had a habit of choosing young brides. Was a marriage with Astra simply to ensure Skadi's obedience, or was it much worse than that?

Skadi shivered and her hand tightened around the hilt of her sword.

No, she would not do it.

There was no point in offering herself as a bride to any other prince or powerful chieftain. After seeing forty winters and only producing one child despite such a long marriage, it was clear she was no longer seen as a desirable match. Besides, no one would want to challenge King Sven by marrying her.

She needed to hold out against Agnar, Sven and any other petty king who sought to overthrow her, at least until Astra was old enough to marry. Then she could negotiate and find an alternative that suited everyone.

Changing the subject, Skadi asked the one question that had been playing on her mind since Oddmund's return. 'Heimdall…was he holding his sword when he died?'

Oddmund nodded. 'Yes, even in death he held it tightly.'

Gritting her teeth against the sudden and unwelcome grief she felt for a man she had loved and lost years ago, she turned and said loudly, hoping the curious ears of the nearby warriors would hear her, 'That is a relief. He always said he wished to die in battle. Tonight, our King feasts in Valhalla!'

Murmurs of approval followed her as she made her way down the wooden staircase to the ground. Morale would be important if it came to a siege.

She spotted her daughter in the distance. Astra was running down the wooden path that snaked like a river through the town from the golden hall at the top of the hill. Brenna followed swiftly behind her, the hem of her skirts raised to her knees so she could run after her. Astra was a handful and thankfully Brenna had the patience and youth to deal with her daughter's excess of energy.

Astra's pale-blonde braids flew behind her as she ran, her face flushed and her blue eyes bright with excitement. Skadi smiled as she approached, pleased that her daughter seemed to be accepting the loss of her father better with each day that passed. She supposed it was because Astra had barely known him anyway, considering how often he went raiding or hunting.

'The cat's had her kittens!' yelled Astra, skidding to a halt in front of her, before grabbing her hand and pulling Skadi along to follow.

'How many?'

'Three!' exclaimed Astra. 'Is your work on the defences done? Can you come see them?'

Skadi nodded, giving Oddmund a meaningful look over her shoulder. 'Rotate the watches regularly. I want to know as soon as any ships are spotted.'

Oddmund inclined his head in silent agreement and Skadi allowed her daughter to lead her away.

Astra was still so young and barely understood the threat, which was a blessing. She had only seen ten winters. A lively but sensitive child. Astra had always tiptoed around Heimdall whenever he was here.

In a way, it was a blessing that he was dead.

Heimdall had not been a cruel father, but neither had he been particularly loving. Astra had already disappointed him by being born a girl and, thankfully, she would never have to face his disapproval again.

Skadi listened to Astra chatter about the kittens most of the journey back to the hall, but she focused her attention on more than her daughter, giving reassuring smiles to traders and craftsmen huddled in doorways as she passed, as well as brief nods of approval at the warriors sharpening their swords and axes with whetstones and grim expressions.

Preparing for battle was never easy, but it was always worse when you faced it at home, as it put your family and loved ones at risk. Fear could end a siege quicker than a breach of the walls. She'd already spoken to the people after Oddmund's arrival, but she decided to do more tonight to reassure them.

Skadi wished she could scream up at the gods, cursing the names of all the men who had wronged her. Agnar, Sven, Heimdall—they had all threatened her kingdom, although Agnar was the greatest villain currently.

Why could he not be satisfied with his life with the Rus? Why come for her kingdom as if it were his right? When he'd barely spent more than a week on her island!

She'd only met him twice. Although both times had been seared into her memory.

The first time he'd been a young boy, holding his mother's hand tightly, while he formally asked for her hand in marriage. He'd been no more than five years old at the time, but he'd not stumbled over his words and he'd gazed up at his mother proudly after finishing. In contrast, Skadi had seen fifteen winters then and was more than a little depressed at seeing how much younger her future husband was. That was the same feast when she'd started hoping for Heimdall. A fine warrior in the prime of his life had seemed a far more appealing prospect than a little boy.

The second time she'd seen Agnar, he'd grown into a lanky youth of eleven or twelve winters, and she'd been a grown woman, eager to begin her life—preferably without a child as her husband. Agnar had seemed a sombre boy, with a mop of dark hair that had almost covered his startlingly green and wild eyes.

His mother had heard of Skadi's father's death and had immediately sailed with her son to demand they marry. Skadi had not been surprised by that—Agnar's mother was known as a She-Wolf in Sven's court. But the change in Agnar had surprised her.

Standing up to men three times his size, he'd demanded Thrudheim's crown and her hand in marriage without a hint of fear, displaying the confidence and arrogance of a much older man. Skadi had been afraid for him that day and had almost wished she hadn't encouraged Heimdall into asking Sven for her hand.

But she'd also seen how swiftly the petty Kings had descended upon her father's death. Each offering their respects with charming smiles, while hoping to snatch Thrudheim for themselves. Heimdall had seemed the wisest choice, her father's second, and well liked by King Sven.

What could a thin boy of eleven winters offer her?

Only war.

Dissolving the betrothal with Agnar protected both of them. But she hadn't realised how bitterly it would affect Agnar and his mother. She'd simply wanted the best for her kingdom.

Had Heimdall's cruelty that day sealed his fate all these years later? If he'd been *kinder*, would things have been different?

Heimdall's words and actions that day still tormented her. She should have known then that Heimdall was not the honourable man she'd first thought. But it had already been too late.

'The bastard Prince demands a bride? He hasn't a hair on his chin, yet he thinks to wear a crown! Come then, boy! Take it!'

But when Agnar had stepped forward, eyes filled with determination, with a cautious hand on the pommel of his sword, Heimdall had kicked him square in the chest, so hard that Agnar's feet had lifted from the floor. She still remembered the way his dark head had snapped back as he fell and cracked against cold stone. The scream of Agnar's mother as a bloody pool seeped around his head.

'There's your crown!' Heimdall had snarled in disgust.

King Sven, his own brother, had offered no words of comfort. He'd simply shaken his head wearily. 'I blame your Rus mother for filling your head with lofty ambitions!'

Skadi hadn't been able to bear it and she had begged Heimdall for mercy. To take pity on the boy and allow him to leave freely with his mother. Perhaps if she had not interfered, if she'd allowed Heimdall's anger to flow, then Agnar would already be dead and not on his way to threaten her home and daughter now.

The death of one child in her past could have saved her own daughter in the future. Fate was a twisted and brutal creature, but she was already well aware of that. A soft and passionate heart had always been her downfall. Thankfully, over time she had cooled her impulsive nature.

Skadi sighed miserably and Brenna gave her a worried glance, but didn't say anything. She wouldn't, not now at least, when Astra was so close.

The Great Hall drew closer and Astra ran forward, eager

to see her kittens. Skadi paused and looked up at the huge imposing building. She had lived in this hall, this island, her entire life. The mountain rose up behind it, its slate-grey edges topped with trees and circling birds, the frosted peak proclaiming the onset of winter.

Thrudheim had to come first... And, even though she'd chosen Heimdall unwisely, he had still been a better choice than Agnar.

There was no point regretting the past. She was Queen of Thrudheim, daughter of an unbroken line of Kings. She was a strong and just ruler—her husband's absence over the years fighting and raiding with Sven had proven it.

Heimdall's death had changed very little about her daily life. It was other men who had thought him important, not her.

For all of Heimdall's faults, his male presence had kept the ravens and snakes away. She'd chosen a grown man and a seasoned warrior to be her husband, not a child prince who had lost everything.

It had been the wisest choice.

Now, it was her turn to face Agnar, but, unlike Heimdall, she had nothing to apologise for.

He had no *right* to her throne!

Chapter Two

After Nattmal, Skadi took Astra on a procession along the battlements, the full moon and torches lighting their way in the dark. The late autumn sun had only just slipped beneath the horizon and, as Skadi listened to the crashing of waves, she wondered what would await them at daybreak.

King Sven would arrive, or Agnar would attack. Both possibilities worried her, although for different reasons.

Greeting the fighting men and shieldmaidens along the battlements served to reassure her daughter that they were well defended. But their presence also encouraged morale among the warriors—proving to them that the royal family was strong and faithful. Skadi had planned many offerings to the gods to win their favour, placing each offering at several points along the battlements. She had always appreciated tradition and ceremony, it gave her people pride in their home and in her.

Astra walked and greeted the warriors with more confidence than Skadi would have had at her age. No mother could have been prouder than she was of Astra that night.

Her daughter was the perfect Princess, wearing a snow-white-and-silver-embroidered apron dress, as well as a blue cloak trimmed with snowy owl feathers. It was pinned to her shoulders with large silver turtle brooches and she even had a ceremonial curved dagger strapped to her belt. Skadi had dressed her in the outfit of a queen, while she wore her armour ready for battle, their silver crowns glinting in the firelight. Her father's old crown was attached to her helm, the other a pretty circlet she had worn herself as a child.

Astra walked with her back straight and smiled innocently at the people as she passed, carrying the holy flame reverently from the shrine, through the town and up along the battlements. Carefully lighting each offering after her mother's prayers were said.

Each offering had been placed along the battlements, representing a God or Goddess. *Astra will make a strong and benevolent queen one day.* It was Skadi's job to ensure that she did.

As they came to the final offering, the wind picked up, whipping back Astra's hair and cloak. But the Princess quickly shielded the flickering flame with her spare hand to stop it from being blown out. Despite her young age, she realised that it would be a bad omen if the flame were to be extinguished before lighting the last of the effigies. She wore leather mittens to protect her hands, so at least there was no danger of her burning herself on the oil lamp.

Skadi stepped forward and raised up the carved effigy, made of pine and dressed in a woollen gown with a necklace of seashells and branded runes. The doll depicted Rán, the Goddess of the sea. It was clear who she was by her hair, which was woven into a long net—Rán used it to pull souls down into her kingdom.

Drowning was one of the few deaths Norse men feared, because it lacked glory and meant a watery afterlife surrounded by monsters. But Rán was also very important, because they depended on her calm seas for trade and raiding.

Her effigy had been placed at the last turret between the

mountain, the hall and the rocky shoreline. It was where the natural landscape protected them the most from attack. No ship could land here, the whirlpools and rocks were too dangerous. The mountain cliffs too sheer and treacherous to climb.

Skadi lifted the effigy up to face east. 'Goddess Rán, with this offering, we call upon you and your nine daughters to protect us in our time of need. Raise your waters, ready your net and drown our enemy! Ensure that our island is safe from usurpers.'

As Skadi lowered the effigy into the logs of the brazier the wind howled up and over the battlements. For the first time, Astra looked frightened and she cupped her mitten even closer around the flame as it spluttered and flickered for a second time.

'Come, Astra,' Skadi said firmly and her daughter obeyed, covering the flame right up until it caught on the net of Rán's straw hair. Relief washed over Astra's face as she stepped back. But then another gust of wind rushed over them, causing the young flames around the Goddess's head to be snuffed out.

Before the crowd had time to realise what had happened. Skadi snatched the oil lamp from her daughter, not caring when the hot oil splashed on to her bare hands. In one quick motion, she threw the entirety of it including the pottery dish on to the brazier. The effigy was immediately consumed in oil and flame.

The crowd below roared with approval. 'No one saw,' reassured Skadi quietly and the men around them wisely looked away.

Wrapping an arm around Astra's trembling shoulders, she turned them back towards the crowd. 'My people, rest and hold your loved ones close. Warriors, you know your duty—watch the seas carefully and be prepared. Our enemy is coming and we will be ready for them!'

The crowd answered with another cheer, their loyalty unwavering.

'My family has ruled this island for as long as there has been a Thrudheim. We will not lose it now!'

Shouts of agreement rose to greet her and she smiled. Turning to Oddmund, she announced, 'I will take the Princess to bed and then I will join you for the second watch.'

Oddmund nodded and she took Astra's hand and helped guide her down the stairs. Brenna awaited them at the bottom and they made slow progress through the crowd back to the hall, as many of her people stopped to offer words of loyalty and comfort. Some even touched her cloak or Astra's hair for luck.

Skadi thanked them all by name—she knew her people well and was glad to have their support.

Back at the hall, they swept through the main chamber with its many lamps and braziers, the protective runes carved into the walls and pillars flickering in the candlelight, alive with magic. A few of the servants were still clearing up the evening meal and preparing the main hall for the guards and servants who slept there. They walked towards the back of the cavernous room, past the trough of flames from the central fire, followed by the raised dais that held the two carved thrones of Thrudheim.

The huge carved stone chairs were cold and uncomfortable to sit on without plenty of furs and embroidered cushions. She smiled as she remembered her sweet and long-dead father once saying, *No crown is comfortable to bear...especially on the bottom.*

In the chambers beyond, she passed her daughter's room, as well as Brenna's, then her own.

'Will we be sleeping in the King's chamber tonight?' Astra asked.

Skadi nodded. 'Yes, and every night until this threat leaves us.'

The King's chamber was a huge room at the very back of the hall. It had its own latrine and treasure room either side of the huge, elaborately carved oak doors. They were already open, a woollen curtain shielding the chamber from draughts, the light of the small central fire kissing the edges of the fabric with a warm and welcoming glow.

Brenna pulled aside the curtain and Astra tiptoed in, as if her father were still alive and she hadn't been granted permission to enter. Skadi pulled the doors shut with a thud, but didn't bother to bar them as she would need to creep out later to take her watch. Brenna began to tend to the fire while Skadi joined Astra, who was already removing her mittens and cloak.

'Well done, sweetling,' said Skadi, helping her out of her clothes. Brenna then came to wash Astra's face and hands in a bowl of warm water she'd prepared. Skadi brushed out her pale-blonde hair, while Astra rubbed her teeth clean with a strip of linen.

After she was done, Astra clambered into the large bed in her shift. 'The stones are still warm,' she declared cheerfully, wiggling her legs further down the bed and then pulling up the blankets and furs to her chin.

'Good,' Skadi said, allowing Brenna to help her with the removal of her armour. There was a lot to take off: her helm with its ornamental crown, the heavy chainmail byrnie, the thick quilted tunic beneath, as well as the leather guards, boots and trousers. It took some time before she was down to nothing more than the short linen shirt. It reached to her mid-thigh and was perfect beneath her armour and quilted tunic. Brenna helped brush out her hair. Skadi then washed her face and rubbed her teeth, while Brenna righted the room.

'Thank you, Brenna,' she said, before climbing into bed and turning towards Astra. 'Are you not going to complain about my cold feet?' she teased.

Astra hesitated before whispering with a worried expression, 'I am sorry, Moma…about the flame. Did I ruin it…the sacrifice…?' Tears began to gather in her blue eyes. 'Have I put us in danger?'

'No,' Skadi said firmly, stroking her daughter's cheek and then gathering her daughter close and kissing the top of her head. 'You did very well, you kept the holy flame burning. I just helped Rán catch it… Burning an offering to the goddess of the sea is always difficult—she does not like flame, remember. I am proud of you, sweetling. You did very well.'

Astra took her hand and patted it gently. 'Does it hurt?'

Surprised, Skadi looked down at the red patches on her skin, remembering belatedly what had caused them. 'They are not bad burns, just a splash of oil.'

Brenna stopped what she was doing and came over to the bed with the medicine chest. 'Shall I put some salve on them, Your Highness?'

Skadi shook her head, but thought better of it when she saw the concern in her daughter's eyes. 'Just a little, to take away the redness. Brenna, can you take a seat by the door? I will need you to wake and dress me when Oddmund comes for the second watch… Then I want you to rest beside Astra for the rest of the night…' She gave her a meaningful look and Brenna nodded with understanding.

They were taking it in turns to guard the Princess. Brenna had been her servant and friend since they were children, there was no one she trusted more to look after her child.

She kissed the snowy top of Astra's head before settling

down to sleep herself. Exhausted by the days of preparation and training, despite her fears, it didn't take her long to drift off.

'Your Highness!' Brenna's terrified scream woke her with a jerk.

Sitting up, while simultaneously comforting the startled Astra, Skadi watched Brenna as she flew into the chamber and slammed the door behind her, desperately struggling to pull down the bar across the door. 'Agnar's attacked! The eastern wall was breached! They came from the mountain side! They're fighting at the doors!'

Several things ran through Skadi's mind in a single blink.

If Agnar was here and he'd come from the east, it meant his ships had landed on the other side of the island. The sneaky trickster had climbed over a mountain to attack them from behind—a feat she would have thought impossible until tonight. The majority of her men were placed at the front of the settlement. On the port and gate turrets, it would take them time to turn and reach the hall.

Shouts and screams of pain came from beyond the bedchamber doors and she knew that Agnar had already breached the Great Hall.

Skadi leapt from the bed and ran to help Brenna. But before she even made it halfway across the chamber, the door was kicked open, throwing Brenna several feet away. She screamed as she hit the ground and skidded a couple more feet to land beside her.

Skadi grabbed her sword and shield, then strode towards their attackers with a roar.

The first man trying to enter was forced back into the hall and received a slash to the gut for his trouble. The second stumbled over the falling body of his companion and she was able to slice his arm. He howled in pain, but then came back with a fiery rage, battering her shield with heavy blows of his axe.

Get them out! her mind screamed and, with a grit of her teeth, she angled her body to better brace against the rain of his attack.

More men were coming down the hallway. A red-haired warrior was battling two of her guards. She took a step forward, pushing her shield forward with all of her might, and her attacker grunted and faltered. Surprise widened his eyes and then narrowed with anger. His gaze lowered to her bare feet and a cruel smile revealed rotten teeth.

The crunch of his boot as it slammed into her foot made her yelp with pain and she stumbled back. She cursed and tried to recover her position, but the man with the rotten teeth surged forward through the door and the red-haired warrior followed closely behind. They then both stopped, hesitating as if unsure of what to do next, now that they had broken in.

Glancing behind her, Skadi was relieved to see that Brenna had had the wisdom to pull a large sea chest out. She was now crouched behind its open lid with Astra, fumbling to string a bow and arrow.

It was a good defensive position, but Skadi knew she wasn't trained with the weapon and was unlikely to hit anything with it. She imagined she was using it more as a deterrent than anything else. Which was proven correct when she raised it awkwardly towards the red-haired warrior who was trying to approach her from the side.

He immediately brought his shield to the front of his head and upper body. 'Think very carefully before letting that arrow fly—you could hurt yourself!' he said calmly and the man with the rotten teeth laughed nastily.

Brenna's hand trembled a little, but with a glare she spat

back, 'And *you* should think very carefully before coming another step closer! I might not hit your heart, but there are plenty of *other* parts I may strike—especially at this range!' For emphasis she pulled the string of the bow tighter.

Skadi positioned herself further back, so that she was closer to her daughter and Brenna. There was no point trying to get them out now. She had to pray that the rest of her warriors would arrive in time to save them.

'Put down your weapons and beg for mercy!' snarled Rotten Teeth with a wicked smile and Skadi's back stiffened. He seemed familiar. Perhaps he was one of the group of men she'd banished from Thrudheim for stealing from the mines… It made sense that such a wretch would return with Agnar.

'I am the Queen of Thrudheim and I kneel for no man!' she replied, keeping her tone heavy and calm. She lunged forward and smacked his sword with a mighty blow that made him stumble back a few steps with a curse. But she dared not risk following him to take advantage of her blow, in case it put Astra in danger from the redhead.

She kept her gaze sweeping between them and her voice steady. 'When my warriors arrive, which they will…*you* will be the ones begging for mercy. Now, either come and fight or accept defeat. I grow tired of your cowardice!'

The redhead sighed, unbothered by her goading, but Rotten Teeth spat on the ground and began to walk forward.

'No,' snapped the redhead. 'Agnar's orders…we *wait.*'

Rotten Teeth paused and glared at him, before lifting his bleeding arm. 'The bitch cut my arm *and* she killed Gro!'

The redhead shrugged before repeating, 'We wait. Besides…you cut her, too. I cannot wait for Agnar to see that!' The redhead's eyes twinkled with amusement and Rotten Teeth made a bad-tempered huffing sound.

Agnar probably wants to kill me himself.

Skadi's thundering heart slowed, and she took another step back, wondering if it would be worth trying to kill them and escape out of one of the shuttered windows.

The redhead seemed less keen on fighting, but he was also closer to Brenna and Astra. If she attacked and killed Rotten Teeth, she might be able to charge the redhead in time, or Brenna might wound him with her arrow… Still, it was a terrible risk.

Warmth trickled down her leg and the pain that had been muffled by shock lanced through her. She glanced down to realise that Rotten Teeth had managed to slice her thigh—that must have been what the redhead was referring to. It wasn't a deep wound; the brute had merely been lucky enough to catch her in a low sweeping strike. In her armour it wouldn't have even pierced her skin.

Heavy boots beat down the hall towards them and Skadi's heart began to thunder once again, preparing for a fight. She took another step back, as a group of men entered led by a scarred, half-naked giant with long dark hair and piercing green eyes.

Agnar!

His sword was stained with blood and it dripped on to the stone floor in thick crimson drops, reminding her of the last time she'd seen him. Except the man who entered was no longer a child.

Agnar was now a fully grown man, handsome but with ugly scars all over his face, arms and bare chest. A wolfskin was draped over his head and shoulders. The beast's muzzle snarled over his head with glass eyes that matched its owner's in colour. She read the runes that were branded on his chest and shivered—*Hagalaz* and *Nauthiz*, wrath and endurance, promises of vengeance burned on his skin by his own hand.

She swallowed down the cloying fear that had gathered in her throat. He took one look at her with those narrowed serpent eyes and she knew immediately that she was in danger.

He hates me...

Chapter Three

Pure fury pierced Agnar like lightning, burning its way down through his body, from his head to his toes.

Blood had been spilt, *her* blood.

Things had not gone according to plan and that always irritated him. But the flash of scarlet had caused his heart to beat wildly in his chest and he had to adjust his sword grip to stop himself lashing out.

Queen Skadi was wounded and looked more like a wild animal trapped in a corner than the serenely beautiful woman he remembered. He would need to tread carefully.

Curse Gro and Beske! They had refused to follow orders more than once already. Too keen to seek treasure and mayhem rather than obeying their commander.

It had taken longer than he would have liked to breach and seal the Great Hall. But he'd had to do it, to ensure his plan succeeded. He couldn't allow time for Thrudheim's army to reach them before he'd captured Queen Skadi.

All of it would be for nothing if he didn't force the Queen of Thrudheim into an agreement immediately. Not only the struggles of the last few days, but also the long years he'd fought for this one chance and his mother…his poor mother… had given everything, including her own life, for today.

Surprise and speed were his only advantage. As predicted,

Skadi had prepared for a frontal attack from the sea. His plan to travel with a small war band across the mountain had worked. They'd breached the wall swiftly, climbing it without alerting the rest of the town, at least until they had reached the Great Hall.

Even now, there was only a handful of men from the nearby turrets clamouring at the door. But they were shouting and beating their shields, alerting others. Reinforcements would soon arrive and he would be outnumbered when they eventually broke through.

The waiting, the suffering, the loss of his birthright and the sacrifice of his mother—all wasted if he failed to convince Skadi to accept him.

She *had* to accept him.

Even after preparing himself for the sight of her, she still took his breath away. A long and proud face, with blonde hair so pale it was almost white. Blue stormy eyes that observed all around her like a hawk. She was as uncompromising, beautiful and regal as he remembered.

Skadi was the embodiment of his ambition, pride and peace, filling him with desire, hope and disgust, the conflicting mix of emotions churning with grief and bitterness. But she was finally within his grasp.

Of course, she was older now, had filled out since he'd last seen her—she'd been much younger then, still not confident in her womanhood or her decisions. She was curvier now, had matured and ripened with motherhood. Rounded hips, thicker thighs, heavier breasts and muscular arms.

Strong and womanly—after all, she was a seasoned shieldmaiden as well as a queen, which unfortunately appealed to his baser instincts. He'd hoped to find some distance between them—that seeing her again would soften some of the raw emotions he'd always felt when he'd thought of her… It had not.

If anything, she was more beautiful now. She'd become a mother since he'd last seen her, but she still trained regularly by the confident way she held her sword and shield. She had grown from a confused princess into a formidable queen.

She'd killed one of his men…one whom he cared nothing for, but he had to admire her ability, considering she was in little more than a short shift. He'd been worried that he couldn't trust Gro and Beske to follow his orders. They were not men he knew well and had asked to join with him only recently. They'd said they'd once worked in the mines of Thrudheim, so they knew the mountain well. Still, he regretted giving them the chance to cause havoc.

He allowed his hungry eyes a moment to devour the sight of her. To reassure himself that he was finally here, ready to claim her. But then his eyes had locked on to the splash of blood across her thigh, the slow trickle of crimson running down her naked leg to pool on the stone floor.

He needed her alive! That was the reason for his anger, surely?

He should have thrown both Gro and Beske off the cliff once they'd shown him the way. They had put his whole plan at risk and he could feel the murderous rage pricking along his sword arm, his muscles contracting, thirsty for blood. But he knew in his heart it was more than that. He was possessive of her, despite only seeing her twice in his life.

Skadi remained defiantly straight and proud in her stance. So at least it wasn't a deep wound. He forced his shoulders to relax as he sought the gaze of his second, Vali, whose head shifted subtly to nod at Beske, informing him without words who had harmed her.

Rage built within him, each moment he spent in Beske's company sparking new anger, like oil dripping on to flame.

But he would have to deal with that later. Currently, he had a murderous warrior queen facing him with a weapon in hand. Behind her, a loyal servant crouched behind an open chest, holding a trembling bow and arrow. A small white-haired girl was crouched beside her who looked just like her mother.

Skadi rolled the sword with her wrist, drawing his eyes back to her—*as if they needed much encouragement*, he thought bitterly—but he could see that she was wary of his focus on her child. A man never came between a mother bear and her cub, not if he wanted to live, and Agnar straightened his spine, trying his best to calm the fire in his heart.

'You know who I am,' he said.

'Agnar Bjornsson,' she replied coldly. 'I remember you...' A bittersweet smile twisted her lips. 'You've grown into a man...finally.'

Her words were both painful and sweet to hear, like honey on a bad tooth drawing out the sad and poisonous truth. Reminding him that his only failure had been that he had been born too late.

Well, he was no longer a child. He sucked in a deep breath and her grip tightened on her sword as she shifted position, putting her wounded leg behind her and turning a little so that she could see all three men clearly. 'I know who you are, but not *why* you are here.'

'For my birthright.'

'Your *birthright*?' She laughed with disbelief, a throaty and rich sound, the voice of a woman who wore jewels and bathed in spices and rose petals. Her eyes hardened as she met his. 'You were lucky to leave this place alive. Do you remember *that*?'

Finally, she spoke the words that opened the door on their mutual past and he stiffened at the shameful memory. How he hated her for reminding him of it. Of his helplessness… his weakness and humiliation. Everything he had fought to overcome. She had witnessed it and had turned away, breaking her promise, ruining his life and that of his mother's, with sweet and wicked words: *'Leave him be, Heimdall...'*

'I remember.' He would never forgive her for it.

'You forget your current position, woman. We have you trapped!' snarled Beske and he took a threatening step forward.

Skadi responded with a defensive position, raising her sword and shield high. Her voice was calm, 'You are also trapped…with me!'

'Beske, speak again and you will regret it!' Agnar interrupted loudly, losing patience with Beske, who seemed to have forgotten that Agnar was his master. 'Queen Skadi, I want…*only* what was promised to me by your father…and by *yourself*.' He came to stand beside Beske, lowering the foolish man's sword with a firm press of his palm on the flat of the blade. Beske obeyed, but he felt the man's resistance and that only angered him further, especially when Skadi showed no regret for her broken promise.

Where was her tearful apology? Her guilt?

'My father did not expect to die so soon. He thought there would be time for you to grow into a man. That he would see us married and settled before he left this mortal realm.' Her hand tightened around the hilt of her sword, her knuckles turning as white as her hair. 'As it was… I had to make a choice, for the good of my land and my people.'

'Heimdall was a *terrible* choice!' The words roared from him like thunder and he struggled to rein in his temper. A whimper from behind the chest forced him to control himself.

To his surprise Skadi didn't argue with him. Her jaw clenched and her chin lifted. 'I have no regrets.'

Fury burned his gut like a brand and his head began to pound.

How could she not regret Heimdall? Youthful lust had clouded her judgement back then, but surely she realised now what a terrible mistake she had made?

It wasn't until he saw the flicker of unease from Vali out of the corner of his eye, that he realised the pounding wasn't in his head after all—someone was using a battering ram against the Great Hall's doors.

Skadi took a deep breath, then asked impatiently, 'Tell me your plan. Do you honestly think that by defeating me you will be allowed to rule Thrudheim freely? I have an alliance with King Sven and he will have you killed! It does not matter that you are his half-brother, he does not care for you. He will bring an army down upon you and call it revenge for the death of his friend, *King* Heimdall.'

She shook her head, as if mystified by his reasoning—or perhaps this was all a delaying tactic to give her men time to break through. 'What do you hope to gain from this?'

'A *queen*,' he answered coldly and without hesitation.

She stiffened, as if she'd been struck, and lowered her sword slightly for the first time. He might have thought it acceptance, except for the disgust on her face. 'Astra is too young to marry.'

Confusion swept through him. 'I do not want Astra.'

Her eyes hardened. 'I have seen forty winters and after twenty years of marriage with Heimdall I could only produce one child. I doubt I can bear another…even if I *wanted* to…which I do not.'

Agnar shrugged. 'We shall see… Either way, it does not concern me.'

A storm of anger seemed to rise up within her and she yelled, 'It concerns me, *Usurper*! Astra is my heir!'

Beske chose that moment to grumble, 'Kill the bitch and take the child! She will be a good enough hostage for now!'

Agnar had had his fill of Beske. His gaze met Skadi's and then, without hesitation, he twisted his body and plunged his sword into the man's abdomen. As smooth and as quick as the strike of an adder.

The man inhaled one shocked gasp and then began to gargle phlegm, his eyes bulging before rolling back. Then his body dropped towards the ground, the knees buckling, the dead weight of him slipping the sword free with a wet slither. He fell with an undignified thud flat on his face. A just end to a corrupt man.

Skadi stared down at Beske's body in horror, the blood draining from her face. 'You would kill your own men?'

'I would do much worse than that.' *Better she meets the beast now and understands what he is truly capable of.*

As usual, Agnar felt nothing at Beske's death, no pity or shame… Nothing. He had killed so many men over the years that their deaths did not rattle him.

It was a convenient kill that simply served his purpose. He knew that Skadi had fought occasionally against petty chieftains who thought to raid Thrudheim. So she must have seen men killed in battle, or even by accident. A man could die in a drunken challenge, or at one of the many feasts throughout the year. But Skadi looked at him now as if he were a monster, for dispatching a man who had been an obvious threat to her… *How odd.*

But perhaps he could use her fear of him against her?

The continued banging at the door forced him to decide.

'I *always* keep my word,' he said absently, lowering his sword without bothering to clean it, allowing it to stain the floor with its ugly paint. 'I told him that he would regret it if he spoke again… He did.'

Another bang reverberated from the front of the hall, this one louder than before—perhaps they had a cart now?

He stared her down. 'I want my birthright. I want what I was promised. But more than anything… I want *power.*' His eyes met hers and the green serpent swirled within him—it was the rage and vengeance that had always kept him company. She shivered, obviously repulsed by him, and glanced back towards her child.

You created this monster, now look! He wanted to scream, but he held his tongue. He had waited twenty years for this moment, he could wait a few heartbeats longer. Especially when her fate was already certain.

'Astra will come to no harm,' he said firmly. 'I swear it.'

Her eyes flew back to his and she shook her head. 'I do not believe you.'

He could understand her doubt. All men wanted heirs, a legacy to pass on to their own bloodline after death. But he did not… He wanted what he'd been promised and he wanted power, so that no one could ever harm him, or the people he cared for, ever again…and *revenge*, not for himself, but for his mother, he wanted that, too.

He was so thirsty for power and revenge that he would put aside anything to gain it. Including children and happiness. Bloodlines did not matter to him, but he knew they mattered to Skadi.

They were his best weapon against her.

'If you marry me, I will name Astra as my heir and she will remain my heir unless we have a son together. Either way, *your* bloodline will continue to rule this island,' he said firmly, then he pulled at the cord of leather around his throat, yanking it so hard it snapped from his neck. He held it out to her, so that she could see it more clearly.

It was a wedding ring, a silver band of intricate knotwork that shone in the firelight. He had kept it for this moment. 'I swear it, on my mother's ring.'

There was another bang at the hall doors. Some of his men began to shift nervously.

Skadi gestured with her chin towards the doorway, but he'd seen the curiosity in her gaze when she'd looked at the ring. It was meant to be hers, had always belonged to her in his mind. 'My men will break through and they will kill you all!'

Agnar laughed, throwing his head back with a false throaty chuckle. The men joined him, chuckling lightly, the tension in their bodies easing as if soothed by his confidence.

As his head dipped forward again to meet her eyes, his smile fell and his voice dropped into a deadly warning, 'Believe me, you do not want that to happen, my Queen. It would leave me with only one choice.' Deliberately he let his gaze shift towards the sea chest and the two people hiding behind it. The child was no longer visible, the servant must have told her to huddle down. But he didn't need to see Skadi's daughter to make his intentions clear.

When he looked back at Skadi, he saw her confidence had drained away and all that was left was a mother's fear. He knew that look well. He had seen it on his mother's face countless times and he felt no sympathy for Skadi because of it. Her actions had brought her to this moment and she was bound to him forever.

It was fate and neither of them could deny it.

Skadi tried to bargain with him. 'There is another path. You could leave Thrudheim and never return. I will not tell

Sven that you came here. I will not demand retribution for Heimdall. Go back to the Rus and live in peace.'

His smile tasted bitter on his lips. He did not smile often and it didn't sit well with him. Just like his next words, even though he spoke honestly, 'I will have all or nothing. Make *your* choice, Skadi.'

She growled at him through gritted teeth, but refused to answer. She was waiting, hoping for her men to break through.

Hope was a dangerous thing.

He knew he couldn't look away from her. Couldn't have her doubt him for a single moment. He had killed Beske in front of her to prove the conviction of his word. But it still wasn't enough…she still had hope.

His plan was despicable. Corrupt. The words of a dishonourable and cruel man.

But he had never claimed to be good and life was never fair.

He had fought for too long and suffered far too much to give up now. He would have her as his Queen, whether it was by deceit or cruelty, he did not care.

He *would* have her.

Stepping forward, he slowly raised his sword. 'If you do not accept, or delay any longer…the child dies.'

Chapter Four

No!

Denial and fury screamed through her body and, with a strength and speed she hadn't realised she possessed, she flew forward as Agnar took a threatening step towards her Astra.

Instinctively, she knew Agnar was the greatest threat and she hoped to kill him before his second had time to react. The redheaded warrior had looked distinctly uncomfortable with the direction of the negotiations and she knew Brenna had a greater chance at protecting Astra from him than from the beast in front of her.

Charging forward, she threw her shield back at the red-haired warrior, hoping to wound or distract him long enough to give Brenna and Astra more time. Unfortunately, the warrior was able to strike it away with his own and it rolled towards the sea chest.

Perhaps Brenna could make use of it? Unfortunately, Skadi didn't have time to check what became of it because she was already within reach of Agnar.

Leaping high, she held her sword with both hands and struck with all her might, the sweeping arc of her blade ready to cleave Agnar from shoulder to hip. It was a move that had floored or killed other men in moments. But as she suspected, Agnar was made of steel and cunning. He matched her strike with a block of his own, her blade scraping down his sword with a screech of clashing metal as she returned to the ground.

It was like trying to cut down a tree made of stone.

An arrow flew to the side of her, but it bounced uselessly off the red-haired warrior's shield and she realised Brenna was running out of time. She spun away from Agnar and attacked the warrior, striking him hard in the same way she'd tried with Agnar. She ignored the pain of her wounded leg and the tiredness in her arms, landing the blow as if she were trying to fell a tree with one hit.

This time she had better success, although he was still quick enough to raise his shield. It cracked in two, one half falling to the ground as he stumbled away, knocking into the bed. Unfortunately, she hadn't managed to do anything more than stun him and he was already rising to his feet.

She spun back towards Agnar, grateful that the man lacked speed despite his god-like strength. He was closing in, but still a few feet away from her, his sword raised high.

Shifting, so that she could just about see both men, she prepared herself to fight again with a few gasped breaths and readjustment of her grip. Ready to take the terrible blows that were sure to rain down on her, to battle with all her might for her child's survival.

Agnar continued to prowl towards her and she clenched her sword tightly.

Then something unthinkable happened.

'Astra!' screamed Brenna and ice-cold dread pooled immediately in Skadi's guts as she glanced sideways and saw the small figure of Astra clutching her ceremonial silver dagger in one hand and her mother's shield in the other. She was racing towards them, *no... Agnar.* Her little girl was running straight towards her enemy!

Time slowed.

The soft slap of young, bare feet on stone echoed around Skadi's horrified mind, causing her heart to beat loudly in time to the horrible rhythm—she would remember that moment forever. Her entire world running towards certain death.

There was an anguished and terrified scream and it was only afterwards that Skadi realised it had been her own.

Skadi burst forward, desperate to intercept, but despite using all of her strength, her sprint seemed unbearably sluggish. Astra continued to charge towards a man who was easily three times her size.

Agnar turned towards Astra, his eyes widening with astonishment as her child flew towards him. His sword arm reared back, preparing to slash forward, and Skadi's world tilted. She couldn't bear it, but neither could she look away… And then, her child raised her shield and stabbed forward with her pitifully small dagger, her wide eyes stormy with blind fear and incredibly foolish courage.

Agnar lunged, but not with his sword. Instead, his free hand plucked Astra's wrist and twisted the blade up and away from him. With a surprised yelp her daughter dropped her only weapon and it clattered to the floor. Astra tried to hit him with her shield, but he simply raised her off the ground and shook her as if she were a doll. The shield fell to join the blade, spinning noisily, until it finally stopped and dropped flat on its rim with a clatter.

From the corner of her eye, she could see Brenna being wrestled to the floor by the red-haired warrior. The other men in the room were watching their weak attempt at defence with grim satisfaction, but thankfully no one stepped forward to join the fray.

The bang of the ram continued to echo throughout the hall, but the sound only depressed her, because it proved they were still alone.

All is lost...

Skadi fell to her knees, all strength leaving her body in a painful rush. The ancestral sword of Thrudheim dropped from her hand and banged on the stone floor in defeat. Her voice was a broken screech as she begged, 'I will do anything you want! Please, don't hurt her!'

Agnar's gaze tilted away from the struggling child he held aloft like a leg of lamb to Skadi on the floor. His face was as cold and inscrutable as before, but he must have known he held victory in his hand, because he nodded in agreement. 'Then, become my Queen, Skadi. Swear to marry me, make me your King and I will never hurt her… You have my word.'

Astra began to cry, although Skadi suspected it was more from fear and frustration than from actual pain, because she twisted like a hare in a trap.

Skadi nodded, answering quickly, unable to bear it a moment longer and desperate to have her daughter returned to her. 'I swear it!'

There was a moment where he just stared at her, as if he were waiting for something else, and panic erupted from her in a desperate cry. 'You have my word! I will marry you! You will be King of Thrudheim. But, please, Agnar! She's just a child! Please, let her go!'

Agnar's eyes narrowed on her and her heart stuttered in panic, because there was a storm of hatred raging within them and she was terrified he would change his mind. 'I was also a child,' he said, 'when you denied me my birthright and left me bleeding on the floor.'

Horror churned like bile in her stomach and she glanced at Astra, her bare feet kicking out aimlessly. Agnar hadn't been much older when she'd denied his claim and he'd been badly hurt because of it. It hadn't been right, but she refused to lower her head, despite the guilt clawing at her throat. Weakly she answered, 'I thought…it was for the best.'

'For you!' he growled with disgust. 'You were eager to be bedded by Heimdall, you cannot deny it.'

Skadi shook her head, refuting his words, even as hot shame crawled up her neck. 'I did it for Thrudheim.'

Her answer didn't seem to appease him and he hissed out a curse. She was about to beg his forgiveness—or say anything to make him release Astra—when he finally gave a grunt of acknowledgement and said, 'So be it.'

Slowly, and with surprising gentleness, he lowered Astra back to her feet and, when he let her go, Astra ran to her. Skadi burst forward, meeting her halfway and sweeping her crying daughter into her arms. She clutched her fragile body close and tried to reassure herself that all was well by patting her back and whispering soothing words.

She glanced over her head towards Brenna who was still struggling under the redheaded warrior's grip.

'Let her go,' said Agnar firmly and with a bad-tempered hiss Brenna staggered out of the warrior's hold and then hurried over to Skadi. The three of them banded together in a tight embrace. Clinging to each other in a tangled web of limbs.

'Your men are still pounding at the door… Come, let us share with them our good news!' Agnar snapped, striding towards her and offering his hand, although his next word belied any pretence of kindness. 'Now!'

Skadi slowly pushed Astra behind her towards Brenna, still hoping that an intervention by the gods might save them.

'And get the Gothi!' snapped Agnar at his men and they

all jumped, looking like little boys caught sleeping on their watch.

'The Gothi lives in the town,' she interrupted, her mind already searching for another delay.

'I brought my own,' said Agnar dismissively, already shouting orders to his men and hurrying them out into the hall. The bang of the door continued to echo and Skadi was disappointed to see a short time later that Agnar had barricaded them into the hall, even using a hay cart from outside to reinforce the doors from the inside.

Agnar clambered up the rickety defences of tables, benches, and the hay cart, to be as high and as close to the doors as possible. 'I have your Queen!' he yelled and there was silence followed by murmurs beyond the doors. 'She has agreed to marry me and make me your King!'

Loud denials and curses came from her people beyond the doors. Eventually a voice which sounded like Oddmund's responded. 'You lie! You have murdered our Queen! We shall burn this hall to the ground and make it her funeral pyre—with *you* as her offering!'

Skadi quickly shouted back a reply, trying to keep as much pride in her voice as possible, 'I am alive, Oddmund! I have agreed to marry him.' She said nothing more, hoping he would understand that she'd been forced to make this agreement.

Already she was trying to think of a way out of it.

So, what if I am forced to marry him? I can easily become a widow for the second time!

She just needed the protection of her men first.

Agnar turned back towards her and gave her a strange smile, as if he already knew that she wished to end his life and for some reason did not care.

Did he really think this idiotic plan would work?

As soon as they opened the doors, he would be overwhelmed and she would order him killed, regardless of whether they were married or not.

'Where is the Gothi?' Agnar demanded, climbing down the hay cart and landing with a heavy thud beside her. 'We need to be married before we open the doors.'

'Here!' said a woman, who was dressed in the many-feathered cloak of a Gothi. She carried a staff decorated with shells and animal bones. She didn't appear frightened, so she must be a part of his war band, or at least had agreed to this voyage and plan.

Skadi scowled at her bad temperedly and placed Astra, who'd been trembling beneath her arm, back into Brenna's care.

'What kind of Gothi allows a forced marriage to take place?' Skadi grumbled at the woman, who shrugged in response.

'A well-paid one… Besides, is this forced, or did you not agree to it?'

Skadi cursed beneath her breath, but the Gothi's smug smile was answer enough. An unwelcome marriage was different to a forced one and they were both old enough to realise the difference, which was nothing to do with morals and more to do with how other men might judge it.

Skadi turned to face Brenna and Astra. 'Keep hold of her and run at the first sign of trouble,' she said quietly in Brenna's ear as she hugged her, in what she hoped appeared to be a comforting embrace.

Brenna said nothing, understanding the need for secrecy. Her friend had helped bring Astra into the world and she would gladly defend her to the death, as she'd already proven. Skadi was grateful to have such a friend.

Agnar continued to stare at her, obviously growing impatient, but being too proud to demand she join him. Skadi walked slowly to the centre of the hall and stood opposite him in front of the Gothi, who held out her staff in preparation for the ceremony.

A cold draught whispered against her bare legs. Suddenly self-conscious, she crossed her arms over her chest to cover the outline of her nipples and tried to appear as dignified as she could despite the drying blood on her leg, and the fact that she wore so little and was beginning to shiver.

Agnar stared at her for a moment, as if irritated by the sight of her. Then he tossed back the wolf's head that snarled above his eyes with a jerk and quickly untied and removed his wolfskin cloak with a sweep of his muscular arms.

He draped it around her shoulders before she had time to refuse. The musk of wolf and man enveloped her and, although she welcomed the warmth and cover, she felt uncomfortable wearing it. Thankfully, he'd not placed the beast's head on top of her own. She wasn't sure how she would feel about wearing it like that—it would be as if he owned her, had claimed her life, as he had the wolf's.

Her discomfort was only increased when he demanded, 'Give me your hand.'

No kindness or compassion, but then she had never expected any, so she held out her hand, allowing her anger and resentment to show in her expression. 'I warn you now, Agnar. I may promise to be your wife and Queen. But I will not protect you from Sven.'

Not again.

Despite his obvious resentment towards her, she *had* protected him all those years ago. Heimdall would have happily killed the boy who dared demand that he return his bride—and Sven would have welcomed it as well. It had been well known even then that he felt no loyalty or love for his half-brother.

Agnar raised a brow in amusement, then took her hand in his own in a hard grip as if he were afraid she would try to shake him off. 'I do not expect you to protect me from our enemies... That is my duty.'

She snorted at that. 'Sven is *your* enemy, not mine.'

Agnar shook his head with a derisive snort, but didn't answer her. Turning towards the Gothi, he snapped, 'Get on with it!'

The Gothi began the ceremony, shaking her staff and calling upon the gods and ancestors to witness the union of their marriage.

Vali appeared at Skadi's side and held out Thrudheim's ancestral sword. He must have picked it up off the floor in the King's chamber. She took it from him with a heavy heart and offered it to Agnar, the blade flat and resting on the palms of her hands. 'The sword of Thrudheim. It has been in my family for seven generations. Each one of them was a wise and mighty king.' She glared at him over the steel, the runes etched down its centre glistening with firelight. 'Do not be the first to lose it.'

Agnar gripped the sword lightly with both hands and met her eyes. 'I have no ancestral sword to give in exchange. But this will always be safe in my possession.' He took it from her and her heart ached to let it go.

After taking his sword from its sheath and replacing it with the sword of Thrudheim, he removed his mother's ring and took the red woollen cord offered by the Gothi. Threading the cord through his mother's ring, he pushed it on to her finger—annoyingly it fit perfectly.

Another ring was produced, this time a masculine version that looked as if it had been crafted to match his mother's.

Agnar offered it to Skadi and with a roll of her eyes at this ridiculous pretence of ceremony, she threaded it through the same red woollen cord and pushed it on to Agnar's calloused finger.

The Gothi grabbed both their hands and pushed them together palm against palm. The two pieces of red woven cord dangled down between them. Chanting an ancient prayer, the Gothi began to wrap the wool around their pressed hands. 'Agnar Bjornsson, you wed and honour the lady of this hall. You will share your wealth with her and shield her back. Faithfully, you will always honour her with your words and actions.'

She then looked to Skadi, who had heard these vows before and had not liked them the first time. 'Skadi Friggsdottir, Queen of Thrudheim. You bow your crown and sword to your new King. You will obey his commands and share his bed. Faithfully, you will strive to give him happiness with your words and actions. Give me your oaths!' the Gothi demanded.

With one last glare at her new husband, Skadi said between gritted teeth. 'I give you my oath…that I will *try*, Your Highness.'

Agnar's head tilted and his eyes narrowed, but he answered clearly, 'I give you my oath, that I will also *try*, my Queen.'

The Gothi looked between them, obviously wondering if these aggressive and subjective oaths were actually binding in the eyes of the gods. But she must have decided they were, because she banged her staff loudly on the floor and shouted, 'The bond is woven. You are bound together in marriage!'

Their hands parted, Skadi's palm burning as if she'd spilled hot oil on it for the second time that night. The cord snapped and the scarlet threads fell away in a clumsy tangle that she had to shake off.

Agnar walked away, appearing not to care about her reaction. After all it was only a symbolic ceremony—the threads no longer mattered once the words had been said. Grimly Skadi thought to herself that even the words didn't matter. Once Heimdall had made his oath and become King, things had changed between them. She'd never regretted her choice, but she had never been particularly happy with it either. At least this marriage had begun honestly, in an odd sort of way.

'I will send the signal now,' Agnar said to a nearby man, who hurriedly pulled out a large metal horn from his pack, the type used in battles to signal charges and retreats. Agnar took it from the man, and with a deep breath pushed it against his lips and raised his head, bellowing out a deep and rich sound that carried up out of the smoke hole and into the dawn above.

Why had he done that? Was it a signal to the outside town that their marriage was complete? But why would the people care? They were waiting for the doors to open, and the release of their Queen.

Who was the signal for?

The distant sound of an answering horn filtered down from the mountain above, followed shortly by several fainter blasts. As if they were being made on the other side of the island, or out at sea.

Skadi shivered, despite the warmth of dawn shining down from the smoke hole above. Pink and amber clouds drifted across the sky and a raven swooped into the opening. It perched on one of the rafters, peering down at her curiously like one of Odin's messengers, reminding her that the Norns had already woven her fate before she'd even taken her first breath.

She looked to her new husband.

Perhaps her fate would be to kill him, or...perhaps they were destined to be together?

She flinched at the thought.

Agnar lowered the horn and looked at her, a slight curl to his upper lip—the beast's attempt at a smile. 'My army is coming.'

Chapter Five

It was clear that Skadi had not expected him to have so many men and he was oddly proud to have surprised her. Endless years of fighting, joining campaigns and selling his sword had slowly built up his skills and reputation enough to lead a formidable army.

All of his focus and drive had been leading to this moment. The day when he would finally reclaim what had been stolen from him. He was covered in the scars of his ambition and the hundreds of men under his command were the symbol of his hard work and achievements. The Agnar who faced her now was completely different to the boy who had been dragged from her hall in a bloody disgrace.

Had she even wondered what had become of him?

He doubted it and that filled him with a dark rage. Years of suffering and struggle and she hadn't even cared if he lived or died.

But he was here now and she would know. He would force her to look, and understand what she had done. Whether she wanted to or not. She would regret her choice!

Heimdall's death had been the inevitable catalyst and it had set in motion all of his plans. Like an entire village going up in flames, because of a single neglected spark, and he was that forgotten flame.

'Army?' Skadi asked, looking strangely magnificent in his wolf pelt. There was no denying her beauty—it captured his senses like a dazzling snowstorm, obscuring all other sights and sounds in her blinding presence. His attraction was as single-minded as his ambition.

'You thought so little of me?' he asked with mocking disapproval, enjoying the irritation that flashed across her face. He moved to stand closer to her and she stared up at him with a defiantly clenched jaw. Now that they were officially married, he allowed his possessive nature free reign. Compelled by some magic, he reached out and stroked a finger down that imperious jaw, marvelling at its softness despite how tightly it was clenched. 'Did you really think I would come for you with so little preparation? *Everything* I have ever done is to be with you.'

It was strange that he could so passionately hate and desire her at the same time. But he did. The mere memory of her had caused him to raise an army—he was half-afraid of what else she could make him do.

Kill a child? The idea repulsed him, even though he had threatened it not that long ago out of desperation.

'But…' She shook her head, stepping away from his touch, making it clear she didn't want him in return, and he felt a fool. 'Who?'

He folded his arms across his chest, still conflicted about whether to allow his desires to rule him so soon. It was obvious Skadi hated him and would need time to accept him—likewise he needed time to forgive her. 'My mother's people, those who were still loyal to her and my father. There are many that disagree with Sven's…methods.'

'Enemies of Sven! He suspected you would betray him.' Anger flooded her expression and she snapped, 'You will bring war and death on Thrudheim with this madness!'

Agnar's own anger began to rise, although it wasn't just directed at her, but at Heimdall and Sven as well. He tried his best to dampen it, to regain control.

'War was inevitable. You were simply too blind to see it! For too long you have been safely imprisoned here on your island. I had thought you would have realised your mistakes by now. That you would beg for my forgiveness and accept my help. But I see you are too spoiled and stubborn to even admit you were wrong. You are nothing more than a puppet queen, blinded by pride and a young maiden's lust!'

Skadi stiffened, but raised her chin regardless, her tone as haughty as ever. 'Let me see this *army* of yours! Sven may have enemies, but I doubt they are significant in number.'

'Gladly! But first…' Agnar deliberately took his time trailing his gaze down her luscious body, a heady poison of desire and triumph intoxicating him in her presence '…you may wish to get dressed first. Your men might think I have already taken you when they see the blood.'

Skadi glanced down at the stains of blood on her tunic and legs. She gave a guttural snort of derision, declaring loudly, 'I have bled more during my monthlies!' Then she looked up at him with a haughty tilt of her nose, impressive considering she was wearing so little. 'You think too highly of yourself, *young buck*! Remember, I am not some innocent maiden easily shocked or frightened by men. I have already been a wife, mother and widow. I have ten more years of experience than you in all matters…including Sven.'

'Young buck?' he asked, incredulous at her words, if not her sharp tongue, which was as arrogant and quick-witted as he remembered. 'No one has ever called me that before. I hope you are not worried about our difference in age… I may have been a child when I last saw you, but I can assure you that I am now a fully grown man in all ways.'

She gasped and colour flooded her cheeks… *A blush!*

It was the first hint that he affected her emotionally, in more ways than anger and fear.

He stepped closer, pulled by some invisible thread, and it took all of his willpower not to reach out and touch her parted lips. 'You might have chosen me then…if I'd been this *young buck*, instead of a boy… You might have preferred me.'

'I doubt that!' she snapped, but she could not meet his eyes. She continued with a pout, 'I grow tired of your looks and welcome parting from you, even if only for a short time. Perhaps when Sven arrives you will leave me again…' Bravely, she raised her chin and spat her last words with venom, 'This time for much longer!'

After her parting barb, she strode away, her hips and hair swinging, her daughter and servant hurrying after her with equal haughty confidence. A female war band, proudly dismissive of him and his men—as if they were no more than unwanted guests.

Agnar watched her leave until she was out of sight, unable to look away from the riddle of her. He knew he wasn't the most attractive of men with his scars—but had that blush indicated a desire for him? He had hoped for affection in time, and gratitude from saving her from Sven. The latter had proven impossible quickly… But might her love for Heimdall be gone? Would she accept him as her husband? Grant him access to her bed? Or, was he reading too much into a simple blush?

'Agnar, shall we remove the barricade?' asked Vali, looking at him curiously, and he realised his men were staring at him expectantly.

Bristling with embarrassment at being caught daydreaming like a love-addled youth, he snapped, 'No, we need to wait for the signal from the approaching ships—I have said this already. Three short blasts followed by one long one.'

Vali nodded, looking more than a little sheepish as he pointed out quietly, 'Yes, it's…been sounded already.'

Chapter Six

Skadi sat with Brenna and Astra in the King's chamber preparing for Nattmal—it was Agnar's chamber now, she supposed, but it still didn't feel real. Her husband of nearly twenty years was dead and she was re-married to his murderer two weeks later.

It seemed the Norns of fate enjoyed making her their fool.

She had not seen Agnar since dawn. He had been busy positioning his men all over the battlements. Her guards had been removed and she'd not seen or heard of Oddmund since the hall had been opened. She presumed he was waiting for things to settle before he approached her for instruction.

Skadi wasn't entirely certain what she was going to do. Servants occasionally hurried in and out like bees, giving news and progress reports to their Queen.

'*How* many ships?' asked Skadi sharply, when the tavern owner whispered an account that surprised her. The tavern owner, Bodil, repeated the answer nervously, probably fearing the Queen's ill temper was directed towards her. 'Twenty, my Queen…so far.'

Skadi felt as if she'd swallowed a rock and she croaked, 'How many men came over the wall?'

'The first attackers were only a small band of warriors, perhaps thirty men led by Agnar—I mean King Agnar…'

She swallowed as Skadi snorted in disgust at his title. 'And… over two hundred men arrived after the second horn was sounded. However, the longships sailing in are also surprisingly well manned. Perhaps, they left some ships behind on the other side of the mountain? Or, they were able to pack all of their number into the twenty ships… It is possible.'

Skadi shook her head. The number was far greater than she could have imagined and, in fact, more than the number of men used to defend Thrudheim. Heimdall had taken half of the men with him raiding—when and how those men would be returned to her, she wasn't sure. Most were young without families or fortune—it was why they had chosen to go raiding. But it also meant a lack of loyalty to Thrudheim… *Would they never return?*

However, that was not her most pressing concern. 'But… *how*? How does he have so many men? I do not understand it!' She gave Bodil a firm look. 'Find out where they have come from. Who are their chieftains? Why did they join with Agnar? What do they hope to gain? And, most importantly, can they be bought? Find out all you can.'

Bodil nodded and dipped respectfully. 'Yes, Your Highness. My tavern butterflies are working the men as we speak. I suspect to learn more after the feast tonight…they will be merry from drink by then.'

'Thank you.' Skadi nodded, comforted by her words. Bodil's women were all pretty and intelligent. They could wrestle secrets from men while removing their boots…as well as other items of clothing.

She turned to Brenna and asked quietly, 'Anything from Gudrun?'

Brenna nodded and slipped a tiny bottle from beneath her sleeve. The glass was murky and stoppered with a circle of cork. 'Your new perfume? Yes, I have it. Although that *damn Vali* follows me everywhere I go!' She glared at the doorway and Skadi presumed he stood guard outside by the way she raised her voice.

Brenna turned back to her and whispered, 'Here it is. You may wish to put it in your purse, be very careful with it.'

Skadi took the bottle from her hands and placed it within the drawstring purse attached to her belt, carefully making sure the stopper was firmly in place. 'Good.'

She glanced towards Astra, who was playing with some dolls quietly in the corner. She was putting them to bed and singing to them softly… She was so young. Despite her bravado against Agnar, she was still a babe who played with dolls and wooden swords.

I will do everything in my power to keep you safe, my darling.

Agnar had had the opportunity to kill Heimdall's only heir and he'd not taken it.

Why?

The most likely conclusion was that he did not want his new wife to hate him. But that didn't guarantee Astra's safety forever. Many an 'accident' had killed a legitimate heir in the past, allowing room for a usurper or second child to take their place. Agnar had said Astra would be his heir unless Skadi gave him a son. But the likelihood of that at her age was small and most men wanted to continue their legacy, to leave something behind of themselves.

Surely she could not trust him to honour such an oath in the future?

Which left her with a difficult choice. Did she honour her marriage vow? Accept him as her husband and pray that she gave him a male heir to secure Astra's safety? Or, should she break her oath for a second time?

Defeating him in combat had failed and now, with the

greater number of his army against her, she couldn't see a way to regain control…at least not openly.

King Sven had always described Agnar as a nuisance, a banished half-brother who bothered him much like a fly might bother a horse's ears. In fact, she had heard very little about Agnar since he had returned to his mother's people. She'd presumed it was because he was no longer deemed a threat.

Had she been lied to? Did the outside world really see her as a puppet queen?

The thought was disconcerting. She had always focused on the needs of Thrudheim first, but had that been a mistake? Should she have learnt more about the wider world from people other than Sven and Heimdall? If she had, she might have realised that Agnar was a threat.

She had barely heard anything about him until Oddmund had returned and informed her of Heimdall's murder. She frowned, thinking again how strange it was that she had heard nothing of Agnar's growing power until now…and yet he had an army and spoke of war as if it were inevitable between Sven and the Rus. Such a war would place Thrudheim in great danger, as it was a strategic alliance that benefited Sven greatly—his enemies would want to break it. She didn't want to drag Thrudheim into a war that had nothing to do with them.

Should she ask her uncle for help in defeating Agnar?

King Olaf, was her mother's brother. She'd not heard from him in many years as his kingdom was far north of Thrudheim. But he would at least be able to support her if Thrudheim found itself dragged into war with the Rus. His support might even allow them to remain impartial…if she were able to rid herself of Agnar first.

Perhaps, once she knew Agnar's army better, their motives and loyalties, she would be better placed to decide about her new husband. His order to feast tonight to celebrate their marriage was enough to ensure a busy household, which suited her plans.

Brenna, Astra and Skadi were the only ones not granted permission to leave without escort. Most of her servants could come and go as they pleased—all in the name of preparation. Her messengers flew back and forth between the hall and the town like sparrows. Vegetables, meat, flour, wine, beer and all manner of demands were veiled with another purpose of gathering information and making plans. The latest was the herbalist and spice seller, Gudrun, who had given her the small vial of 'perfume'.

Skadi gave Brenna a pointed look. 'Did she understand… that I wanted the *same* perfume that her husband Kar enjoyed?' Gudrun was a widow and it was well known that he had died suddenly, and also that he had deserved it.

Brenna nodded. 'She understood. It's exactly what you wanted. She says it is potent. Even a drop will do and it will linger for five to six hours before doing its…work.' Her expression became pinched and she whispered, 'Are you sure about this? I'm afraid for you…'

Skadi squeezed her arm lightly and forced a reassuring smile, although there was nothing she could say to ease her worries.

The tiny bottle wasn't a perfume, it was a weapon. One Skadi would never have imagined she would be willing to use. But with all other noble actions lost to her, she was determined to do all in her power to protect her daughter and her crown.

Even if it was through deceit and cowardice.

The tiny bottle felt as heavy as lead in her purse and her

chest tightened at the prospect of using it to kill a man. But her daughter's safety meant far more to her than any morals.

'I am ready,' Skadi said, rising from the stool where her kohl makeup had been applied to her eyes. She did not want to look beautiful, but fierce. So she had insisted on plenty of it around her blue eyes, knowing they would appear more cat-like and brighter because of it. She wanted to enthral Agnar enough that he did not look too closely at his cup, or what she was putting in it.

Her jewellery was equally captivating and added to her elaborate gown. It was her favourite, a sapphire, close-fitting apron dress with a matching cloak lined with northern fox fur and trimmed at the hem and sleeves with Byzantine embroidered silk. Even the embroidery thread on her dress sparkled in the firelight, as it was woven with thin strands of silver. Her slippers were also made with the same silk and the same silver embroidery.

She wore her decorative silver crown with a sapphire in its centre and tall spikes coming up from the base like icicles. The decorative knotwork around the band was so intricate it looked as if it had been embroidered.

Her entire outfit showed off the trading links, craftsmanship and wealth of her island. Her kingdom might be small, but it was powerful and not without friends. She picked up four blades and attached two to her belt, one as an eating blade and the other as a ceremonial dagger. Then she lifted her leg on to the stool and strapped the third to her thigh. As she was in the process of strapping on the other, the door burst open and Agnar stormed in.

'What is taking you so long, my men are hungry!' he snarled impatiently running a hand through the mess of his dark hair. He stopped dead when he saw her thigh and stared at it as if he'd never seen a woman's naked leg before. The knot of his throat worked as he swallowed and slowly raised his eyes.

Skadi wasn't sure what to make of his lust-filled gaze and was surprised when a shiver of pleasure ran down her spine. But she dismissed it as pure vanity. Heimdall had grown bored of her over the years—it was flattering to be considered beautiful again…even if it was by her enemy.

With a bad-tempered huff, she finished buckling the weapon and then dropped her leg, sweeping the fabric back into place with a flick of her wrist. 'I am ready.' She glanced meaningfully at Brenna who nodded, subtly patting her own leg, where her blades were also hidden. Surrounded by their enemy they had to be prepared for anything.

They had agreed already that Brenna would sleep with Astra in Skadi and Astra's old room tonight—she would not eat with them. Brenna would be responsible for all of Astra's meals and care, as her unofficial personal guard.

Already, Agnar's second, Vali, had moved his things into Brenna's old room, so it had seemed natural that Skadi insist her close friend sleep with Astra and not lose her place of respect within the hall. The room also had a small shuttered window high up by the roof, which could be reached with enough chests stacked on top of each other—Skadi had moved many into the chamber claiming they were Brenna's possessions or linen storage. The linens could easily be tied together and used to carry them down to safety…*if things went wrong, they would have an escape route.*

She shuddered at the thought.

But at least Brenna's orders were clear. Defend Astra with her life, and get her to Gudrun. The herbalist knew the forests well, she could hide Astra there if needs be, and there was also the whaler, who had offered to take Astra and Skadi anywhere they wished.

One thing was certain. All of Skadi's people would help her—many had already pledged their allegiance, whispering vows of loyalty among the deliveries.

After careful thought, Skadi had decided that Astra would be safest with King Olaf in the far north—her mother's people. But honestly, she wasn't even sure if that was the wisest choice. If there was going to be a power struggle among the petty kingdoms—her uncle included—perhaps King Sven was a wiser choice after all? Although it made her stomach churn…because Astra would still be a hostage regardless… or worse, married off while still a child.

No, she could not risk such a thing!

'Is Astra not joining us?' he asked.

Immediately Skadi shook her head. 'Astra is too tired.' She didn't bother glancing back at her daughter, wanting Agnar's focus to remain on her.

Agnar was a few feet inside the chamber and any embarrassment he might have felt at seeing her naked skin was immediately forgotten. He examined her in the same way she might check the quality of a piece of jewellery, or a sword. No admiration, just a cold sweep from crown to slippers. She almost preferred the embarrassed flash of lust…at least that had felt human.

This cold assessment reminded her of how Heimdall had behaved towards her after their marriage, as if she were nothing more than a trophy that had lost its charm and beauty once it had been won.

I am a queen! she reminded herself firmly.

Ignoring Agnar's offered arm, she strode past him and out into the main hall, adjusting the silver arm-ring that she always wore out of habit. It had been her mother's. Perhaps, she should give Astra the arm-ring, in case she had to send her to Olaf? It would be a reminder and proof that they were kin. She vowed to do so tonight after the feast.

She'd not seen King Olaf, since her wedding... *My first wedding*, she corrected, the thought chafing at her neck, making it hard to swallow.

But then she passed her throne and saw row upon row of benches filling the cavernous space. Hundreds of people quietened as she entered, many of them familiar faces, but a disturbingly large amount were strangers—all armed men.

Every torch was lit, painting the hall in a golden and welcoming glow. Embroidered runners ran down the tables, sapphire blue on white linen, the colours of Thrudheim. The banners of Thrudheim were also hung from the beams, but they were interspersed with the black head of a wolf on a scarlet background, presumably Agnar's banner.

In front of the two thrones, a beautifully carved table had been placed. It was set up as if for a special occasion. Usually, she sat at the front of the hall on a similar bench to those of the crowd, although facing towards them, in case they wished to speak with her or Heimdall—if he were home. Oddmund, Astra, Brenna and whomever they wished to favour that night would also sit with her.

But tonight, it would just be Agnar and herself, alone on the uncomfortable thrones. She walked around the dais to reach the steps and then climbed them. She was used to being the centre of attention and over the years she'd become accustomed to it, taking her time with everything, she did so to not make mistakes or appear uncertain.

However, when she saw the two thin cushions placed on each seat, she had a petty desire to be vindictive. Agnar was walking at a slower pace behind her, so she took the opportunity to snatch his cushion from his seat and without a glimmer of shame added it to her own.

Agnar was staring at her as he stepped on to the dais, probably wondering why she would steal something so insignificant as a cushion from him. But he said nothing. To demand its return would seem pathetic and, of course, like all men, he was too proud to request another cushion in case it made him appear weak.

So, he sat down without comment…and then shifted, and shifted again, like a bear trying to scratch his back. He tried to do it subtly, but if anything, the frequent small movements only proved his growing discomfort and irritation.

Skadi smiled.

Chapter Seven

'You seem pleased with yourself,' Agnar said as the hall began to bustle with servants delivering platters of steaming food to the crowded tables. An entire suckling pig was placed down in front of him, lying flat on a silver platter, stewed apples glistening around it, a carving knife placed at the piglet's little feet.

His stomach clenched, as he remembered Astra running towards him bare foot. He'd been bluffing about harming the child, had only said it to ensure Skadi's obedience. But when Astra had flown at him from seemingly nowhere, he'd had a moment where his instincts had almost caused him to do the unthinkable.

Thankfully, he'd realised in time and had been able to stop and disarm her safely. But, Odin's teeth, *what if he hadn't!*

He tried to shrug off the unnecessary guilt that plagued him. The child was safe and Skadi had agreed to marry him. He'd achieved a goal that had once seemed impossible.

Tonight, he would allow himself a small celebration, because tomorrow the hard work would begin.

More dishes were placed on the table until the linen that covered it was no longer visible.

Did they expect them to eat everything?

It was a lot for two people and he hated waste. Too many

days of starvation had left him with a deeper appreciation of plenty and going forward he would insist on proper management of their supplies. He would have to ensure the servants were using leftovers wisely and providing for those less fortunate than those allowed a seat within the hall.

*Although...*he probably *could* manage most of it, after the events of the past few days. His mouth watered at the sweet and salty smell of the roasted meat. He hadn't eaten properly in months. Had he lost weight? Was that why his rump hurt so much on this throne?

'It is hard to be pleased, considering my position,' Skadi replied tartly, followed by a sly and mockingly innocent question, 'Does the seat of power disappoint you, King Agnar?'

He would have smiled, if he wasn't so uncomfortable. It felt as if he were sitting on a bag of broken blades. The throne's seat hadn't looked that rough, cold possibly, because it was stone, but the seat had looked reasonably flat.

Until, of course, he'd sat down…

Still, there had been many times over the years when he'd almost doubted ever achieving his goal of returning to Thrudheim as its king. An uncomfortable chair seemed a small price to pay for attaining it.

'Did all of your ancestors have rumps of steel?' he asked mildly, not bothered by her teasing. It was clear she did not welcome his arrival. But the deed was done and in time she would realise it was for the best.

Skadi turned a little in her double-cushioned seat to see him better. It was awkward to speak to one another in such fixed chairs and it seemed as if Skadi would find fault with everything he said tonight, because she declared, 'These thrones were carved seven generations ago from the same mountain cliffs that shield us today. They were a gift from the first King of Thrudheim to his bride, Queen Estrid.'

'He didn't like her much, then,' grumbled Agnar with another shift of his buttocks.

The amusement seemed to die in her eyes and she answered sombrely, 'I suppose not.' Lifting the glass jug, she poured wine into two equally ornate glass chalices, the blue matching perfectly with the Thrudheim colours. The banners on the battlements had all been replaced with his own, but the tablecloths, tapestries and some of the hall banners remained in the blue-and-white stripe of her family.

'What do you think of my banners in your hall?' he asked. For some reason he wanted to antagonise her enough to bite back at him again. He preferred her spitefulness and amusement to the sad expression that had graced her face a moment ago.

Had Heimdall not been kind to her in their marriage, or did she simply miss him? Both thoughts were alarming in different ways. He'd hated the man, but he'd thought he was at least kind to Skadi. He'd spent a long time wooing her by all accounts.

Why he should care about her sadness was beyond him. *Perhaps his vengeance wanted her to suffer more?*

He had to admit that he'd expected more regret from her once her anger had settled. At least an apology for what she had done all those years ago. But it appeared she had no regrets for the great suffering she had caused. Which only infuriated him further.

Unconsciously, his hand shifted to the small throwing axe he always kept at his side—the touch of the old blade often comforted him when he was frustrated. It reminded him of his purpose and goals. Unfortunately, his goals and purpose were exactly what was infuriating him right now!

'They look…' She paused, sipping her wine with apparent boredom as she examined the black wolf-headed banners on a blood-red field hanging from every beam in her hall. Even Agnar had to admit the number of them was a little excessive. Finally, Skadi answered him with a disappointed sigh, *'Ugly.'*

At his burst of laughter, she raised a single pale brow in question.

Had she thought to offend him? Probably.

But even he could see the colours clashed badly with the serene blue, white and silver of the rest of Thrudheim's decorations.

Did she hope to intimidate him? He chuckled at the thought and her eyes narrowed further. She looked strange with the dark kohl painted thickly around her eyes—sharp and cruel. Tonight, he suspected she was testing him again, with her wit rather than her sword.

He was willing to rise to her challenge.

She had grown into a formidable queen. The woman in front of him today had worn her crown for so long that it was no longer a costume, but a second skin, deeply ingrained in her every word and action. He doubted she would, or even *could*, admit that she'd been wrong…that she'd made a terrible mistake.

When he'd last seen her, she'd been naive and frightened—easily led by the men in her life, tentatively playing the role of Queen, a young maiden's desires clouding her judgement. Things could have been so different for both of them, if only he'd been a little older.

What had he expected from her? Part of him had imagined the same beautiful, frightened girl to welcome his vengeance. As a youth he had fantasised about freeing her from Heimdall and Sven's imprisonment, that she would run to him with tears of repentance and fall on her knees, begging him for forgiveness.

A fanciful notion!

The formidable woman beside him regretted nothing, not even her mistakes. He'd realised it straight away when she'd fiercely defended her child and crown with sword and shield—she would not bend until she was broken.

Skadi was, and had always been, a volatile creature…he supposed that was why he was so obsessed with her. The flaming jewel he could never possess.

Belatedly, he realised she'd been waiting for his answer as she placed his wine closer to her silver trencher with a thud. He picked up the glass absently, pleased by the surprising weight of it, and sipped from it slowly. Partly to rile his bride, who was obviously waiting for an answer, and partly because he'd never drunk from a glass before and was half-afraid it might break if it knocked against his teeth.

'I agree,' he said. 'The Thrudheim blue clashes with the scarlet of my banner.'

'It does.' She nodded. 'Red is such a garish colour. I have never liked it.'

'It is cheaper to produce than blue. Especially *that* shade of blue.' He flicked a wrist towards her banners.

'Indeed…' She smiled wickedly before delivering another verbal slap. 'I suppose that is why you picked it, because it was cheap.'

'Do you think me ashamed of my past?' he asked, a little irritated that she'd struck home with her poisoned arrow.

She shrugged. 'I think it would be a disgraceful waste to destroy hundreds of years of Thrudheim tradition on an *ugly* red banner.' She then sipped her wine and smiled pleasantly at the servants positioning the final dishes to their table. He was surprised they'd managed to fit much more on.

'Is everything to your liking, Your Highness?' asked one

of the girls, looking nervously towards him and then back at their mistress as if uncertain.

Did he look annoyed?

He didn't really care too much about the banners, although, he would like his insignia present—the wolf's head meant a lot to him. His mother had been known as the She-Wolf and, as he'd grown up, he'd grown to have more in common with the snarling beast than his father's corrupt side of the family.

A self-conscious thought rattled through his head. *Did she think him as ugly as his banners?*

The battle for revenge had not been kind to his face. He was covered in scars and women tended to be afraid of him—despite him hardly ever approaching them.

He was significantly younger than Heimdall at least, something which was finally in his favour. But perhaps she had truly loved her husband—she'd certainly been infatuated with him as a young woman. Uncomfortably, Agnar realised that if he'd been the same age as the handsome Heimdall, Skadi might still not have accepted him, regardless of their betrothal. She was certainly far too beautiful to be besotted by someone with his face.

'It looks delicious, thank you,' Skadi said sweetly to the servant, before turning back to face him, and adding quietly, 'It is customary for a king to serve his Queen first and then for him to eat the first bite… A small piece of bread will do if you are not hungry. Otherwise, no one else can begin…'

Chapter Eight

Was that true? Were they all waiting for him to take the first bite?

It seemed so ridiculous, but he supposed it made sense and all of the hall's eyes were watching him expectantly. He'd been so wrapped up in speaking with Skadi he'd not noticed until now.

When he did nothing, she continued with an exasperated expression, 'I would not wish for the food to spoil. You insisted on a feast, but we will be limited this winter without more supplies coming from outside, Sven provides our winter grain…or, at least, he used to.'

He reached for the circular loaf of bread. The top was dusted with what looked like a colourful burnt yellow spice that would cost more in weight than his leather and fur-lined boots. A flower motif had been cut into the dough before baking, the petals rising up, as if seeking the sun like a waterlily.

He glanced at the other side dishes and noticed they were presented in similar ways. The honey had been poured into an elaborate gold and rock-crystal jar, designed to look like a beehive, the gold spoon crafted into the shape of a bee, with an extra-long stinger as its handle.

The roasted vegetables were in pottery dishes made to

look like wicker baskets, as if they'd come straight from the field, and arrived at their table already cooked and drizzled in an herb-infused oil. The braised cabbages with bacon were in pottery bowls shaped and painted like cabbage leaves. Even the butter had been moulded into a silver cup shaped like a butter barrel, the blunt knife stabbed in its centre looking like a churning oar.

Whimsical and ridiculously extravagant.

But he supposed this was what came of idle hands. Skadi might not realise it, but she had been kept prisoner for nearly twenty years. A willing prisoner, but still a…captive.

He tore off a petal from the bread and reached for the honey, the silver stinger thin and fiddly in his hands. But he persevered, drizzling a small amount on to the tip of the delicate petal. The salt dish was nearby and, of course, it was shaped into a sapphire flat fish. He pinched a little of it and sprinkled it on to the honey.

He glanced at Skadi and her face was tight and pale as she watched his movements. He wondered if it was the tradition of sharing bread and salt that bothered her—as by the laws of hospitality, it ensured no harm came to a visiting guest.

But, of course, he was not a guest. He was Thrudheim's ruler and now her husband.

No, it was obvious, what bothered her was that he knew how she liked her bread and honey. Or…at least, how she'd used to eat it.

All those years ago, on that terrible day when he had arrived to claim his betrothed, he'd watched her in fascination at the evening meal, as she carefully added a tiny sprinkle of salt to her bread and honey. It had confused him and he had tried it himself immediately, surprised by how the sweetness seemed to intensify with the sprinkle of salt.

He lifted the petal and held it in front of Skadi's lips.

Her eyes widened but, with a quick glance at the watching crowd, she opened her mouth and bit into the bread with pearly white teeth.

The crust of the bread crunched with a soft crack and then she pulled away delicately, chewing the bread and wiping the crumbs away with an embroidered napkin. His entire body stiffened with longing and he wasn't sure what had aroused him. Was it the secret knowledge they both shared, or the sight of her lips so close to his fingers, willingly opening for him?

He shifted in his seat, for once grateful for the discomfort as it brought him back to his senses. Over half of the petal was left and he popped the entirety of it into his mouth and chewed.

The spell was broken.

The awaiting crowd immediately began to eat, with a tide of clattering dishes and cracking of bread, the sounds running from the front to the back of the hall in a noisy wave, although most of it was from his men. Thrudheim's people were solemn after their quick and unexpected defeat. The locals did not care to speak with his men, as if they were still uncertain and afraid of his arrival. He could understand that—he'd tried to limit the damage of his invasion, but there had still been a handful of deaths and plenty of injuries.

He carved the suckling pig, for the first time confident in his task, and grateful that it meant he had to stand up. There was a large silver trencher beside it and he laid the slices of meat and crackling on top. After he'd filled the trencher, he turned to Skadi, who was watching him thoughtfully while sipping from her glass of wine.

'Is that enough?'

'I should think so,' she replied tartly, then nodded to a nearby servant who lifted the remainder of the suckling pig and took it to a nearby table to add to their offering. It was torn apart in moments by his hungry men—they'd not had fresh meat in months. The sheer glut on display was overwhelming, each table had mutton stews, or some kind of roasted joint available. They crammed it in their mouths as if afraid they would never taste it again. He knew that feeling well and smiled, which only made Skadi look at him with further disgust.

He sat back down on the cursed throne. It was somehow even more uncomfortable than before. Had she made an offering to the house elves, asking them to place tiny thorns in the stone? He swore his trousers snagged on the seat as he shifted awkwardly for the hundredth time. He offered the trencher of meat to Skadi, who stabbed at it with her eating knife and picked up one small slice, before laying it carefully on her plate.

He was sure she'd taken so little just to make him appear foolish.

'I can get the rest,' she said firmly. 'There is no need to serve me every dish.'

It felt like a rebuke, although he had no idea what he'd done wrong. He had thought to show her respect. Irritated by her ill humour and his own discomfort, he began to serve himself in silence, heaping the variety of food on to his platter and then eating it with relish. He hoped that some sort of inspiration for conversation would soon flow.

Had Thrudheim become his prison now?

After everything he and his mother had sacrificed to regain his birthright, was a miserable marriage his only reward?

This was not the marriage he had imagined. No, he'd thought it would be a little awkward at first, as he would have to learn to forgive her, but he'd hoped in the end they would be comfortable together. Except, she'd not asked for forgiveness…and it was clear she *hated* him.

He'd been so focused on getting to this point—of finally winning back Skadi and Thrudheim, that he'd not actually considered what married life with Skadi would be like.

You have everything you ever wanted...and you are still not content?

But what did he want from her? Love? Such things were for lust-addled youths, not grown men and women. Besides, what could he possibly say to charm her?

Condolences for your dead husband...the one whom I killed.

Better to be practical—she would understand him in time. 'You should make a speech to your people. Reassure them that all is well.'

Skadi stopped chewing and stared at him as if appalled by the suggestion. 'Is it? Is *all* well?'

'Yes, as I have said before, you and your daughter are safe with me.'

Skadi leaned in close, and he caught the scent of her perfume, which was also extravagant and whimsical, like her array of pretty dishes. One of the many requests she'd made today had been to order a special perfume made and brought to her personally by her handmaid. He'd taken it—perhaps wrongly—as a sign that she might be more willing to welcome him as her husband.

However, he'd not felt particularly *welcomed* since sitting down to eat with her.

Which was proven even further, when she hissed back at him, '*Safe?* You broke into my home and forced me to marry you!'

'It was necessary,' He shrugged, dismissing her outrage. In his mind, he'd done nothing wrong and, eventually, once she began to trust him, his Queen would feel the same... *He hoped.* 'Your perfume smells nice,' he added, hoping a compliment might ease her anger.

'I'm not...' She blinked, confused by his awkward flattery—she wasn't alone. He was beginning to wonder if he would fail at the one task he'd thought would be easy...being happy. Her mouth snapped shut for a moment, before she huffed, 'You had no right to do any of this!'

'I do and you know it.' He kept the statement crisp and calm, not wanting to rile her, but wanting to make his point clear. Fixing her with a heavy look, he added, 'We were betrothed. I stood right there...' He pointed at the bottom of the dais with his eating knife. '*Twice!* Once to ask for your hand in marriage—which was *granted*!' He barked the last word sharply. He might have only seen six winters the first time, but he remembered it clearly. 'And...well, we all know what happened when I came to claim you for the second time after your father's death.'

For the first time, while speaking to him, her eyes softened with genuine sympathy. 'You were too young.'

'As were you.'

Her spine stiffened and her black-rimmed eyes narrowed with fury and indignation. 'I did the best for my people and for myself! A ten-year-old boy could not rule Thrudheim, or even be a true husband to me for several more years! The petty Kings were planning to overthrow me! Do you have any idea what I was facing?' Her voice had risen, but he knew it was fuelled by guilt as well as rage. She *had* doubted her decision, he was now certain of it, and it gave him a glimmer of hope for the future.

'I understand why you felt that way.'

Her face reddened, but after a quick glance at the watching and curious crowd—who'd become significantly quieter since the start of their argument—she lowered her voice. '*You understand?* Yet you still judge me for it! Killed my husband—Thrudheim's King—and for what? A promise given to a *child*? You threatened the life of my daughter and forced me to marry you, all so that you could be King! Have you even considered that *perhaps* the reason my daughter does not wish to attend our wedding feast is because you *murdered* her father! A father she has not yet mourned, because he died only two weeks ago!'

By the time she had finished her rant, she was breathless and he realised how much Heimdall must have meant to her. His hope died just as quickly as it had flickered to life. He could not find the words to answer her.

'Do you deny killing him?' she snapped.

It was clear she would never forgive him for killing the man she loved. He met her eyes and sealed their miserable fate. 'I do not deny it.'

'You have *no shame* for what you have done?'

'None. And I would do it again.' Turning away, he picked up his glass chalice and was about to sip from it, resolved to the grim future that lay ahead.

A knife clattered to the dais floor, metal on stone. Skadi must have dropped her eating knife. He glanced between the two thrones, but saw nothing. Skadi was staring at him expectantly, her hands clasped tightly in her lap, the knuckles white as bone.

'My eating knife... I think it landed by your feet. Please can you get it for me?' she asked politely, which threw him far more than anything else she'd said tonight.

The thrones were made of heavy stone, so he couldn't push back his seat to take a better look.

Putting down his chalice, he nodded and crouched down beneath the heavy tablecloth. On the dais floor he saw the knife lying on the ground a couple of feet away. It was further from their feet than he would have expected.

However, crawling beneath a table was far more pleasant than facing her accusations or that awful seat, so he shuffled around until he could reach it, then clambered back out with as much dignity as he could muster. He took the time to wipe the blade with his own untouched linen napkin.

At least it had given him a moment to consider his next words to her, 'I am not sorry about Heimdall, but I am sorry about Astra losing her father at such a young age. We both know the pain of that.'

Skadi continued to stare at him with a red face. She didn't even thank him as he handed her the knife. Instead, she stared at him intensely and then surprised him by asking, 'You must have had help to grow such an army. Have the petty Kings decided to revolt against King Sven?'

'Many are not happy with him, but very few have the courage to go against him.'

She frowned. 'But you convinced some of them? King Leif? If you think he will support you against King Sven, then you are mistaken. The man lacks warriors and a spine.'

'Not him.'

'Surely not King Erik?'

'You think all of my men are gathered together from an assortment of disgruntled petty kings, with no real alliance to speak of?' He laughed, picking up his glass chalice and gesturing to his men with it. Her shrewd eyes followed his movement like a hawk.

'Are they not?' she asked the question just as he was about to drink, reaching out her hand to rest it on his elbow to stop him. The touch surprised him, and he lowered his arm to see her better. The heat of her palm soaking through the cloth of his tunic raised goosebumps along his arms.

'There were a handful of mercenaries who sought glory—but they proved themselves to be unfit.' He frowned as he remembered the men who had attacked Skadi in her chamber. 'Half of my army is made up of the men I fought and trained with in the east.'

Her hand tightened on his elbow and his lower body stirred with desire. 'The other half?'

'King Olaf.'

He smiled at the shock on her face, and lifted the glass to his lips, trying to pretend he was not affected by her touch, despite feeling lightheaded. Why did her touch unsettle him? His heart seemed to leap into a running beat whenever she was close. Gritting his teeth against the intoxicating scent of her, he opened his lips to drink.

Suddenly, she jumped, or thumped his arm—he wasn't sure which—and the chalice spilled scarlet liquid down his tunic. Thankfully, his reactions were quick and he managed to save the precious glass from falling…or at least he would have, if her hand hadn't then flicked out a second time to knock it out of his hand.

It smashed on the stone floor beside him, and he stared at the shattered pieces and spray of wine on the dais floor in shock, as an uneasy thought slowly crept in.

Poison.

Chapter Nine

One of her servants, Inga, hurried forward. 'I will get a bucket and broom to clean it up, Your Highness.'

'Bring some lye soap, too… I don't want the floor to be stained,' said Skadi, although honestly, she didn't care if the floor cracked in two. She was more worried about Inga, considering the subtle strength of the poison she'd almost served to her new husband. It was bad enough to kill a man she hated, but to kill an innocent by accident?

There were some things even she couldn't stomach.

Agnar hadn't moved since she'd swatted away the poisoned chalice and she had avoided his eyes for fear that one look at her guilty face would be enough to condemn her. Instead, she tried to brazenly act as if nothing had happened, nervously picking at her food and swallowing it down even though it felt like gravel in her throat.

Inga returned moments later with two buckets, one filled with soapy water and a scrubbing brush, the other containing some straw and ash. Diligently Inga spread the straw and ash over the spill, pressing down with the brush to soak up the wine, and then began to sweep it up into the bucket.

Skadi called out to her again, 'Inga, be careful with the glass! Throw both buckets in the rubbish pit after and be sure to wash your hands thoroughly…' She could feel Agnar's stony gaze on her and she added weakly, 'Glass shards can be very dangerous and wine will stain your fingernails.' She turned to another servant, trying to ignore the wild pounding of her heart. 'Please fetch a new chalice for the King.'

She turned back to Agnar and swallowed when she saw the cold fury in his eyes.

He knew.

'What was in it?' he snapped, his voice far too loud for Skadi's comfort. She was sure Inga had heard him. A couple of the tables at the front of the hall had also stopped what they were doing and had now turned to stare at her accusingly. She recognised one of the men as his second Vali, the red-haired warrior who Brenna hated—for good reason.

'Nothing.' She busied herself by picking up her chalice. She took a sip and realised it was empty. Not bothering to wait for a servant to refill it, she poured herself more wine from the jug and took a large gulp.

Will he kill me now?

It would be the perfect excuse to dispose of her…

How could she send word to Brenna to escape? Would it be obvious? She suspected her people would revolt at her death. But would Astra and Brenna even make it out alive?

Her hand began to tremble. Agnar grabbed her chalice and put it firmly back on the table with such a heavy thud that the wine spilled over the rim, staining the white-and-blue linen with a splash of scarlet.

A dark omen. Not unlike the horrible splashes of oppressive blood-red hanging all around her.

She stared down at the stain, guilt churning like a whirlpool in her stomach. She had tried to murder him. Slipping a drop of the poison into his wine, while he rooted around under the table for her knife. The fact he'd even agreed to do that still surprised her.

Even worse, she still wasn't sure if she'd done the right thing by saving him. But she couldn't deny the doubt and hesitation that had plagued her for those last few moments. When he'd raised his glass to his lips, she'd found herself finding any excuse to question him, to delay her crime.

Why had she done that? Guilt? Curiosity? Regret?

And, then he'd revealed that her uncle, the only person she thought might protect her, had worked *with* Agnar. She couldn't kill him until she knew why her uncle had given him aid. But had she put Astra and herself in danger by doing so?

She couldn't understand her actions, and neither could Agnar by the sound of it…although, for different reasons.

'Why did you strike it from my hands if there was nothing in it?' he snarled, looking a lot like the fierce wolf's head that roared across his banners. But there was something else behind his anger…a flash of hurt and betrayal. It was the same look she had seen all those years ago when she'd hurried Heimdall away from his bleeding body.

It was a stark reminder that he was a man and not a beast.

She forced herself to look at him, to truly see him. He was an unusual-looking man, strong rough features marred by many nicks and scars, serpent-green eyes that were deep set and brooding. No beard, but plenty of stubble instead, suggesting he did not care to shave or groom a beard like most men. Yet his hair was long, shiny and, when combed, as it was now…extraordinarily beautiful.

Why was she noticing this now?

Probably, because it will be the last thing you see!

'I saw a fly,' she mumbled, her chest so tight she was almost tempted to loosen the ties of her gown.

'A fly?' He glared back at her and she shrugged, reaching for the bread and tearing off another petal, desperate for a distraction.

'We had a pestilence brought about by a swathe of flies last year… I did not want to see such a devastating illness return.' It was the most feasible excuse she could think of for her behaviour and she hoped it would be enough.

It was not.

Agnar's voice bellowed out to the rest of the hall. 'Vali! If I die quickly and with no obvious reason…' His jaw hardened and his next ominous words chilled Skadi to the bone '…you *know* what to do.'

Vali nodded, stabbing his dagger forcefully into a chunk of meat and picking it up to take a large greasy bite. Skadi wasn't sure what would happen if Agnar died suspiciously, but she was certain that she wouldn't like it.

Skadi swallowed nervously, as the sound of Vali's chewing seemed to fill the silence.

She couldn't kill Agnar with poison. Not until she knew the truth about her uncle's involvement. A strange relief washed through her and she realised she had not wanted to stain her soul with murder…even if it was justified.

Now that she knew her uncle had helped Agnar in his quest to take Heimdall's throne she had to claim ignorance and learn more about her uncle's feelings on the matter.

Why would he help Agnar, if he were happy with Heimdall? And, why wait all these years to give his support to Agnar now? None of it made sense! She rallied her thoughts and feelings to calmly ask, 'Why would I want to kill you *if*, as you say, King Olaf, my uncle, supports you?'

'He does support me,' replied Agnar, placing his hands in his lap. He didn't reach for any more food or drink and she couldn't blame him for it.

'Surely, not until recently, or you would have come sooner,' she laughed, but the amusement died in her throat when she saw the seriousness of his expression. 'Why would he support you? The Rus are a threat to all of us!'

'A threat?' he chuckled bitterly, but gave a strange nod of agreement. 'Sven is the only one threatened by them and only then because of their connection with me. Your uncle, values trade with the east and would prefer a fairer agreement than the one currently provided.'

'But…' her mind struggled to accept his words '…why has he never spoken of it? I know I haven't seen him for many years. But we are family, he could have sent word to me about his grievances.'

'He sent several messengers to Heimdall about it, but was always ignored. Did Heimdall not tell you?' Agnar's question was said with a knowing look that made her anger flare.

She scowled at him, but answered politely, 'Unfortunately not. I suppose I will have to take your word for it.'

'The very presence of his men under my command is proof enough that I speak the truth.'

She tried her best to ignore the smugness of his tone. 'My uncle approved of my match to Heimdall. I am simply…surprised that he would change his mind.'

'Things have changed… For one, I am now a grown man. Your uncle realises that what suited both of you then is no longer of benefit to him now.' His jaw flexed as if even acknowledging the truth of it irritated him. 'He supported me in challenging Sven and becoming King of Thrudheim. He wishes no further interference from Sven in the running of this important and strategic kingdom.'

'Sven does not rule Thrudheim.'

'But he told you to marry Heimdall and Heimdall has always agreed to his demands.'

She stiffened because that much had been true. King Sven had been the one to tell her that she could not rule alone and had even suggested Heimdall as a potential match, explaining that she would need a warrior husband, or her kingdom would fall under attack from the petty Kings or the Rus—who threatened him daily. 'I married Heimdall because I was vulnerable.'

'Being a young and unmarried woman wasn't what made you vulnerable. Back then, you had enough support from the petty Kings to remain secure in your position. Sven manipulated you into thinking otherwise and then over time took all of your forces from you. *Now* you are vulnerable.'

She didn't like how true that sounded, but she couldn't argue it. The forces of Thrudheim *had* diminished over the years. Raiding and mining was dangerous work and had stolen the lives of many of Thrudheim's young men. 'You are King Sven's half-brother. Surely it would have benefited him more to have a close relative like yourself as ruler of Thrudheim rather than a warrior with no connection like Heimdall.'

To her surprise, he shook his head. 'No, it would not. It would distance you further from him. I am his half-brother. If I married you and we had children, he could not marry them or take you as his bride. He wanted you to remain under his thumb, while also providing a possible match for him or his sons in the future. Heimdall was the perfect choice—he paid him well to court and support you. He feared that he would be surrounded by powerful Rus families on both sides of the sea if you married me.'

Raw embarrassment and pain flashed through her. How dare he comment on her life as if he knew everything! And, yet, describing Heimdall's deliberate 'seduction' of her felt brutally close to the truth.

But she still had her pride and refused to admit her past mistakes to someone who was so blinded by his own lust for power. 'You know nothing of my marriage. It is clear you hate Heimdall and King Sven. I would be a fool to trust you, especially with the life of my child at stake. You say you will claim her as your heir. But I do not believe it. No normal man would willingly give up his name, his legacy, for another man's child, especially his enemy's!'

'Perhaps I am not normal,' he admitted with an amused smile that made her want to scream. 'But marrying you and ruling Thrudheim has always been my goal… I have never thought to have another.'

She stared at him, trying to distinguish between the lies and the truth. Unable to be certain of either, with a sniff she said, 'If King Olaf believes you are Thrudheim's future, then there is little I can do about it—he was my last hope for Astra's safety…from both you and Sven! I suspect war will be the only rotten fruit of your scheming with my uncle. But I will have to accept it for now.' She pushed away her trencher, her appetite all gone.

'It was inevitable,' he replied. 'Are you done eating?'

She swallowed a sudden knot in her throat.

Did he want to bed her now?

'Yes, I have instructed a bard to tell the story of Thrudheim—I thought it best you learn some of our history. Let me call him forward.' She lifted her hand to get the bard's attention, but with lightning speed Agnar grabbed her wrist and lowered it back on to the table.

'Not tonight. Another time, perhaps,' he said and his hand flexed around her wrist, almost as if he didn't want to let her go. It was as rough and as calloused as his face, but warm, so hot it sent a wave of goosebumps up her arm.

'This will be a poor feast without entertainment.'

She was trying her best not to seem too obvious in her delaying tactics, but Agnar merely shrugged. 'My men will entertain themselves.' His fingers shifted, a subtle touch that was almost a caress.

I will not be your entertainment!

Twisting her wrist, she broke his hold easily. 'I would rather not witness such revelry. I will retire for the night, but do enjoy drinking with your men.' Loudly so that all could hear her indignant fury, she said, 'If any harm comes to my daughter, I *will* kill you. This I vow before all my people and the gods!'

She rose from her seat, but to her dismay Agnar followed her, until they stood side by side.

Unlike her first wedding feast, there were no jokes or cheers, no bawdy pushing of the bride and groom towards their bedchamber. Her people looked up at her with pity and dismay in their eyes and she swallowed the weight of their gaze.

I have disappointed them. The thought cut her like a knife and she balled her fists, hating every moment of her shame. Tonight, she would be bedded by the new King and she'd never felt less human.

Once again, she was a trophy to be owned and coveted. But this time she was fully aware of it.

With as much dignity as she could muster, she raised her chin and turned away from him. She heard him follow her, his footsteps heavy and calm. She refused to glance back as she made her way off the royal dais. She walked in front of the benches, her people lowering their gaze as she passed, while Agnar's warriors smothered looks of amusement.

It was a slow and humiliating walk out of her hall, leaving as a queen, but knowing the following day she would return as a wife…*lesser*. Her discomfort didn't ease as she continued down the corridor to the King's chamber. Heimdall had carried her on their wedding night, his men making lewd comments, until he'd been forced to kick them away and rush them into her chamber with a laugh.

In contrast, Agnar followed her like an unwelcome shadow, the darkness of the corridor closing in on her as she headed towards the open doorway of the chamber. A couple of torches were lit within, the curtains pulled aside, the bed as imposing as it had always been.

Heimdall's bed.

She turned quickly in the doorway of the chamber, almost knocking into Agnar who she hadn't realised was quite so close. Her hands instinctively pushed against the soft wool of his tunic, a scarlet red that matched his banners and the stain of poisoned wine.

'Is there any need for this?' she whispered, glancing back down the corridor, grateful to see no guards or warriors watching them.

A muscle jumped in Agnar's jaw and his green eyes softened with sympathy, almost giving her hope until he said firmly, 'Yes, there is.'

Chapter Ten

Skadi's head lowered, her hand not leaving his chest, her fingers splayed open in a desperate plea that he'd immediately denied. 'I had hoped never to do this with another man,' she said quietly and his heart dropped like a stone.

The heat of her touch was spreading across his chest, like the roots of a tree, sending out threads of awareness throughout his body. His senses answered like the wind in the trees, swaying towards her with desperate yearning.

Did she realise how powerfully she affected him? Her words cut deeply to the bone, even as he leaned into her touch, wanting more of her. His chest tightened and he clenched his fists at his sides to stop from pulling her back, as she turned and walked into the room with a miserable sigh.

Yes, he had been foolish to think she would welcome him.

After meeting her again, he'd realised how pragmatic and proud she could be. He'd not expected her to relish the prospect of sleeping with him, but hearing her say that she'd hoped never to do this with another man had affected him far more than he would have imagined.

It reminded him that Heimdall had been her husband for nearly twenty years—most of his lifetime—she had slept beside Heimdall, became a mother to his child… Agnar had taken that peace from her and, for the first time, as he followed her into her husband's chamber, he actually felt as though he deserved the nickname Sven had given him: *Usurper.*

A handmaid rose from a stool in the corner and put down some needlework. She hurried forward as Skadi sat in front of a table and began to gently remove the Queen's crown from her head.

Stubborn and sanctimonious! Spoilt and brazen!

So many insults came to mind when he argued with her, but he couldn't seem to find the courage to say them. He'd seen the flash of outrage and pain earlier when he'd called her a puppet queen. Did she truly not realise how badly Sven and Heimdall had manipulated her?

Part of him was reluctant to hurt her again.

Which was oddly ridiculous—she had caused him and his mother so much heartache that he should hate her. Any other man would have cut off her head and certainly wouldn't have lowered himself by marrying her.

The hard work, the risk, everything he and his mother had done to ensure his success, all of it had come to fruition and he should be celebrating his triumph.

Instead, his feast had been as sombre as a funeral and his bride had tried to poison him mid-meal.

But then…had he honestly thought she would welcome him with open arms as her saviour?

Yes…he had. Even when she'd tried to distract him by dropping her knife, or had touched his arm, he had stupidly thought that each touch held a secret meaning. That she might want him as much as he wanted her. *Idiot!*

The handmaid used a cloth and cleansing balm to remove the kohl from Skadi's eyes, the black softening to a messy smudge. It reminded him of his mother, who had used the ash from his father's funeral pyre to smear her face and show her grief, not only for her husband's passing, but for the loss of her son's protector.

Was that why he felt no ill will towards Astra? Because he'd also been a fatherless child, his inheritance and safety also threatened by grown adults who should have protected him?

Was Skadi grieving for Heimdall? He hated the idea, but he knew it was likely. *Would he be as callous as Sven had been to his mother? Demand she forget her husband and move on immediately?*

It seemed wrong. But he also needed to consummate their marriage and, of course, he wanted her. Desperately, as if his body yearned to have her as much as his obsessive mind had been fixed on reclaiming his birthright.

'Leave us,' he snapped at the handmaid and to his annoyance she waited for Skadi's nod of agreement before leaving.

He glanced at his unopened sea chest at the bottom of the bed. It looked ugly and battered surrounded by so much luxury and, of course, it was the only object in the room that belonged to him.

'Am I safe to sleep around you, or will I find a knife at my throat?' he asked mildly. It was a pathetic attempt at humour, but he'd never been able to charm those around him. He commanded loyalty by being true to his word and fair, not by being likeable.

His throat tightened and he moved towards two matching bowls of water set out with cloths and combs in one corner. He took off his tunic and laid it on a nearby stool, before washing his hands and face.

Skadi answered him with a bored sigh, 'I imagine, if I did kill you in your sleep, my own death would follow shortly after.'

'That would be the most obvious step to follow,' he answered, rubbing the linen cloth down his face and chest to dry himself. It wasn't true, but he wouldn't tell Skadi that. If he died, Vali's orders were to take Skadi and her daughter to King Olaf unharmed.

He glanced back at Skadi. Her spine was as straight as a spear and she was gently applying a salve around her eyes to remove the last of the kohl, which was now almost gone. To his surprise he realised she was watching him curiously in the polished bronze plate that was propped up on an iron stand.

Was she admiring him? The thought was ridiculous, he'd fought many challenges and battles to command such a large army. His body was covered in the proof of it, ugly scars and burns to cauterise his wounds. His hair was too long—it swept around his shoulders, tickling his lower ribs. He should probably cut it off, as it made him look like an unkempt beast no matter how much he combed it.

Her eyes flicked away from him and she began to wipe at her eyes with a strip of linen, as if she were unbothered by his presence.

It irritated him that she found his presence so easy to ignore.

'Where is the poison?' he asked, wiping the last droplets of water from his face and neck with one of the linen cloths, the colour of Thrudheim blue. He tossed it down on the table with a flick of his wrist, the smack of the cloth drawing her attention to him.

It had to be on her, as he'd drunk from the glass previously with no effect. She must have added it when she gave him that ridiculous task of crawling beneath the table for her knife.

She'd made him behave like an absolute fool!

'It was nothing,' she snapped, primly wiping the last of

the balm from her eyes, as if she weren't the most deceiving witch to walk the lands of Midgard.

Striding over to her, he grabbed her arm and lifted her up. She gasped in outrage, but he ignored her, inspecting her dress until he spotted the small purse strapped to her belt. With one hard tug he broke the leather tie holding it in place and then let go of her to open it.

Inside was a tiny corked bottle. 'Your perfume?' he asked with a mocking raise of his brow.

She smiled cruelly, not a hint of shame on her beautiful face. 'Try it for yourself and see.' Had she smiled like that when she'd agreed to break their betrothal and marry Heimdall?

Ignoring her, he took the purse and its contents straight to the brazier and dropped it in the flames. When he returned, she was rinsing her face in the bowl of water he'd not used. She even dried her face with a fresh cloth, refusing to touch anything that he might have used.

'It appears you are even more dishonourable than I thought, Skadi. Such cowardly tactics are beneath a true queen.'

She raised a pale brow at him and lowered her drying cloth. 'Strange, I have not thought of you at all. At least… not until a couple of weeks ago, when I heard you had *murdered* my husband. Is it true you stabbed him in the back? How amusing that you would call *me* dishonourable!'

Agnar was stunned, he felt as if he had run head first into a wall. 'I did not stab him in the back!'

She walked to a seating area screened off with a little steel brazier. There was more furniture in here than last night, he noticed. Did she normally sleep in another room? Or was that another foolish wish of his?

She settled herself into a large chair beside the brazier

and folded her hands in her lap. 'The men that returned to me before your attack say otherwise!'

Red-hot anger flooded his veins, and he moved to stand in front of her leaning down to glare into her face, not caring how intimidating he might seem. 'Then send for them. I will hear these lies said to my face!'

Skadi gave a derisive laugh. 'And have you kill them for it? No, I will not.'

'Then tell me what they said, word for word.'

'Only if you stop raging at me like a wounded bear,' she snapped, gesturing to a nearby chair. He grabbed it, thumping down in it to face her, their knees brushing against one another and causing Skadi to squirm back in her chair.

'Well?' he growled between gritted teeth.

With a roll of her eyes, she explained, 'Heimdall had finished a successful raid.'

'Raid? He slaughtered an entire village of unarmed peasants,' Agnar corrected, his blood running cold at the memory.

Skadi's eyes widened. 'His…back was turned and he was overwhelmed by your men—'

'He was attacked by a group of men. But they were not mine.'

'Convenient.'

'True.'

They glared at each other for a moment, neither one of them willing to back down, until Skadi leaned forward to ask, 'Why are you contesting this? You told me yourself that you killed him! That you *wanted* to kill him!'

'I did.'

She shook her head and threw up her hands with an exasperated huff. 'Well then!'

'I challenged him to a death match, *openly*, and he couldn't deny it. I am a man of power now, with my own army behind me. It was the only reason I was there, to meet him honourably, away from the walls of his kingdom. The only way I could win back my birthright, without attacking Thrudheim directly. The day was set, and then Sven asked him to plunder the village to the north.

'I suspected Sven was trying to delay the challenge, so I followed. When I arrived at the village, Heimdall had made bloody work of the Saxon peasants and appeared to have travelled onwards, even further north. When I caught up with him, his men had been ambushed. Heimdall lay bleeding on the ground, crawling towards his sword. I gave him the mercy of a quick death and allowed him to face me sword in hand. It was far more than he deserved.'

Skadi had been staring at him with exasperated disbelief, right up until he'd described Heimdall's death. Then her expression had faltered and he'd seen doubt in her eyes, the same uncertain expression he'd seen all those years ago, right before she'd asked Heimdall not to kill him. He still remembered her words of supposed mercy, *'He is no one, Heimdall, just a child...leave him, he is no match for you and never will be.'*

The same words had spurred him on to defeat Heimdall twenty years later, to demand his birthright and to show Heimdall that he was not only an equal match...but *better.*

But then her stubbornness flared to life and she haughtily informed him, 'That is your recollection. I am sure Sven would have another tale to tell.'

'I am sure he would. King Sven is not and has never been your ally.'

She bristled, rising from her seat and walking towards a wooden screen at the side of the bed. 'No one is! According to you!' she hissed the words, although this time, her voice was more tired than aggressive and he decided against riling her further. She would realise the truth in time—or perhaps she had always known it? And had lived all these years in denial of her mistake…that was far more likely.

He heard her fumbling with clasps and ties.

'Do you need help?'

'You dismissed my handmaid, remember!' she grumbled back, and there was more huffing and straining from beyond the screen.

Impatient with her obstinance, he walked around the screen to find her with a dress half over her head as if she were caught in a sack.

Smiling to himself at the absurdity, he allowed himself a moment to enjoy the sight of her ridiculous struggle, because for once she appeared fallible. But he knew she would not thank him for it, so he lowered his smile and helped yank the tight-fitting gown over her head. There was a small tearing sound and he was sure a seam had split somewhere.

She emerged from the bundle of fabric red faced and irritated.

He handed her the gown and stepped back around the screen. 'I'm sure you can manage the rest.'

An unwelcome tide of emotion rushed through him and he struggled to regain his control. He had wanted to keep going, to rip every elegant seam and shield from her armour. To strip her bare.

Why did the thought arouse him so much? He'd had Byzantine courtesans dance naked in front of him at the Emperor's palace. They'd fallen into his lap like ripe fruit—paid, of course, and used as a temptation by the Emperor to try to entice him to remain as part of his army in Constantinople. But even so, he'd been less intoxicated by their blatant invitations than he had been by the sight of Skadi's furiously wriggling body.

The soft sound of her dress tearing had filled his mind with wicked possibilities, of him ripping the remaining shift from her body and ravaging her against the wall. To have her powerless under his control. Not with fear, but with passion.

He had never wanted a woman more…and yet, he loathed her. Hated every ignorant, spoilt and stubborn thing she had ever done.

Why, then, did he want her so badly? Would taking her satisfy his ambition, soothe his pride? Symbolise a final triumph and victory? Would reclaiming her ease the heartache of the past? Console the hurt and frightened child he'd once been?

Did he need her to finally see him as a man?

To want him as a man?

Ridiculous! He had to control himself, or he'd risk looking a fool.

Chapter Eleven

Skadi wasn't quite sure what would happen next. She had heard him climb into bed, *Heimdall's bed*... That was an unsettling thought.

Would she be taken by Agnar in the same bed she'd lost her virginity in?

She thought back to that first night with Heimdall when she'd been young and nervous. She'd tried to act as an adult, to laugh along with the bawdy jests at the wedding feast. But that night she'd realised how naïve and innocent she truly was.

It had been an awkward and humiliating experience. Heimdall had tried to be gentle and patient with her. But, lying beneath a man while he sweated and pawed at her, had quickly soured the adoration she'd felt for him.

Afterwards, she'd always thought of this bed as Heimdall's, not her own. He'd taken it and the throne of Thrudheim with a few measly drops of blood.

Of course, things had improved with time. But her youthful adoration had died that night, replaced by a far more practical acceptance.

Heimdall wasn't a terrible lover. Eventually, she grew comfortable enough to enjoy their couplings. But her sweet infatuation with him had never returned and he did not behave towards her as he once had. He no longer gave her compliments or whispered sweet words and she suspected he had never loved her despite his previous flattery.

The crown was all he had wanted and she had been a fool to think otherwise. She had not blamed Heimdall for it. After all, she had chosen him not only because of her attraction, but because he had been the best choice for Thrudheim.

Despite Agnar's accusation, love and lust had never been her only guide.

Marriage with Heimdall had been simple. He'd snored terribly and it had been the perfect excuse to sleep elsewhere. Whenever he wanted her, he would say *he wished to speak with her in his chamber.* Afterwards, she would go back to the comfort and privacy of her own chamber. It had suited both of them.

Her duty and task had always been very clear and uncomplicated. It was true that he'd asked for her less and less over the years. She presumed he was growing bored of her, especially as she hadn't given him a son and was getting older.

But Agnar was a younger man—would he require her every night?

Hopefully not!

She stared down at her linen night shift. This one reached to the floor and billowed around her neck and arms, revealing very little of her shape.

How had it come to this?

Last night she had fought him with sword and shield. Now, she was like an obedient wife submitting to her duties.

Should she not rebel? Fight and deny him?

I am Queen of Thrudheim, she reminded herself firmly. The statement had always given her courage before. But her confidence was crumbling, she felt attacked on all sides.

King Sven, who she'd always suspected of manipulating

Heimdall for his own benefit, might have ordered her husband's death. If she believed Agnar, which she still wasn't entirely sure she should.

The hardest news to digest had been King Olaf's support of Agnar. He was the last of her family and he had chosen Agnar over her own wishes. There had not been a messenger from her uncle in twenty-five years, but now he sent her an army and a husband? Unless Agnar spoke the truth and her uncle had tried to contact her, but had been denied…

Either way, without King Sven or King Olaf supporting her, Thrudheim was vulnerable to invasion and her daughter's life and crown were also at risk.

Should she lie down next to Agnar and submit to him, then?

Accept him for Thrudheim's benefit, as she had with Heimdall?

Or... Should she straddle him and take him instead? As she'd liked doing occasionally with Heimdall when she was in the mood? Part of her liked the power play of such a move. To no longer be the submissive victim in other men's plans, but a force of nature instead.

Perhaps it would intimidate Agnar?

She quickly shook her head.

Nothing would intimidate Agnar and that behaviour would only suggest to him that she *wanted* to be intimate… as if she secretly *wanted* this marriage… Which she did not!

Wouldn't it be better to show her disapproval of the match? To fight him, scream and claw at his already scarred face? But that seemed reckless and senseless, and could even put Astra at risk. Despite his saying he didn't want an heir, he might still hope for one. Of course, a few potions from Gudrun would easily ensure against that possibility…

Another thought suddenly occurred to her and a chilling humiliation ran down her spine.

What if he doesn't want me?

After all, Agnar had said he wanted only what was *promised* and that had been the crown of Thrudheim. He had that now, with or without her. Was taking her tonight his final triumph?

I want power, he had said, and now he had it. Marrying her had simply given him validity in his claim. She was older than him by ten years and close to the end of her childbearing years. It had never concerned her before—even when Heimdall began to lose interest in her, she hadn't been overly bothered. Especially as she'd also grown bored of their couplings, and was confident Astra was strong and healthy enough to live past the dangerous early years.

Why should Agnar's lack of attraction bother her?

Because you do want him.

She flinched at the dark whisper in her mind. It was true, she had found Agnar attractive—in an oddly dark and sinister way. But that was probably just curiosity and the drama of their first encounter after so many years apart. He had changed from a boy into a man. If it hadn't been for his green eyes she might not have recognised him.

A creak of Heimdall's bed reminded her that she'd been worrying about it for far too long. She decided the best course of action would be to neither encourage nor discourage him. Sometimes it was better to do nothing and see what came of it.

Skadi strode out from behind her screen, trying to appear confident, but her steps faltered at the sight of Agnar. Naked from the waist up, he sat with his back against the headboard, the blankets and furs draped over his lap. The scars on his chest and arms were numerous, but his muscles were well defined and his stomach as flat as marble.

His long silky hair fell around his shoulders in a soft contrast to the hard masculinity on display. The runes of wrath and endurance that covered his heart rose and fell steadily with each breath. She had seen him bare chested before, but she'd been about to face him in battle then. Now, he seemed to be waiting patiently for her, as if he cared very little about what would happen next.

Would he be better or worse than Heimdall?

He would certainly be very different and facing the unknown always made her nervous.

At her arrival, his eyes swept slowly up towards hers, taking in the long linen shift as if he were looking at a dull tapestry. His sable brow lifted with amusement, 'You wear more tonight than last night.'

'I was preparing for war. The shorter shift was to accommodate my armour.'

The amusement didn't leave his face. 'I would like to see you in armour.'

Was he mocking her?

'You seem comfortable considering,' she said mildly, staring down at him, reluctant to climb inside the bed. She would wait until he insisted—that would grant her some dignity. Showing reluctance on her part, without making a foolish scene.

To her annoyance, he didn't insist, and her feet began to chill on the stone floor.

'What?' he asked, weary irritation causing his forehead to crease.

She took a deep breath. 'Are you truly comfortable sleeping in *my Heimdall's* bed?'

He dropped his head against the wooden headboard, the

carving of a serpent-like monster roaring open mouthed beside his neck. 'He's dead. Why should it bother me?'

'Some people might not want to sleep in a dead man's bed…especially not one that he'd killed. I thought warriors were superstitious. I imagine most would baulk at the idea…' *Probably more so than the thought of sleeping with a dead man's widow*, she thought bitterly.

Agnar shrugged. 'The dead do not have opinions.' Then he looked up at her and asked, 'Does it upset you?'

'Upset me? Why should it? I have nothing to be ashamed of.' Skadi bristled as if he'd called her a coward and with a flick of her wrist, she spread open the covers. She'd done it a bit more forcefully than she'd intended to, though, because the length of Agnar's naked leg and hip were revealed and she gulped, grateful that the gods had been kind enough not to embarrass her with his *full* nakedness.

As if bored, Agnar's gaze flicked down to his displayed flesh and then back up at her again. 'Are you getting in or not?'

'I just thought you wouldn't want to take me in the same bed I shared with Heimdall!' she snapped. 'But I am sure you care very little about such things.'

She climbed into the bed, her body stiff as a plank of wood. The ropes beneath the mattress creaked like the sails of a ship, as she squirmed down beneath the covers, her toes like blocks of ice, and she wiggled them to get the feeling back.

Silence filled the space between them and she stared up at the ceiling, waiting for him to roll towards her and begin. She wasn't a frightened virgin, perhaps she might even enjoy it? If she could just focus on the act itself and not who she was *doing* it with.

'I will get a new bed,' Agnar declared. She heard him

shifting down beneath the covers to lie beside her, close but not touching. The heat radiating off his big body was like a fire trough along her side. A moment later, he added, 'Try not to kill me in my sleep… It will only irritate me and I have a lot to do tomorrow.'

Skadi took a peek at him from the corner of her eye and, sure enough, Agnar had turned away from her and was apparently going to sleep. Untroubled by the lack of consummation in their marriage.

He doesn't want me.

'I will go and sleep in another chamber,' she said briskly, opening the covers and about to get out, when he grabbed her by the arm and pulled her back into bed with such speed she gave a little cry of surprise.

Not content with scaring her witless, he hauled her towards him, the covers bunching up between them, as his big body arched over her. He thrust her wrist above her head, his stomach pressing against her belly, as her breasts brushed lightly against his chest. The thin fabric of her shift was not enough to stop the sensation from causing her nipples to tighten with sensitivity. Her heart began to pound and she was ashamed to admit it, but wanton liquid heat pooled between her legs.

'No. You sleep beside me, *always*,' he commanded, the words snarled into her face, and she shrank away from the possessive fury in his eyes. 'Do not be mistaken,' he continued, with a hard expression. 'I *will* bed you. You are my wife and my Queen… Just not tonight. It has been a long day.'

She tried to twist her wrist out of his hold, but unlike before it didn't budge, and the heat and closeness of his body made her dizzy.

'And…' he growled, looking almost feral in the dwindling light of the brazier, 'I will take you in a bed made for us…

thoroughly.' The final word was spoken like a promise and then, finally, he released her.

Trying to appear unbothered by the easy way in which he had overpowered her with both action and word, she flapped the covers and huffed, doing anything to distract herself from the burning heat and excitement of his touch, until she'd finally settled herself under the bedding.

'I hope you do not snore. I cannot bear snoring!' she grumbled before turning away from him.

'Go to sleep, Skadi.'

She shifted further away, trying to make herself more comfortable without falling off the bed. But she suspected it would take her many hours to relax enough to fall asleep in the company of her enemy. She only hoped her fidgeting disturbed Agnar and he thought better of his command to *always* share a bed.

Chapter Twelve

Agnar rose early the next day, as was his habit. He'd slept surprisingly well, a short but deep sleep, despite the murderous woman beside him and the fact he lay in Heimdall's bed. He supposed the strain of the last few weeks was finally catching up with him.

That it was Heimdall's bed had not bothered him until Skadi had mentioned it. Which was odd, but he supposed he had not liked to think of her sharing anything with Heimdall, especially in the bedchamber.

Agnar held little value or sentimentality to objects—with the exception of his mother's wedding ring and his axe. Possessions could easily be lost or broken, attaching meaning to them was ridiculous. But it had obviously bothered Skadi and that had disturbed him far more than the dead man's bed.

Had she loved Heimdall?

It enraged him to think of her loving Heimdall, of calling out his name in those sheets, or gripping the headboard as she orgasmed beneath his enemy's touch.

Why would such affection matter to him? The old man was dead. Agnar did not mind that he'd had to agree to Astra as his heir. If bloodlines truly mattered, Sven would never have turned away from him.

Besides, Agnar had made a promise to Skadi's father when

he'd accepted their betrothal, *to continue the unbroken line of Thrudheim rulers*. Skadi's family was the beating heart of the kingdom and his duty as Skadi's husband would be to ensure the next generation to rule Thrudheim was from her bloodline.

Oddly, he remained loyal to that vow, just as he had expected Skadi to remain loyal to their betrothal. Instead, her head had been turned by Heimdall. *Was he jealous of a dead man?*

Had she loved him? At first, he'd not been sure. Certainly, she had been infatuated with him as a young woman, but he'd hoped things would have changed since, that she would have realised the truth.

Skadi had not shed any tears in his presence over the man and had spoken pragmatically of his demise. But he knew her pride meant a lot to her, so she would be reluctant to show any distress in front of him, or anyone for that matter, he imagined, but did he really know her? He had thought so, but last night's trick with the poison had made him question his assumptions about her.

Regardless of whether she had loved Heimdall or not, she needed to forget about that serpent-tongued deceiver and look to the future for the good of the kingdom and themselves. Admittedly, his threatening her daughter's life had not been the most auspicious start to their relationship… But that had been necessary.

In time, Skadi would realise his threats had been nothing more than a pretence.

Today he planned to scrub out every last trace of the man who had stolen his future. Rising from the bed, he dressed quietly. Skadi was snoring lightly, curled up in a ball on the very edge of the bed. It had taken her a long time to fall asleep and for some reason he didn't like the idea of disturbing her.

Maybe it was because he didn't wish to fight with her so early in the morning? He snorted with amusement as he tightened the buckle of his belt.

Skadi frowned in her sleep and grumbled before settling down again with a sigh.

*She snored...*only very lightly, but it still made him chuckle. He was certain she would not thank him for mentioning it. So, of course, at some point he would.

He went over to her table with its lotions, salves, kohl pots and brushes. Feeling like a thief, he quietly opened the jewellery chest and hissed with disapproval at the excess within. Then he reached for her comb and began to run it through his hair. His mother had loved his hair because it had matched her own colouring and, to honour her, he left it long most of the time—at least until it became unbearable.

He dragged her comb through the tangles and then tied up half of it. His hair had mingled with a few strands of hers in the teeth of the comb. Black and white entwined like lovers. He pulled them out and tossed them on the floor, embarrassed that she might realise he had used her things. But his own comb had more missing teeth than an old warrior and he hadn't had a chance to get another.

Once he was dressed and ready for the day, he made his way out into the hall. Vali was eating porridge at a nearby bench with the rest of the men. Nobody appeared tired or sick, which meant there'd been little celebration last night after he'd left with Skadi.

He couldn't blame them—the fact their commander had almost been poisoned to death at his own wedding feast would not fill them with confidence about their victory.

Vali's head raised as he approached and he stood up. 'Good morning, Your Highness.'

'You don't need to call me that.'

Vali shrugged. 'It might be best that I do. At least until things are settled here. The people are uneasy around us… unsurprisingly.'

Agnar grunted in agreement.

'Shall I get a table set up for you?' Vali asked cheerfully, gesturing towards the dais and its thrones.

'Odin's teeth, no! That throne is damn uncomfortable!'

Vali grinned. 'One of the servants mentioned that Skadi usually takes her meals at a table in front of the thrones. It seemed strange to me, but now it makes sense.'

Agnar looked around the hall thoughtfully. 'Remove my banners, but add the wolf's head to the Thrudheim colours.'

Vali inclined his head. 'A wise choice.'

A serving woman hurried over with a bowl of porridge for him and he recognised her as the same girl from last night who had cleaned up the broken chalice. He inspected her for a long moment, to be certain she didn't show any sign of illness.

Unfortunately, she misunderstood his staring for suspicion, because with a gulp, she hurried to explain, 'The porridge is fresh, Your Highness! Straight from the cauldron, look!' She pointed to a large pot suspended over the fire pit, a long line of people waiting to be served from it, his own men as well as Thrudheim folk.

'Are you well?' he asked and was surprised when she jumped at the sound of his voice.

She nodded quickly. 'Yes, Your Highness. I… I did everything the Queen asked of me.'

'She should have scrubbed the floor herself!' he grumbled, taking the bowl from the servant's trembling hands.

To his irritation and surprise, she said, 'Our Queen is wise. I would gladly do anything she asked of me.' Then, with a respectful bob of her head, she hurried away. He sat down beside Vali, who had returned to eating his own porridge.

Agnar ran through all of his tasks for the day. 'We need to order the silversmiths to change Thrudheim's coin mark to that of a wolf. No one is to accept Heimdall's likeness in payment. I do not want to see that man's profile ever again!'

Vali looked up and nodded with agreement.

'And order a new bed made for me. I want it as soon as possible… something whimsical and intricate like the pottery the Queen favours. But also matching our new banner of Thrudheim… Skadi will be pleased with that if nothing else.'

Vali nodded again, this time with a small quirk of his lips. 'You didn't sleep well?'

'I slept fine.' To avoid further conversation Agnar began to eat his porridge.

'I have that perfume seller here, if you wish to speak with her?'

'Did she tell you anything?'

'No, but I learned a little about her from some of the men in the taverns.'

Agnar waved his spoon. 'Go on…'

'Gudrun has provided the settlement with medicines, soaps and perfumes for years. A family trade I believe passed on from her mother. A few years ago, she had a husband called Kar. He used to beat her daily and spent her silver in the taverns. One day, he beat their little boy instead of Gudrun—broke his nose and arm. Apparently, it was the first time Kar had turned on anyone other than her. Within two days he was dead.'

'I see,' Agnar replied grimly, losing his appetite for the porridge and stirring it absently.

'There were mutters of poison from some of his friends and Heimdall almost ordered a trial. But Queen Skadi said that she had been visited by the Goddess Frigg in a dream. She was told by the Goddess that Frigg herself had struck him down for his cruelty and bad behaviour. Gudrun hadn't been present with him at the time of his illness and none of the friends he'd been drinking with had become ill—despite being with him at the tavern all day and night. *So, how could he have been poisoned?* Skadi then called for witnesses—and there were several who had heard him drunkenly cursing the gods and his wife.'

'So, Heimdall pardoned her, because of his wife's pleading?'

Vali shook his head. 'Skadi declared her innocent. It seems Heimdall did not rule at home.'

'That explains his constant need to go raiding. Either that, or he was trying to avoid being poisoned himself,' Agnar replied, an odd relief and satisfaction easing the tension in his shoulders. 'Release Gudrun. Punishing her for my wife's crime is pointless and will only encourage further resentment among the people. But keep an eye on her and her son. Any more *perfumes* or medicines are forbidden from entering this hall without my permission.'

'There are other ways she could bring *perfume* in,' Vali said thoughtfully. 'That Brenna is a most cunning servant… I will keep a watch on her at all times.' He snorted with amusement. 'I imagine it will drive her mad—she thinks very highly of herself.'

'*You* think very highly of yourself,' Agnar pointed out. 'But I doubt Skadi will try again. Besides, my order has made it clear who to blame if something should happen to me. She won't put her daughter at risk.'

Vali's eyes widened and he leaned in to whisper, 'You cannot know that!'

'I do,' Agnar said firmly and strangely he did. He'd seen the hesitation in her eyes, even before she'd learned of her uncle's approval of him. She'd had doubts.

It wasn't simply her reluctance to kill him—after all, she was a warrior at heart. A shieldmaiden who would do anything for her daughter or her people. He'd also seen their devotion towards her—such loyalty was not given easily. She loved her people and they loved her back. She wouldn't risk their safety without a good reason or certainty of success.

Vali did not appear convinced, by his words. 'I will still keep a close eye on her handmaids.' His eyes shifted to the side and Agnar noticed it was Skadi's dark-haired servant, Brenna, and Astra seated at the opposite side of the hall. The child seemed to be trying to feed a cat in a basket some of her porridge and the servant stopped glaring at Vali a moment to scold her lightly.

Agnar nodded. 'I am sure you will. As will I.' He scowled at the oddly soft and lingering gaze of his second in command as he looked at the servant. 'We cannot allow our judgement to become clouded by…other things.'

Vali nodded quickly. 'Indeed, I shall keep a careful watch.'

'Hmmm…' replied Agnar, unconvinced when he realised Vali had gone back to staring at Skadi's servant.

Chapter Thirteen

Sven's fleet was spotted just after midday, the yellow-and-black sail matching the egg-yolk sun spilling golden rays across the cold sea. The unseasonably good weather was an auspicious arrival for what Skadi hoped would be her saviour.

She had heard of his arrival from her flock of spies and rushed to the battlements, climbing the ladder two steps at a time to reach the top. Unfortunately, her enemy-husband had also been made aware and was currently scowling at the ships that sailed not far from the mainland.

'Open the gates!' snapped Skadi, slightly out of breath by the time she reached him. There was no point ordering the warriors at the gate, as they were Agnar's men and not her own. None of the men guarding the battlements were hers and she was rattled to see so many unfamiliar faces.

'No,' said Agnar, scowling at the horizon and barely glancing at her as she approached. Only infuriating her further.

'Whatever your feelings towards King Sven, he *still* has an alliance with Thrudheim. An important one! We sell a good portion of our silver to King Sven. In return we receive trade links, security and, most importantly, *grain.* Without him, we would starve... Winter is almost here. Do not be a fool!'

'For too long you have relied on him for your safety and comfort.'

She gritted her teeth and tried to remain calm. 'That's because he *ensures* it!'

'Not for much longer,' Agnar grunted, turning away from her as if he were about to climb down the steps. She grabbed his arm to stop him from leaving and he stilled, but only to stare down at the way she clutched his sleeve.

'Whatever your grievances with Sven, you cannot ignore him.' She glanced back at the sea and squinted into the light, gesturing with her other hand in exasperation. 'See!'

Slowly, Agnar raised his eyes from the sight of her clutching his arm to the distance, then he shrugged off her touch with a bad-tempered huff. 'One longship is coming. The rest remain where they are. He thinks to negotiate.'

She tried to ignore the pinch of embarrassment when he shrugged her hand off.

Was she truly so awful to him? Was that the real reason he had avoided bedding her? She bristled at her insecurities; she was no longer a young woman affected by the fickle nature of men. Why should she care if he did not desire her? She should be thinking about how best to get rid of him! An unwelcome thought suddenly struck her… *What if he wished to get rid of her first?*

Was that why he did not want to bed her? In case he inadvertently killed a potential heir? She had been so busy considering how to make herself a widow, she hadn't thought that he might feel the same way towards her. She'd only worried about Astra, but perhaps hurting her daughter was not his intention after all? A young princess would be far easier to manipulate than a grown woman—she knew that well enough.

Did he want to kill Skadi and then use Astra as his puppet?

But then, why had he not killed her already? Yes, he'd

needed her to open the gates of Thrudheim to his army. But after that…he could have easily killed her on their wedding night, especially when she had tried to kill him.

But he hadn't. Am I the one at fault?

She blinked, shaking off the thought. Agnar had no right to claim her hand and kingdom. Straightening her spine and trying to appear larger, she blocked his view of Sven by moving to stand in front of him, although she wasn't quite as tall as Agnar…few were.

Absently, she realised, he looked…better today. His long hair had been combed, half of it pulled into a knot at the back of his head to keep it out of his eyes, the rest flowing down his leather armour like black silk. It highlighted his square jaw and piercing green eyes, which seemed more rested than the previous day. She bristled at her foolish thoughts. Why should she care?

'Good,' she said, 'Negotiation would be the best for everyone. He might offer you a better solution than demanding Thrudheim's throne.'

Agnar met her eyes with a bored expression. 'We are married. Nothing can change that.'

Your death can...or mine, she thought grimly, not liking the deceitful prospect of either.

But, of course, Skadi didn't say that, or even remind him that divorce was also a possibility. *Why bother?* A king was more likely to take another wife than divorce an old one… *Would Agnar do that?* She would definitely kill him then. 'Let us welcome him with a meal and discuss what steps to take to ensure a peaceful future for all. Surely you realise Thrudheim cannot thrive in isolation and we need King Sven.'

Agnar began to climb down the ladder. 'I will not break bread with him and he will not enter Thrudheim. I will speak with him at the gate, as I would any other aggressor who thinks to visit with a fleet.'

Skadi hurried down the ladder, half-afraid that he would leave without her. 'He had the same number of ships with him when he stopped here on his way to raid the Saxons. It is hardly an act of aggression, simply a friend and neighbour checking to see that I am well. I will remind you that I did not open my gates or agree to marry you willingly! Of course, he will be concerned about Thrudheim, as am I!'

She'd had to use her longest and quickest strides to keep pace with him and she was startled when he stopped walking to face her. 'You should not come with me.'

Crossing her arms, she said firmly, 'I *will*! Do you think Sven will be appeased without seeing that I am safe and well?'

'I do not care whether he is appeased or not.'

Fury swept through her like a wave of flames and she lifted her chin higher before declaring, 'I will join you, or you will have to drag me away by force!'

With a roll of his eyes, he continued on and she was pleased when he didn't argue with her further. She was even a little pleased with herself when she was able to match him step for step towards the huge gates.

Oddmund began to walk a few steps behind her and she was glad of his support, although she'd not seen him since the night of the attack and wondered if he'd been kept from her by Agnar and his men. She would not have been surprised if he had.

Agnar nodded to his men and they unbarred the smaller door set into the huge oak doors. He strode through seemingly unconcerned and she quickly followed with a small guard, all of whom were Agnar's men, apart from Oddmund.

King Sven's ship had rowed up to one of the jetties and

a gangplank lowered on to the wooden boards with a bang. King Sven strode from his longship like a barrel on stick legs. He had dirty-blond hair that he lightened with lye, which was pulled back at the top into a short braid and shaven beneath. The gold crown encircling his head shone brightly in the light, as did his silk-trimmed tunic and fur-lined cloak that seemed to swamp his thin lower body.

She'd always found the Danish King a peculiarly shaped man, but she composed her features to greet him in her usual polite and friendly manner. It was strange to think that the wolf beside her was related to him—the only likeness between them was the intelligent green eyes of their father.

King Sven wasn't known for his skills as a warrior, although he was a strong sailor and he was unmatched as a tactician. He'd won most of his battles from the safety of his war tent. He was followed by several burly warriors who, in contrast, looked as if they'd fought in many wars and lived to tell the tale.

'Greetings, King Sven, I hope your raids were a success,' she called out, hoping to slow the King who was striding towards them with a severe expression on his face.

Agnar and Sven looked at her as if she had decided to lift her skirts and dance in front of them. But it was King Sven who spoke first.

'What is the meaning of this, Agnar?'

'King Agnar,' barked Vali, from the side.

Skadi had learned the redheaded warrior's name from Brenna, who still held a deep and understandable dislike of Agnar's second. Skadi didn't like him, either, he was Agnar's most obedient dog. She wondered how best to remove him as a threat…perhaps Bodil's butterflies could help? Most men had a weakness…

She stared at King Sven as he approached. She had always

known his weakness...*greed.* But she had been able to manage it in the past, had even used it to her advantage at times.

King Sven didn't even blink at Agnar's title, so their marriage had not come as a surprise.

A prick of awareness ran down her spine, although she wasn't sure why. After Agnar's attack on Heimdall, it was obvious that he would seek Thrudheim's crown and the easiest way to do that would be through marrying her.

Still...why had Sven not come to her defence earlier?

King Sven's top lip curled with disgust. 'Marrying the man who killed your husband is unseemly of you, Skadi.'

Skadi clenched her fists. *Was that all he had to say to her? A condemnation?*

'*Queen* Skadi,' Agnar interrupted with a deadly expression that made King Sven grit his teeth.

It surprised her to hear Agnar defend her honour. But perhaps it was only to assert his authority as Thrudheim's ruler? She had no idea what Agnar's weakness was and that frightened her.

'I had very little choice in the matter,' Skadi said, all smiles gone. 'Especially without my men or further aid. Oddmund tells me only one of Heimdall's ships could return. Why is that?'

King Sven pointedly ignored her, his eyes fixed on Agnar, and she remembered how often he had spoken to Heimdall over her as well. She'd always thought it was because they were friends, but now she realised the truth of it. He had never respected her in the same way.

King Sven declared loudly, 'Open your gates, or face retribution. It is clear Skadi has been forced into this alliance. Once I have spoken with the other petty Kings, they will join with me to take it back. Save yourself bloodshed now and surrender!'

'My Queen asked where the rest of her ships were. Why do you not answer?' asked Agnar with a bored expression.

King Sven shrugged. 'Oddmund was sent to tell you of Heimdall's death by the Usurper—it is a shame you did not heed his warnings. The rest of Heimdall's men are with me, ready to avenge their master and liberate Thrudheim from Agnar's clutches!'

Agnar had the audacity to chuckle. 'It is well known that I was the one originally betrothed to Queen Skadi. It is also known that I openly challenged him for my birthright. Do you honestly think the petty Kings will support you in attacking Thrudheim now? I do not. In fact, I suspect they will be grateful to no longer have to deal with you when trading for Thrudheim silver.'

King Sven stiffened, but then his eyes narrowed. 'King Olaf will live to regret his alliance with you, *Rus scum*!'

Agnar shrugged, but did not answer.

For the first time, King Sven turned towards Skadi and said coldly, 'You should never have let him in! He will kill you and your daughter before the end of the month and replace you with a Rus princess. I am aware, Agnar, of the other match presented to you! You could have had a young and fertile Rus princess…' he glanced at Skadi and gave a dismissive snort '…but instead you chose—'

Agnar stepped forward, his hand braced on the top of his throwing axe and shouted, 'Enough!'

The guards on either side bristled and placed their hands on the pommels of their swords. But Agnar was not done and he glared at King Sven, before snapping, 'You have denied me for too many years as it is! I am married to Queen Skadi, I am the King of Thrudheim and I accept Princess Astra as my heir.'

King Sven's gaze had not shifted from Skadi and she

knew he saw the doubt and fear in her eyes, because his voice softened to a serpent-like persuasive tone, 'We spoke about a betrothal for Astra. Consider her safety, as well as the upcoming winter without my grain… If she leaves with me, she will be safe.'

Skadi's fists clenched and unclenched. She could not trust either man. This was the first time she had heard about a Rus princess and she began to worry about what that could mean for herself and Astra. Agnar had not denied it, but then, would Astra be safe with Sven? She doubted it… She would be his hostage and a way for Sven to reclaim the throne of Thrudheim at a later date.

'My daughter remains with me until it is her time to wear the crown. She will remain on this island and rule it, as I have done, and as all her ancestors have done before her.'

'A kingdom requires a king to rule it!'

Agnar replied coldly, 'This kingdom has one. Perhaps you should return to yours?'

King Sven gave a disgruntled huff and turned away with a parting hiss to Skadi, 'You will regret this!'

He left with a swish of his cloak and the clatter of his armoured guards hurrying after him.

Skadi still wasn't sure if she'd just snubbed the only man left who could possibly help her. But she could not waste time regretting her decision, so she turned on her heel and left.

Hating all men and their selfish plans.

Vali came to stand beside Agnar as he watched King Sven's longship row out of Thrudheim's harbour to rejoin his fleet.

'Did you count them?' Agnar asked quietly.

'Yes, we outnumber him. But I will wait for the man we

sent to higher ground to confirm if any were hidden from view.'

'I doubt it. He wanted to show his fleet. He hoped to intimidate me, but King Olaf's support has now been confirmed to him. He will not attack openly... At least not yet.'

'What are your orders?' Vali asked, his eyes squinting into the distance as the fleet sailed eastwards.

'Keep a close watch on Astra and her handmaid. King Sven wants Skadi to give her up to him... Be sure she doesn't.'

'Do you think she will let her go to him willingly?'

Agnar shrugged, turning away and walking back through the gate, Vali following close behind. 'I doubt it. But there may be men and women loyal to King Sven here. Keep an eye on that Oddmund, too... I do not trust anyone Sven knows by name. Especially one I have heard nothing of until now.'

They made their way through the smaller door of the gate and, with a silent nod from Agnar, it was barred and locked.

It seemed Skadi hadn't made it that far back to the hall, as she was now speaking with a woman on the wide cart road that led to the market.

'Who is she speaking with?' asked Agnar curiously and Vali peered at the woman before answering.

'Hmmm, I believe her name is Bodil and she runs the brothel. Their tavern also supplies the ale for the hall—I've seen her delivering it.'

'Why would she be speaking with a light-skirt?'

'Perhaps, she's getting tips on how to please you?' Vali said with a mischievous wink, which soured under Agnar's glare of disapproval.

'No? Well... I suspect the girl is giving her information about us.' Vali shrugged. 'A lot of our men have been spending time there. A couple had the wit to notice the ladies were very interested in where we've come from and why.'

'I presume they told the truth.'

Vali nodded. 'They were under no orders to do otherwise. She will be telling your Queen that half of your army is Rus and the other are King Olaf's men, just as I imagine you have already told her.' He turned a little, a curious look on his face. '*Should* they have said otherwise? It is not as if King Olaf wants his men returned quickly.'

'No, King Olaf wants assurances Thrudheim is secure from Sven before I return his men,' Agnar replied and they continued onwards, passing the Queen just as she said goodbye to the young woman.

'Thank you, more ale would be most welcome, Bodil. Especially with the Yule festival fast approaching.'

Skadi fell into step beside him, which surprised him far more than the feigned request for more ale to be delivered. She asked quietly, 'Who is the Rus Princess Sven mentioned?'

Agnar smiled, amused that she would be immediately threatened by Sven's words. The man was a serpent who liked to twist and manipulate all around him. 'Princess Irina is one of my distant cousins. She will probably marry a prince—her father wishes to strengthen his links to the Byzantine empire.'

Skadi sniffed the air, as if she smelt something foul. 'King Sven seems to think otherwise.'

Agnar stopped walking, gripped her arm, turned her to face him and looked her in the eye. 'Even now you trust his word over mine?'

She blinked, then jerked out of his hold. '*Even now?* When have you *ever* given me cause to trust you?'

'How about when Sven decided you were no longer Queen of Thrudheim? Did that not strike you as odd?'

She stiffened and he could tell that his words had struck true.

He began walking again and she joined him, matching him step for step. 'He has never considered you anything more than Heimdall's wife. Here you have the security of your bloodline and the respect and loyalty of your people.' He tipped his head to the side, gesturing at the gates behind them. 'But out there… Nobody respects that. They believe you are a vassal of King Sven, a puppet for his amusement. Your only purpose is to ensure the smooth delivery of *his* silver. Your alliance with him is now broken—there will be no grain, support, or security from him.'

'You are wrong! We have dealt with Sven for many years, but I am no puppet! He will come around eventually,' Skadi replied, the colour high on her cheeks. She was obviously struggling to accept the truth of his words.

'You think so? When he comes to your shores with a fleet and makes it clear he disapproves of your marriage to me?'

Her eyes narrowed. '*I* disapprove of our marriage! And how are you any different to Sven? You also want to control me, to make me your puppet! If what you say is true, then I am simply replacing one tyrant for another!' She strode away, lifting her skirts above the muddy path and walking at quick pace up the hill towards the great hall in the distance.

Vali, always the fountain of wisdom, commented sagely, 'She still doesn't like you very much. Shall I ask the whore to give *you* some tips?'

Agnar almost choked on his outrage. 'We have been friends for many years, Vali. But if you overstep like that again, I will beat you senseless.'

Vali gave an infuriatingly thoughtful nod, as if Agnar

hadn't just threatened him. 'Ahh, so that is the way of it—you wish to break her in gently.' Agnar was about to throttle him when he added, 'But that might not be the wisest course. In fact, bedding her well might help her feel more secure in her position and help you gain her trust.'

Agnar stared at his friend, wondering if the man had lost all of his wits. 'How?'

Vali gave him a sly teasing smile. 'Well, she's an experienced, mature woman and you are a man in his prime—if a little inexperienced in the art of love. If you please her, she might forget her grievances against you and give you peace. A happy wife leads to a happy life…or so my father used to say.'

Agnar was one step away from ripping off Vali's head and kicking it over the battlements—their years of friendship be damned! 'Say that again and I will rip out your tongue.'

'And…' Vali added cautiously, taking a couple of steps to the side so he was out of Agnar's reach, 'if you fill her belly with another child, she will *know* she is safe.'

Agnar rolled his eyes. 'Idiot! She is afraid for her eldest child.' He thought of the herbalists with all of her potions. 'She will not give me another willingly—for fear of disinheriting the first.'

Vali spoke as if he'd not heard him, 'Make sure you keep trying until she bears a boy. Surely, if she'd given Heimdall a son, he would have become heir over Astra.'

'She doesn't want any more children.' Agnar wasn't entirely sure why he was allowing this conversation to continue, but as they climbed the path towards the hall, he found himself desperate for guidance. He'd planned everything to ensure his successful claiming of Thrudheim, but he'd not thought much past achieving his goal.

'Why not?' Vali asked, confused.

'She is ten years older than me.'

'Is she? She doesn't look it,' said Vali. 'I mean…you look older than her.'

Agnar couldn't argue with that. 'Unlike me, she has lived a pampered life. She knows nothing of true hardship.'

Vali for once didn't tease or laugh at him. 'I remember when you first came to Aldeigja, my father presumed you were escaped thralls at first, you looked so wretched and wild… At least until your mother spoke to him.'

'And?' asked Agnar, confused as to why Vali would mention it. Vali's father had been the chieftain of the Rus trading town. A man sworn to his mother's royal family.

'You must have thought I was pampered,' said Vali thoughtfully. 'The third son, without a scratch or hair on his chin. And, there you were, with your wolf cloak and wild ways.'

His *wild ways* were an understatement—Agnar had been almost feral by the time they'd reached Aldeigja. After struggling to survive for so long, he'd learned to hunt and move like a wolf. The journey back to his mother's homeland had been brutal and his mother had been so broken by it that she'd died shortly after their arrival.

Agnar gave a guttural huff of acknowledgement. 'I remember you following me around like a noisy shadow, scaring all the prey away… What of it?'

Vali shrugged. 'Only that some things are beyond our control. Both the good and the bad. I saw how you were and I knew that, if I followed you, I would find adventure and excitement—which I did.'

'And?'

'Sometimes happiness is a choice. You should try being happy.'

Agnar stared at his friend, then thumped him in the arm. 'You are an idiot!'

Vali grinned. 'But I am a happy idiot!'

Chapter Fourteen

That evening, they ate on a table set out in her usual style and Skadi was surprised Brenna and Astra were joining them.

'Why are you here?' she whispered to Brenna.

Brenna was quick to answer, nodding towards Agnar and Vali who stood talking with some of the warriors at the far end of the hall. 'King Agnar asked the servants how the tables were usually laid out and he requested the same for tonight. He also insisted Astra eat with you at the head table as normal.'

'I see,' Skadi said with a frown, before forcing a smile and asking Astra about her day.

'I played with the kittens and then went to help feed the animals with Brenna and Vali,' Astra said cheerfully. 'Then I practised writing my runes and counting with the priestess. I am getting much better! I can write the whole of the Futhark now, and recite most of their meanings—I only forgot three!'

'Well done, you've worked very hard on your writing and I'm proud of you,' she said. 'Let's play a game after dinner, we haven't thrown the dice in a while.'

Astra's eyes brightened at the prospect. 'Yes, please! And, can we train tomorrow?'

'Of course!' Skadi nodded enthusiastically, trying to

smother the squeeze of guilt that locked around her chest like rusty chains. So much had happened in the last two weeks that had taken her away from her daughter. Heimdall's funeral, preparing Thrudheim for war—all of it had distanced her from her child when she'd needed her most.

Looking around the hall, she noticed that every Thrudheim banner had been removed—the golden walls and beams looked bare without her colours. Brenna had mentioned to her that the women were busy altering them to a new design chosen by Agnar. She didn't have the strength to check on their progress—the thought of her beautiful sapphire banners being butchered to incorporate the scarlet-and-black wolf filled her with dismay.

Out of the corner of her eye she spotted Agnar heading towards them and she made her way to the central chairs. Thankfully, these wooden thrones were far more comfortable than the stone thrones and had cushioned seats. The carvings were of the cliffs and forests of Thrudheim, but were smoothly polished and smelled of beeswax.

She took her seat and waited for Agnar to join her, although she tried to appear as if she wasn't, and continued to talk with Astra about her training and what skills she needed to develop further. Skadi was determined to speak with her about her attacking Agnar. She couldn't allow her daughter to make such a fatal mistake again, but she also didn't want to frighten her further about what could have been.

When his big body sat down next to hers with a creak, she took her time to acknowledge him. She shifted back into her seat and turned towards him. 'May I ask about your plans for Thrudheim?' she asked politely. Even though she hated to do so, she knew from experience that she'd learned more from Heimdall when she'd been meek.

Her change in attitude seemed to surprise him because he raised a brow at her polite tone. 'What do you mean?'

She bit back an exasperated sigh, and gave a tightly pinched smile. 'I mean…we have a shipment of silver ore for Sven almost ready. What do you plan to do with it, or all of the others that follow for that matter?'

Frustratingly, he shrugged. 'I would imagine that Sven is no longer expecting any shipments from us. So, it really does not matter.'

She wanted to scream, but managed to control herself. 'It *will* matter, especially, when winter comes along and we have no grain… We import barley and wheat from Sven.'

'I am sure others can provide it.' Before she had time to argue with him about the higher price and difficulty of procuring grain from other kingdoms, he added, 'I would like you to show me Thrudheim. I want to see the farms, forests, mines and landmarks of my new home.'

She swallowed her indignation. *Now he wants to see it?* After conquering her kingdom, he *now* thinks he should learn about it? 'I see… Well, I am sure one of my men can give you a tour of the island.'

'I want *you* to show me,' he said firmly, reaching for the bread and peeling off a petal. She watched with a knot in her throat as he prepared it just the way she liked it, with honey and salt—just like her father used to do.

He offered it to her and she was so surprised by his request that it took her a moment to react. 'Why?' she asked, taking a small bite, as she'd done the previous night. Was it going to be an oddly intimate tradition between them now? She wasn't sure how she felt about that.

'Because…' He paused, his eyes almost black in the firelight, a stormy green circling the pupil. *Was he staring at her mouth?* 'You know Thrudheim better than anyone.'

'I will not argue with that,' she said and he popped the remaining crust in his mouth and chewed it slowly.

The rest of the hall began to eat, but she didn't notice. She was distracted by the thought that Agnar might actually be attracted to her. He'd stared at her bare thigh when he'd interrupted her dressing and during the meal his eyes had lingered on her touch—just before she'd tried to kill him. Not the most auspicious start to a seduction.

Did she *want* to seduce him?

That was a surprising reversal of fortune. For her to be the manipulator instead of the victim. She knew she wasn't ugly, but she was certainly older and had presumed any interest he had in her would be mild at best.

But...was she wrong? Could Agnar desire her? He was such a difficult man to read, his emotions tightly reined in. The only real emotion she'd witnessed had been anger.

She pushed aside her wild thoughts and focused on their conversation. 'The island is surprisingly large. The silver mines are to the west of here, as are the pig and sheep farms. But to reach the largest mine, you have to travel through the forest up the mountain. Then beyond the ridge is the flatlands—going over the mountain is the only way to reach them, as the cliffs are a sheer drop into the sea on that side of the island. It would take at least a couple of days to visit each site.'

'That doesn't concern me,' he replied, ladling a portion of fish broth and placing the bowl in front of her. It was one of her favourite pieces, a fish head-tapered bowl, with large gaping jaws as if it were reaching for a worm on a hook. He ladled another bowl for himself and then stared at the dish with a wrinkled brow, his spoon poised in his hand, obviously realising his spoon would not fit in the narrow entrance. 'Why are all your dishes like this?'

Skadi looked at the fish head and smiled. It was more like a large cup than a bowl and could be a little tricky to eat from. She picked up the dish and sipped from it. 'You use it like a cup, it's only a thin broth, so doesn't really need a spoon.'

'What nonsense!' he snapped, placing his spoon down and drinking from the fish's head as she had done.

'I like them,' she said quietly, setting it down gently. 'I appreciate their beauty and the skill that has gone into making them.'

'You think gaping fish heads are beautiful?' He looked at her with genuine bewilderment.

Skadi laughed. 'Why not? I find all nature beautiful in its own way.'

He snorted with disbelief. 'Next you'll be saying my scarred face is handsome!'

She frowned. Was he trying to trick her into complimenting him? *Well, she wouldn't fall into that trap!* Silence stretched between them, and he reached for the skewers of pork, placing two on her trencher, before taking some for his own.

'As I was saying,' she said, clearing her throat and trying to break the awkwardness that had developed between them. 'It would take several days. Oddmund used to be my second and he knows the island as well as I do. I can get him to show you around.'

Agnar bit off a large chunk of meat, and spoke through a full mouth. 'I want you to show me. A few days is nothing.'

Exasperated, she snapped, 'I cannot leave Astra, even if it is only for a few days. The last two weeks—'

She had been about to argue her point, when Agnar interrupted her with a shrug. 'Of course, Astra will be coming with us. I am sure she already knows the island better than I, but it will be a good opportunity for us to get to know one another.'

Shock rattled through her. *Why would he be so open to having Astra join them?* Was it because Astra was a hostage and too valuable to leave in the palace alone? Or, did he *actually* consider her as a part of his household…his heir?

He leaned around her to call out to Astra. 'What do you think, Princess? Shall you show me all that there is to know about Thrudheim?'

Astra nodded hesitantly, staring at him wide-eyed, much like the fish head in his hands. Her daughter was understandably still uncertain about the stranger who had married her mother less than a day ago and under less-than-willing circumstances.

Skadi flinched at the uncertainty in her daughter's eyes. She was still afraid of Agnar…and for good reason, as it wasn't long ago that he'd held her up by her wrist and disarmed her as if he were shaking out a fleece.

Skadi leaned closer towards him, blocking her daughter from view, a deadly warning hissed between her teeth, 'Do what you will with me. But do not toy with Astra, she is still a child.'

His head tilted. 'I have told you. Astra has nothing to fear from me. I gave you my word. Thrudheim is stronger with me at your side… Have I not already proven that with Sven? You are my Queen, not my hostage.'

Skadi felt like throwing up her hands and marching from the hall, but she managed to control herself enough to say, 'Only time will reveal the value of your word. But I feel as if I have made many concessions, least of which is agreeing to marry you. Perhaps you should make some allowances of your own? Although, if Astra is to come with us, I suppose we can leave tomorrow afternoon. If you are sure that Thrudheim is safe from attack in the near future?'

To her surprise, he smiled. 'No one will attack us within the next few days. Of that I am certain.'

She supposed he was right; Sven had left with little more than disgruntled and vague threats. No war had been declared, but that did not reassure her. She suspected that Sven would be speaking with the petty Kings and ensuring that no one traded grain with Thrudheim. Why declare war, when he could weaken them with starvation?

Soon, Agnar would realise that they could not survive by ignoring Sven and she would unfortunately have to deal with repairing the alliance. A partnership that Agnar had so recklessly cast aside. The prospect of grovelling to Sven filled her with melancholy and she went back to eating her meal in silence.

After Nattmal was finished, she played dice with Brenna and Astra, then they practised their needlework, embroidering ribbons together. The kind that Astra wore in her hair. Several times she noticed Agnar staring at her from where he sat drinking ale with his second, Vali. It reminded her of the way he'd stared at her mouth, with a fascinated sort of longing. She wondered if her earlier thoughts about his attraction to her were not as fanciful as she'd first thought.

Why hadn't he taken her, then?

Was it more than the superstition of bedding her in Heimdall's bed? Did he truly think himself ugly with his scars? Was he giving her time to grow accustomed to him? It seemed a foolish thought for a man in the prime of his life...but not impossible.

The chief seamstress came into the hall, a sapphire banner draped over her arm. She went to speak with Agnar who immediately gestured towards Skadi.

'Yes, Gunhild?' she asked as the woman approached.

Gunhild dipped respectfully. 'The King would like your approval of the new Thrudheim banner.'

Skadi raised a brow at that supposed display of respect by Agnar. 'Show me, then.'

Gunhild carefully rolled out the banner. It was the same Thrudheim blue background as before, but instead of the strip of white down its centre, there was a black wolf's head.

She sighed. It was ugly, but not quite as bad as she'd thought it would be. At least the blue remained and there was no clashing red. Still, it felt wrong to change it, these had been the colours of Thrudheim since the very first King. Why should it change now, when it had not changed under Heimdall?

You are my Queen, not my hostage. His earlier words came to mind and she wondered if she should at least try to accept him. Even if only in the short term. *Choose your battles, Skadi*, her father's voice reminded her firmly.

After a moment of consideration, she gave her instruction. 'I do not like the black. Make the wolf's head white.'

The seamstress rolled up the banner and with a nervous look headed back to Agnar. Skadi sat back and watched him, wondering what he would make of her command. She had relented, if only a small amount, but she wondered if he would see it as that, or judge it as another defiance.

Would he deny her?

As he listened to the seamstress speak, his eyes shifted to meet hers, and Skadi raised a brow in question. He then nodded at the seamstress, approving her suggestion, and a glow of triumph warmed deep in her belly.

He had agreed to keep both her family colours and she

had agreed to use his symbol. Could this bode well for them in the future? Or, was she going mad to even hope for peace with her previous husband's killer?

She shifted uncomfortably at the thought and returned to staring at her needlework.

Should she not wish to avenge Heimdall, the father of her child?

Except, a lot of what Agnar had said sounded genuine. She had known Heimdall twenty years, he had been obsessed with raiding and the hopes of entering Valhalla. She imagined he would crawl for his weapon, even in the last moments of his life…and that Agnar, who despite hating him, would still offer him an honourable death because of it.

She sighed miserably, snapping the thread of her embroidery by accident. What if Agnar was claiming an interest in her kingdom and manipulating her emotions, all so that he could overrule her in the future?

It wouldn't be the first time she'd been easily misled.

She went to bed early that night and took one of Gudrun's sleeping draughts that she kept in her medicine chest. She wanted to ensure a deeper sleep than the one she'd had the night before and also hoped to avoid any awkward conversations with Agnar. Or, any further discussion about when and where he would bed her.

By the time Agnar entered the King's chamber, her eyelids were so heavy she could barely keep them open and she barely noticed the shift of the mattress as he lay down beside her.

Chapter Fifteen

The next morning, she woke up later than usual, the exhaustion and sleeping draught from the night before having knocked her out.

Groggily, she turned on to her side, slightly disorientated to find herself in the King's chamber. It took her a moment to remember where she was and why. Then she noticed Agnar fully dressed on a nearby stool, sharpening his blade on a whetstone, and she bolted upright with a startled gasp.

His eyes lifted from the shiny blade to her face and he asked mildly, 'Are you well?'

'Of course,' she snapped, squinting up at the smoke hole and realising the sun was higher than she had expected.

'You were sleeping like the dead.' He glanced pointedly over at her bone cup and spoon on a nearby table, which she'd used to mix her sleeping draught.

'Did you think I'd poisoned myself? Sorry to disappoint you, but I would never leave my daughter willingly.'

'True. But for a moment, I wondered…' he admitted and she scowled at his lack of concern. 'But then I heard you snoring like a drunk and knew you were fine.'

Horrified, Skadi threw aside the covers and got out of bed with an outraged shriek. 'I do *not* snore!'

'If you say so…' Agnar gave a wicked smile that caused

flames to rush up the sides of her neck. He stood up and left without further comment.

So much for him finding her attractive…although, had he really been concerned about her?

Confused, she stomped behind the screen and dressed in her training clothes, a thick blue-wool tunic over a linen one, with matching soft woollen trousers and brown fur-lined boots. She didn't bother with a cloak, as her training would keep her warm, and she belted her practice sword around her waist and strode out into the pleasant autumn day. She doubted there would be many dry and sunny days left—when winter came to the island it was always swift and brutal.

She'd agreed to meet Astra at the training yard with Brenna, so after eating a quick breakfast she made her way there, knowing Astra would have already started without her.

The training area was a fenced-off square, a few hundred feet from the hall. The ground had been flattened and covered with a layer of sand. The armoury building was also within the square and when she walked through the gate, she nodded at many of her warriors, who were training within. She suspected they were bored.

Many of them were locked in combat with one or two others, using wooden swords and shields, while others practised archery with straw targets or wrestled bare-chested. They were accustomed to her presence and knew not to stop training just because she'd entered the yard.

Agnar's men still lined the battlements and took turns taking the watch. She wondered if she should speak with Agnar about re-introducing her men into their defences. There was no way of knowing how long Olaf's men would remain with them and it would be unwise of Agnar to not use the local warriors, especially as bored young men often left to seek new adventures and very rarely returned.

That had been the problem with Heimdall—he'd insisted on going raiding every summer with Sven. But his travels had put a strain on her own defences, as the young men always left with him and often settled in new lands or died in battle.

In contrast, Agnar seemed keen to learn about the island and, if it hadn't been *him*, she might have been impressed to have a husband so willing to ensure the survival and prosperity of Thrudheim… Except that had always been her domain in the past and she was unwilling to give it up.

It took a moment to spot Astra and Brenna among the warriors. Usually, Brenna embroidered or knitted while Astra practised her sword swings. But today, the basket of crafts was left ignored on the floor, and Brenna stood anxiously wringing her hands.

It didn't take long for Skadi to realise why. Astra was wearing her usual helm and similar clothing to Skadi's training outfit, but she usually practised her sword swings and shield blocks on the large fighting post.

Today, she faced Agnar and he looked like a giant against her daughter.

Skadi broke out into a run.

'What are you doing?' she demanded, only slightly relieved to see that Agnar was no longer carrying a steel blade, but a wooden sword and shield. However, he still had a weapon strapped to his belt, the throwing axe he carried around with him everywhere he went. Its presence made her nervous, despite the blade head remaining firmly in its leather holder.

Brenna's shoulders visibly dropped with relief when she

arrived. 'He insisted!' she declared, although there was anxiety and apology written in worried lines all over her face.

Agnar's eyes locked with hers and he shrugged. 'I am teaching her how to protect herself against a bigger opponent.'

Skadi's jaw tightened and she was about to yell at him when Astra declared cheerfully, 'Look Moma!' and she stepped forward, her shield raised high, and Skadi's heart stopped.

Agnar gave Skadi what she assumed was meant to be a reassuring smile, then he swept his sword down to smack Astra's shield with a force that Skadi was far from comfortable with. To her surprise, Astra shifted out of the way at the last moment and struck down with her sword point against Agnar's boot.

'Ouch!' Agnar grumbled, hopping up and down with far more energy than seemed realistic for the light blow he'd suffered.

'Sorry!' giggled Astra, without a speck of regret, and Skadi forced herself to smile.

'Well done, Astra. That is an interesting technique. I had thought to move on to counter-attacks when you were confident with holds and swings.' She gave a meaningful glare at Agnar, hoping he would understand that she'd intended Astra to be confident with the basics, before she moved on to complicated defensive manoeuvres.

However, Agnar seemed oblivious to the importance of her process, because he said dismissively, 'What is the point of her knowing all the thrusts and strikes when she doesn't have the power to use them? Much better to teach her wit and cunning, so that she can disarm her opponent quickly.'

Skadi frowned. 'At *her age*, I do not want her fighting an opponent. We are learning the basics with the sword and shield. We will move on to more complicated things when she is strong enough to handle them.'

Agnar shook his head, oblivious to her growing temper. 'She will be dead in less than a heartbeat if she gets into a true fight. Those techniques are useless without strength and height. You saw how quickly I disarmed her before.'

Astra stared up at him with wide eyes and Skadi saw the fear whisper across her face as she no doubt remembered the way Agnar had easily held her aloft. But to Skadi's surprise and considerable pride, Astra's chin rose and she declared, 'I like Agnar teaching me his wolf-cub tricks!'

'Wolf-cub tricks?' she asked, with a raised brow as she crossed her arms over her chest.

Astra nodded eagerly. 'Agnar used to live like a wolf cub in the wild with his mother. They travelled all the way to Aldeigja alone and most of the way by land, too! Avoiding wild beasts, cut-throats, thieves, and slavers! And he wasn't much older than I am now!'

Skadi blinked, her stomach twisting. Was it true? Or, was it simply a man boasting to a naive child? 'I thought Sven took you and your mother back to the Rus?' she asked, already dreading his answer by the way his eyes narrowed.

'He offered a ship to take us, but only if my mother declared at court that I was illegitimate and had no true claim to either Thrudheim or Sven's kingdom. She refused and we made our own way to the Rus alone.'

Skadi swallowed the bile in her throat.

How had they survived? It was many weeks to Aldeigja by boat—by land it would have taken many months. Had her rejection of him all those years ago set a terrible tragedy in motion?

A sudden and unwelcome thought came to her.

Where was she now? His mother had been the champion

of his birthright…what had become of her? Surely she would have remained at his side when he sought to reclaim Thrudheim? Nausea threatened to overwhelm her as she asked quietly, 'Is your mother still with her Rus family?'

Agnar's jaw flexed. 'No. Unfortunately, she died. Not long after we arrived in Aldeigja.'

'I am sorry… I did not know…'

'Would it have made any difference? Would you have chosen me instead?'

'I…' She couldn't answer him.

A silent and painful acknowledgement passed between them. Skadi had not known about his mother, or the suffering they had endured to escape Sven's clutches. But neither had she troubled herself to check or ask what had become of them. And, of course, she still would have married Heimdall.

Honestly, she was surprised he didn't hate her more. And worryingly, she now couldn't justify hating him either.

Astra glanced between them, before asking impatiently, 'Please, Moma, let him train me. I promise to practise my swings as well.'

Skadi couldn't speak; she merely nodded her agreement. She moved to stand beside Brenna, her hand resting lightly on the hilt of her practice sword as she watched.

Agnar was surprisingly patient with Astra, taking time to demonstrate twists and steps that would move her swiftly out of reach. He showed her the obvious ways a larger opponent might try to disarm or attack her and what she needed to do to thwart them.

They practised over and over until Astra began to do the movements instinctively as if they were dancing. Her daughter laughed and grinned with excitement and satisfaction at grasping the skills quickly.

When it came to demonstrating one defensive technique,

Agnar stopped and asked Skadi to come and join him. 'It will be easier to demonstrate if she can see what needs to be done.'

Skadi came to stand in front of him. Gently he took her shoulders and turned her around, so that her back was to his chest. 'If someone comes at you from behind.' He reached his arm around her waist and tugged her backwards. She tried her best to ignore the heat of his thick arm against her stomach, or the way her bottom pressed into his groin, or even how well they seemed to fit against one another…because her daughter and Brenna were watching them.

'They will try to grab you here.' He gently curved his arm around her, pressing his palm flat against her shoulder. 'Or, here…' His hand lifted to rest flat against the side of her throat—she swallowed nervously as waves of goosebumps ran down her neck. His breath ruffled the baby hairs against her ear, and she had to hold her breath to stop herself from moaning. 'Do you know how to escape me, Skadi?'

She moved slowly, not wanting to hurt him and so that she could explain it to Astra. 'Foot to foot.' She lightly pressed her boot against his. 'Elbow to rib.' She demonstrated again with her arm, deliberately dropping her arm as the elbow connected, and letting her body lean against his. Her bottom pressed lightly against his groin and his sharp intake of breath was the only answer she needed. 'Head to nose.' She tapped her head back, Agnar arching away from her far more than necessary, so they didn't make contact.

His hands immediately dropped from around her body and she stepped out of the stifling embrace, glancing curiously back at him. He looked stunned and uncomfortable, his eyes avoiding hers.

Agnar cleared his throat, reaching for his sword, where he'd left it on the ground. 'Excellent. Now, while you practise your sword skills, I will go and prepare the horses for our journey.'

Skadi nodded and watched him leave, shaken by the ache within her.

She wanted him, enjoyed the feel of his body pressed against hers and longed to feel his lips against her throat. Wicked thoughts spiralled in her mind and she had to take several deep breaths to calm herself. If she allowed this passion to control her, she might as well sacrifice her daughter and kingdom now.

When he was gone, she turned to Astra and asked gently, 'Are you comfortable around Agnar? I know it must be difficult, after what happened with your father.'

To her surprise Astra shook her head. 'No, Agnar explained it to me. He told me you were meant to have married him many years ago, but couldn't. Then, when Father was badly hurt, he helped him enter Valhalla with his sword in hand. He said he was sorry for that, but it's what Father would have wanted… Which it was, wasn't it? Pappa always said Valhalla was the greatest honour any warrior could receive.'

Skadi swallowed the knot in her throat, regret threatening to drown her. Could things have been different if she'd taken greater care to ensure Agnar and his mother had been better cared for? Could she have avoided all of this? 'It is.'

Astra nodded sagely, 'Then I am glad. Agnar scared me at first…especially that first night. But he got down on his knees today and swore with his hand on his heart that he would always protect us.'

Skadi glanced towards Brenna, who nodded. 'He did… in front of all the men, too. He made them stop training to watch.'

Skadi's gaze followed the dark shape of Agnar as he strode out of the training square and disappeared from view. The men watched him as he passed and not with the animosity she would have expected. There was a subtle shift in their attitude towards him—now they watched him with respectful curiosity.

He was her husband and the King of Thrudheim, only his death or hers would change that, and she was beginning to wonder if denying her fate was a pointless waste of her energy.

She was a queen. If her fate was to be with Agnar, then she would mould her future as she saw fit. At least, she understood him better now. He was justifiably resentful of the past, but he *did* desire her. For once, she *could* be the seducer and lead her own destiny.

Chapter Sixteen

Agnar was pleasantly surprised by what Thrudheim had to offer, as well as Skadi's impressive skills at ruling and managing her kingdom. He'd given up looking for signs of her mismanagement. The town and port ran well and fairly, with very little disgruntlement from the traders and merchants.

Skadi might be proud and spoilt, but she was a good queen, and Agnar was beginning to realise that he had been harsh in some of his assumptions.

A larger party of servants and warriors had gone ahead of them to prepare the mountain lodge. They followed with a small group of guards at a slower pace, Skadi occasionally stopping to point out some landmark or introduce him to the loggers who lived within the forest.

The island was large and split by the mountain range that hugged the bay and town like a crescent moon. The perfect mixture of natural and fortified defences. But there was far more to Thrudheim than the small bay. The rest of the island was more difficult to reach and involved climbing one of the two mountain paths that ran through the forest and over the ridge to the flatlands beyond. There was no access to the flatlands by sea, as the sheer cliffs fell straight down and were hazardous to climb.

They'd spent the afternoon riding through the forest,

climbing steadily to the hunting lodge near its peak. The weather was definitely turning, red and gold leaves carpeted the forest floor and were beginning to brown. The bare branches allowed the bitter wind to rattle through despite the sunshine overhead.

The mountain path was wide and he was able to ride his horse beside Skadi's most of the way. He wondered if she was beginning to thaw towards him, as she'd made pleasant conversation for most of the ride and even smiled more than once at him…in a way that almost felt flirtatious.

He must be mistaken; their training together earlier had been an error. He'd had to battle with his lust through each move and touch and then run from her presence like a pitiful coward. Surely Skadi wouldn't have changed her mind about him so quickly? It was simply wishful thinking on his part.

After all, Skadi took such time and care in all of her other decisions. Even now, Astra sat in front of her, Skadi not trusting such a steep and slippery path for her child to ride alone.

'Can I ride my own horse once we've passed the ridge?' grumbled Astra.

'We haven't any spare horses. But we might be able to borrow one between the farms and the crafters.'

'Crafters?' asked Agnar curiously.

'There's a village of them,' declared Astra brightly. 'I like going there, it's fun! I can play with the children or make things: pottery, jewellery, tapestries, and cloth!'

'You have seen their work…they made the fish cup you admired,' said Skadi with a teasing smile that made it obvious she knew he'd thought it a ridiculous piece of pottery. She glanced around at the thick forest either side of them. 'Usually, they alert us to any arrivals coming from behind the mountain. You must have kept your ships hidden from both the port and the crafters to arrive without us knowing.'

Agnar nodded. 'I knew you had settlements on the flat-lands. I had to keep in line with the highest peak so as not to be noticed from either side. Thankfully, Rán was feeling generous and matched the waves to our course.'

Astra stiffened and glanced up at her mother with a worried expression.

'I am sure it is nothing to do with Rán,' Skadi said dismissively and he wondered if there had been some prophecy or fearful omen, before the arrival of his ships—something to do with the goddess of the sea. Either way, Astra had a decidedly guilty look on her face and Skadi seemed determined to ease her worries.

He shrugged, deciding the best way to reassure her would be to accept the good fortune he'd received and explain it as best he could. 'We made many sacrifices to Rán before we left. I am sure she was well pleased with them.'

'Before you left, you say?' said Skadi, patting Astra's shoulder.

He noticed the way they both relaxed when he nodded in agreement. 'Yes, well before.' He thought back to when he'd secured his army. 'King Olaf wanted to ensure my safe arrival in the Saxon lands, so he had a great feast and burned a ship in his fjord.'

Skadi's eyes widened at his words. She knew he'd had help from King Olaf, but not the true conviction of her uncle… The sacrifice of a ship meant a lot and he was certain Skadi hadn't fully appreciated the strength of his support until now. Unfortunately, the men were not a permanent addition to his army. He needed to secure Thrudheim's future and quickly eliminate the threat Sven posed.

'When will my uncle expect the return of his men?' asked Skadi curiously and he realised how similarly their minds worked, as he'd been thinking much the same.

'Once things have been settled,' he said quietly, not liking how close her man, Oddmund, was riding behind them. Skadi had insisted the man join them, as he knew the mines well. Agnar also suspected she wanted Oddmund present as a form of protection for herself and Astra. She might have softened towards him, but there was still a long way to go before she trusted him fully.

He could understand her reluctance. His mother had been equally protective of him as a child. At least she was willing to make compromises, as Astra's presence and the new Thrudheim banners showed.

Whether he could ever fully forgive her for her part in his mother's death…he wasn't sure. He knew he still carried a need for vengeance, but he was beginning to doubt the callousness of Skadi's part in it. She had seemed genuinely horrified to learn of their difficult journey to Aldeigja. It made him wonder what other lies she'd been told over the years.

Skadi was frowning at him and he realised his vague answer regarding his future plans had irritated her. 'You have said that before—I was hoping for something more specific.'

'I cannot be specific,' he answered, glancing towards Oddmund. Skadi's frown turned into a scowl and he had the feeling they'd taken a step back in their understanding of one another and this time it was his fault.

They arrived at the hunting lodge as the sky turned a pretty shade of purple bleeding into a sapphire blanket and sprinkled above with silver stars. A break in the forest showed the cliff drop to the side of the lodge, the sea and sky fading into moody shades of blue and black in the distance. They left their horses to be looked after by the men and were welcomed by a few of Skadi's servants who had been sent ahead to prepare the lodge and evening meal.

Most of the men would be sleeping in the tents set up in the little clearing around the cabin—a campfire was already burning for them. The darkness of the forest was already creeping in around them and Skadi hurried Astra inside.

The smell of warm pine, ash and fur hit him as he stepped inside. It was a good-sized lodge, with enough space for four long tables and benches. The central fire burned brightly and there were a few wall torches among the thick tapestries of hunting scenes and displays of antlers.

Brenna greeted them with a horn of mead and a pleasant smile. 'Your beds are ready and I've put in some warming stones under your blankets. The food will be ready shortly.'

'Did you bring…?' Astra glanced at Agnar with a blush, before whispering, 'Freydis?'

Brenna grinned. 'Yes, Freydis is in your bed already. She has some new clothes, too. Your mother made them.'

The little girl's eyes lit up as she looked to Skadi. 'When?'

'While everyone was packing for this trip and you were busy fussing over those kittens.'

With a squeal of excitement Astra ran to the loft ladder, scurrying up it with incredible speed.

'Her doll,' Skadi explained to Agnar before thanking Brenna and taking a large sip of mead from her horn. 'Ahh, I didn't realise how thirsty I was.' She then glanced up at the loft space, smiling at Astra who was already playing with her doll on her bed.

He followed her gaze to the platform above, which jutted out over half of the hall. It contained one large bed and two smaller beds either side of it. He presumed they would be sleeping there tonight, while the rest of the servants slept on bed rolls, or with the warriors out by the campfire.

It was a family home, he realised, quiet and snug in comparison to the hall's large and luxurious chambers. Skadi's eyes even softened as she looked around her, as if pleasant memories were warming her heart.

He sipped deeply from his own horn of mead. 'Does anyone live here—when you're not using it?'

'No, it has always been used by my family. Although I often open it to guests. Traders and merchants, as well as visiting kings and chieftains who wish to hunt.'

An unwelcome anger rose within him. 'Sven?'

She nodded. 'Of course. He always liked to go hunting with Heimdall when he visited.'

'Have you stayed here often?' he asked, a swirl of jealousy whipping up a storm in his stomach. He realised then that he hated Heimdall and Sven for more than taking his birthright, he hated them for enjoying hunting lodges. And he hated Heimdall most of all, because he'd had a beautiful wife and daughter, while Agnar had spent years fighting for his survival.

He wondered if she noticed his seething, because she gave him a curious look before answering, 'Many times. I prefer the fresh air and privacy.' She moved to sit at a bench close to the fire.

He took a seat opposite her, mainly so that he could see her better. The golden light of the fire warmed the whiteness of her hair and the brightness of her eyes.

He sipped from his own horn and was about to ask her about their plans for visiting the silver mine the next day when she surprised him by saying, 'My father loved this lodge. I spent most of my summers here, at least until I married.'

'Why did you stop?'

'Heimdall used to go raiding or on campaigns with Sven in the summer. I had to remain in the hall close to the harbour, in case of trouble.'

'So…you never came with Heimdall?'

'Very rarely.'

Agnar's jealousy disappeared like a fog, allowing him to see clearly. What a fool Heimdall had been, to have everything and never value it. 'But you came with your father?' he asked curiously.

Skadi smiled and nodded. 'All the time, I suppose…things were safer then. We were less bothered by the petty Kings. Straight after my father died, we began to be regularly attacked by raiding parties. My men and I were always able to defeat them, but sometimes they managed to steal from our harbour and the merchants became nervous.'

He snorted. 'And it miraculously improved after your marriage to Heimdall, and alliance with Sven was agreed… How convenient!'

She raised a brow at his mocking tone. 'You are suggesting Sven was to blame. But my father trusted him and therefore so did I. He'd already agreed an alliance with Sven's father…with our betrothal, remember?'

'A betrothal you did not keep.'

She nodded, still refusing to apologise. But for some reason it no longer bothered him. Perhaps because he finally understood why she had been so afraid. The pressure and responsibility she'd faced back then at such a young age was something he already understood. Although he would still argue that she should never have trusted Sven or Heimdall.

'The alliance was maintained…because Sven *suggested* I break the betrothal. You are probably right about his reasons for doing so. He's asked to be matched with Astra more than once.'

'Astra?' Agnar felt his stomach churn with horror and disgust. Now he understood her fearful words that first night, when he'd demanded the return of his Queen. It hadn't even occurred to him that she would suspect he meant Astra. The little girl who quite rightly still played with kittens and dolls.

Skadi gave him a pointed look. 'And yet you expected the same of me?'

'You were not old enough to be my grandparent like Sven! There is only ten years between us.' But then he glanced at Astra and finally understood what Skadi must have seen when she'd looked at him all those years ago. 'Granted, I was too young then. But all you had to do was agree to the wishes of your father. My mother would have stayed with me in Thrudheim and we could have requested your uncle's support. In a few short years, I would have been more than capable of bedding you and the difference in our ages would have meant nothing, as it does now.'

A pink blush stained Skadi's cheeks and he realised she was embarrassed by his blunt words about bedding her. He was secretly pleased that she no longer appeared disgusted by the suggestion… Perhaps, she was warming towards him?

Eventually, Skadi cleared her throat and shook her head in disbelief. 'I am sure you believe you are simply rectifying a wrong done to you many years ago. But things were more complicated then. I never meant to hurt you or your mother. I thought I was doing the right thing…for all of us.'

Previously, he would have raged at her for saying such a thing, but he found himself accepting the sincerity of her words, even if he did not agree with them. 'Things could have been so different… Your father was a good man. I am sorry he left this world so unexpectedly, it must have been difficult for you to mourn him and defend your throne at the same time.'

Skadi nodded, her expression turning sad. 'I often think about how much *better* things would have been if he'd lived longer.'

Agnar was surprised by her confession and she chuckled at his obviously dazed expression. 'Not because of *you*!' She rolled her eyes dramatically, before sighing. 'Well, not entirely because of you… I would have loved to have been with him for longer…to have learned at his side. I felt as if I were drowning at first, under the responsibility of it all. I thought I'd prepared myself for it, but I hadn't. There was no one to offer me guidance, except for Sven, my mother was long dead—I do not even remember her—and Heimdall seemed like such a…*safe* choice.' She shrugged. 'Hate me for it if you must. But I could hear the beasts scratching at the door and I was afraid that if I didn't act, they would eventually come bursting in.'

'Heimdall was Sven's puppet,' he snapped, unable to hide his resentment.

Skadi sighed. 'And I thought to make him mine. I thought he adored me, that he would have done anything that I wished…'

'And did he?'

She laughed, the sound bitter and cold. 'Of course not. He never loved me. I was the one blinded by desire and foolish pride. But I still do not regret marrying him.' She smiled warmly, as Astra came down the loft ladder with her doll in her hands. 'How could I regret her?'

Astra strode up and placed her doll on the table with a soft thud. 'Look at her new dress! Isn't it beautiful?' she declared and Agnar noted that the doll wore a sapphire gown with a white wolf emblazoned on its front.

The new banner of Thrudheim.

For the first time he truly understood why Skadi refused to beg forgiveness for what she had done. To do so would be to admit that she regretted marrying Heimdall and having Astra.

Skadi refused to regret the past, because it had given her a future. Perhaps he should also let go of the past and *choose* to be happy?

Chapter Seventeen

They rose early the next day, and made their way through the forest to the silver mine. Skadi had been relieved that Agnar had let her have some privacy last night, especially as Astra was sleeping in a little bed next to them. He'd waited until they'd both gone to bed before joining her.

Thankfully the loft bed was large and she barely noticed him in it. It was about as intimate as sleeping next to Brenna, or dare she say it… Heimdall.

The path to the silver mine from the lodge was reasonably flat, winding through the forest of the mountain ridge to the small and unassuming hole in the rockface that was the entrance to the vast network of tunnels beneath the mountain. It didn't take them long to reach it and they quickly dismounted their horses. If it wasn't for all of the tools, carts and the miners' cabin beside it, a person might miss it entirely.

'When you arrived, did you use the path we used yesterday to get to my hall, or did you use that path?' Skadi asked curiously, pointing down to a rocky path that was even steeper than the one they'd climbed with horses.

'Neither,' Agnar said, shaking his head. 'If I'd known these two paths existed, it would have been much easier. We used hooks and ropes to climb up the cliff face from our ships and then hacked our way through the forest down to your gate. It was very…challenging.'

'I can imagine!' Skadi laughed and after a moment he returned her smile. 'But I suppose these paths are not obvious from the sea, sheltered as they are by the trees.'

'Which is a good thing,' Agnar said thoughtfully. 'Every man craves silver, either for a Thor's hammer, or to trade it for goods. Later, we line our burial chambers with it and carry it with us into the afterlife. It is essential to our way of life, yet this is the only place producing a significant amount of silver in the west. The rest comes from the Islamic Caliphates in the east and they expect hordes of slaves and furs in payment. It is why many covet your kingdom, despite its small size. To produce your own silver is to own true freedom.'

'Did you ever travel east?' she asked curiously, wondering what the eastern mines were like so far away.

'Yes, to Constantinople and beyond.'

'What was it like?'

Agnar shrugged. 'Hot and strange.'

She laughed. 'Is that all you have to say?'

Agnar smiled and his gaze lingered on her mouth for a few moments. 'It was not where I wanted to be. As you get to know me you will realise that I am as obstinate as a mule, especially when it comes to my goals, and I saw those places as stepping stones, a way to reach my ultimate ambition…' He paused and his eyes locked with hers. 'I wanted to be here…with you.' As if embarrassed by his confession, he looked away from her towards the mine, his jaw flexing as if he were fighting some inner turmoil and regretted his words.

Skadi's face flushed and she struggled to think of a response.

Surely he didn't mean it like that? He'd been building his army and wealth, not…yearning to be by her side. He'd only been a boy when he'd left—no man would be infatuated with a memory from his childhood, especially for all that time! Perhaps he meant simply that he'd wanted the land and kingdom that he'd been promised. Which meant she was still a trophy to be won and owned… *Yes, that's what he meant!*

Skadi cleared her throat and pretended he hadn't spoken. 'We also produce lead and copper here and in greater quantity to our silver. But it is not without risk or hardship. This…' she pointed to the steep path with its pulley and thick rope '…is the safest way down for the ore. There is no danger of mudslides as there are on the other path. It is too rocky for that, but the path is unbearably steep. We use winches, pulleys and strong mules to safely transport it to the smelting furnaces at the bottom of the mountain. The miners are rewarded well for their dangerous and hard work, but sadly we still lose men occasionally. There's always the danger of a mine collapse, or even bad falls from on the mountain path.'

Agnar moved closer to the steep drop. 'I will not benefit from another man's labour and sacrifice until I have experienced it myself. When things are settled, I will inspect and work these mines to see if there are any improvements I can make to safety.'

A warm glow of appreciation spread through her body. 'That is admirable. I did the same when I was younger, but I welcome any and all improvements to safety. The mountain is treacherous, but it is also our greatest protection. As you learned yourself, the landscape of Thrudheim makes it difficult to sneak up on us, or conquer our lands. You were indeed lucky to do so without coming to any harm.'

'It will be even harder now,' Agnar replied and then explained by pointing up at the peak of the highest mountain. 'I will be creating a series of beacons around the island. Once enemy ships are spotted, they will be lit and it will warn us of any unexpected arrivals.'

'Impressive. I did not have enough men to do that before. It is good that you are rectifying those gaps in our defences.'

Agnar seemed pleased by her confession and he turned towards the entrance of the mine. It looked more like a troll's cave, the area around its entrance dusty and well worn from so many carts being pulled back and forth to the smelting furnaces and workshops below in Thrudheim.

They walked over to the clearing around the mine's entrance. There was a small stone cabin close by for the miners, its timber roof tarred and painted green to keep out the rain and any eagle-eyed Vikings watching from the sea.

The horses they'd ridden joined the stock of hardy mountain ponies in a loosely fenced pen to enjoy the alpine herbs and bushes. The encircled 'pasture' was more of an encircled piece of the forested slope, but there was still a small amount of grass for them to enjoy despite the increasing cold.

Astra was already inside the fenced area, patting the ponies and feeding herbs to the greedy goats. Skadi pointed out the small replica of the cabin with a smile. 'That's for the chickens and goats, so that the miners can have fresh eggs and milk. They have limited supplies up here, but I've tried to give them a few home comforts. I've told them they can return to Thrudheim for winter now. The weather has started to turn and there's no point them carrying on if the frost and snow come.'

She frowned.

'What is it?'

She was reluctant to admit the truth, but she knew it would give her a clear insight into Agnar's true nature. 'We only mine for a short time each year, late spring to late autumn, when the weather is reasonably dry and warm enough to dig. They could work for longer, I suppose, through the winter and spring. But to do so could put the men at risk, especially in the wet and cold months. The land shifts—occasionally we've come back after a stormy spring to find a tunnel collapsed or the path blocked by fallen trees.' She paused, watching his face closely. 'But to mine throughout the year could significantly increase our production…and our wealth.'

She didn't mention that Heimdall had tried many times to convince her of mining throughout the year. She'd managed to avoid it by pointing out, or exaggerating, some recent disaster or struggles the miners had faced that year. Luckily, he'd not been interested enough in running the kingdom to question it.

Agnar's top lip lifted in a lopsided smile and her breath caught in her throat, not only in anticipation of what he would say, but in an unexpected flood of desire. She found his gruff features more handsome every day, particularly when he had that knowing smile on his face, as if he knew some dark and wicked secret of hers.

'Do you not have enough wealth already?' he asked mildly, 'You bathe with exotic soaps, eat honey and spices daily and drink Frankish wine from a glass chalice… What more could you want?'

She stared at him, this scarred and fearsome warrior who so easily dismissed increasing his wealth, when any other man's greed would lead the way. Glory and treasure were the reason Norse men became Vikings, so that they could raid and gather more treasure. Heimdall had not been content with his hoard, he'd searched and raided every year to increase it. Wanting to enter Valhalla with a sword in one hand and the glory of a mountain of silver in the other.

What more could she want? She dared not even think

about it for too long. To do so felt greedy and all she could think of was Agnar's warm arms wrapped around her in the training yard, that lingering look to her mouth just now and his confession that he'd simply wanted to be with her.

What would it be like to kiss him? To make love to him?

She'd hoped that she might be able to seduce him…but was she foolish to think she could manipulate a man with something so fleeting as desire? And was he the one actually manipulating her? She couldn't be sure either way, as her attraction towards him seemed to be growing despite her better judgement.

She turned a little to watch her daughter squeal with delight as the goats hopped on logs and boulders around her.

Agnar was dangerous. She couldn't forget that, or the way he'd held her daughter's life in his hands only a few days ago. 'I want nothing more than my people to be safe and well fed.' She looked back at him, her tone serious. 'Wealth allows that.'

His eyes met hers and the green of his eyes shone with understanding—it was as if he could read her thoughts, her fears and doubts. 'It does… But you are not safe…not yet. However, I can help you with that. Wealth is of no use without that, especially if you are only mining it for another. Please show me everything, I wish to learn.'

His willingness to listen to her was surprising, but she did as he asked. She began to run through the process, reciting what she'd learned from her father. Explaining everything there was to know about the mines and production of the ore. His interest seemed genuine and he regularly asked questions to clarify points, never once appearing bored or disregarding her opinions as Heimdall so often had.

As they were preparing to enter the mines, Astra joined them and she included her in her teachings. It was an important part of Thrudheim that she needed to know as its heir. Although Skadi refused to let her enter the mine without all of them first putting on the battered helms many of the miners wore to protect their heads.

Agnar smiled as he accepted his helm. 'I rarely wear a helm in battle, it feels strange to put one on now.'

'Yes, I remember. You wear a wolf's skin, why is that?' Skadi asked.

'Are you a berserker?' gasped a wide-eyed Astra, her voice filled with awe.

It was a good question, although Skadi suspected Agnar was the type of man to prefer to be in control of his mind during battle. Unlike the mushroom-induced-madness of the berserkers, who believed themselves transformed into strong beasts impervious to pain after taking their magical potions. Skadi had seen berserkers fight on despite horrendous injuries. But she'd never been completely sure if it was due to magic, or simply because of their inability to have any reason or feeling once they'd descended into their bloodlust.

When Agnar answered, they leaned forward to listen. 'I wear the wolfskin as a reminder. My mother was given the name She-Wolf by Sven. It was meant as an insult, but she liked it. In a den of wolves, the females always lead the pack. Unfortunately, while we were travelling to Aldeigja we were hunted by a pack of wolves. My mother had an injury from a previous fall that had begun to fester—I think the pack saw us as easy pickings. We managed to fight them off and I now use their skins to keep me warm and to remind myself that a fight can turn for the better or for the worse in a matter of moments. My mother said it was a good lesson. To always watch your back and protect the pack—even if it is only a pack of two…or one.' His eyes saddened for a moment and Skadi knew he was thinking of his mother's death.

Her heart ached for him, she knew what it was like to be left alone with no family for protection.

'Are we part of your pack now?' asked Astra hesitantly.

Agnar smiled down at her daughter. 'Yes…if that's acceptable to you, my Princess?'

Astra nodded sagely, reaching for Skadi's hand. 'Moma will lead, as she's the She-Wolf now.'

Skadi squeezed her daughter's hand. 'That sounds reasonable. Now, let me show you the different seams of silver, copper and lead. It's a lot of walking and the tunnels are cramped and dark, so keep hold of my hand.'

Astra offered her free hand to Agnar, 'We should stick together, as a pack.'

He stared down at her tiny hand and then, with a nod of agreement, he took it. Skadi tried to ignore the hope blooming within her chest at the sight of his large hand wrapped lightly around her daughter's. She knew she shouldn't, but she was beginning to wish for a future where she and Astra were no longer alone.

Chapter Eighteen

They left the comfort of the hunting lodge bright and early the next day, making their way carefully down the other side of the mountain. It took most of the morning to clamber down the winding path, the majority of the time spent on foot gingerly leading the horses down one at a time. The gravel shifted occasionally, sending a cascade of rocks down the barren mountainside—it was a stark contrast to the forested slopes on the ridge. Eventually, the steep drop levelled out into woodland and they began to breathe more easily, each returning to mount their horses with a grateful sigh.

'It might be as easy to sail around to this side of the mountain,' declared Agnar bad-temperedly. 'Even using hooks and ropes to climb sheer cliffs must be easier than that!'

Astra, who'd grown more and more confident with him, giggled and began to explain with a lot of wild hand gestures why that was impossible. 'The cliffs on the harbour side are much smaller! Here it's all meadows and flat farm land. At the very edge of the island there are no beaches or gentle slopes. The land drops right off into the sea from a very great height.'

She chopped straight down with her hand to demonstrate. 'The cliffs are very dangerous and sometimes big chunks of rock fall down into the sea with no warning! So, you wouldn't want to get close to the edge or try to climb them with hooks.

You'd hit a bit of loose rock and go…' She whistled loudly, mimicking the sound of something falling through the air. 'SPLAT! You're dead!' she shouted, banging her fist against her palm for dramatic effect.

Skadi rolled her eyes at her child's exuberance. *What had happened to the terrified little girl being held up like a leg of lamb?* It seemed Astra was far quicker to forgive and forget than Skadi.

'Be careful you do not spook your pony,' she warned Astra, who frowned back at her, but held her reins a little more firmly. She'd managed to sweet-talk Skadi into borrowing one of the miners' ponies, although Skadi might insist they use it for transporting goods on the way back—Astra could be a little reckless when riding.

Agnar scratched his chin. 'Hmmm, then I won't climb the cliffs… But this is *still* a troublesome region to get to!'

'It is,' agreed Skadi. 'The harvest is brought over by mule to Thrudheim. Or occasionally through a path on the southern ridge, but that relies on the time of year and the tides clearing enough space around the harbour. The journey has to be timed very carefully. It is worth it, though. The flatlands are fertile and the food produced here fills most of Thrudheim's stores with vegetables and meat. Unfortunately, wheat, barley and rye crops tend to fail here, the land is too rocky, the storms too harsh.' She looked pointedly at Agnar, hoping he would remember what she'd said about the grain stores and having to import them from Sven.

He nodded. 'I have a plan for the grain…' Again, he didn't give a full answer and she was growing tired of his lack of openness, especially as she was *trying* very hard to be open with him.

With a sharp glare she asked, 'Perhaps you will deign to tell me of it some time?'

* * *

She kicked her horse forward with a bad-tempered huff and Agnar immediately regretted his words. He kicked his heels urging his own horse to follow her. It only took him a few moments to catch up with her and, after a quick glance behind, he was reassured to see that Oddmund was riding further back.

'Skadi!' he hissed and she eased her horse into a slower trot before glaring back at him.

'Yes? Are you finally willing to trust me with your plans to feed *my* people? I have explained everything you have asked of me.'

He sighed. '*Our* people,' he corrected before adding, 'I hope to make a deal with King Erik. He has an excess of grain and would welcome some silver.'

'I am sure he would!' snapped Skadi, 'It is the exact same arrangement we have with Sven. You are simply exchanging one deal for another.'

'That is true,' he admitted, 'but King Erik has something in his favour that Sven does not.'

'And what is that?'

'His lands lie between King Olaf's and yours. If we ever need help, we can use his trading and fishing routes to notify Olaf. It would put us in a stronger position to trade with your uncle and get aid from him whenever we need it.'

'Sven will not be pleased if King Erik accepts our deal. They have been in disagreement with each other for some time. Sven might even use it as an excuse to try to overthrow him.'

'He might.'

As if she were talking to a child, she said, 'And *that* would leave us with two Kings angry with us and still no grain!'

'No… The other Kings would revolt against Sven for his

high-handed attitude. They do not like him; they do not like how he controls this region with an iron fist. They know that if they allow him to threaten one King, especially for simply trading with another, then they are all doomed.'

Skadi could see the wisdom of it, but she was still worried. 'You play a dangerous game… Let us hope *our* people do not suffer for it.'

They came to a fork in the path, and Skadi halted her horse, standing up in her seat to face Oddmund, who'd managed to worm his way to the head of the group. Thankfully, he was still too far away to hear their conversation.

'We shall pay respect to my father and the ancestors, before heading to the crafters' village. Oddmund, take half the men to the crafters and let them know of our arrival. We will join them before nightfall,' she declared, before lowering in her seat and trotting her horse towards the path on the left.

Agnar followed, being sure to check that Brenna and Vali were either side of Astra before continuing.

'Do not speak to Oddmund of my plans,' he said and she stiffened before turning to face him.

'I have known Oddmund my entire life. He can be trusted.'

'If you want me to tell you more about my plans for Thrudheim's future, you must swear to speak only to me about them.'

'Is that because I am part of your *pack* now?' she teased, but swallowed when his eyes narrowed with anger.

'Yes,' he growled. 'And I do not give my trust lightly. Even Vali isn't privy to everything.'

She turned away from him, but gave a begrudging nod of agreement. 'Then, no one shall hear of your plans from me.'

The woodland path ahead of them opened out into a meadow that overlooked the sea. But that wasn't the most remarkable sight. Awaiting them were two imposing white stones guarding the entrance to the meadow like frost giants. Beyond them were several funeral mounds, covered in grass and flowers. Oval shapes of varying heights covered in turf and encircled by a jagged ring of rocks placed to ensure the shape of the ships lying beneath the earth remained, even as time dragged them deeper down.

They stopped in front of the two stone guards, beautifully carved with painted sea serpents and runic ribbons intertwined. Agnar followed Skadi's example as she dropped down from her horse and let it feed on the meadow, passing their reins to one of the warriors who had remained with them. He then helped Astra dismount, surprised when she grinned up at him and said, 'Grandfather's ship is that one.' She pointed to a large mound a few feet away from the entrance. 'Moma says he wanted to be placed facing east, so that he could always watch the sunrise.'

Agnar looked out at the mound. The sun was high overhead, but he imagined that during sunrise it was a beautiful spot. The curving flatlands and dramatic cliffs of Thrudheim were at your back and the endless sea stretched out in front of you. He wondered if Skadi's father had ever longed to travel, to see what lay beyond the sea.

Agnar would have told him not to bother. There was nothing more than greed and cruelty beyond his lands.

'You wouldn't be allowed to be buried here,' said Astra bluntly and then added with a gentle apology, 'I'm sorry, but only the *true* bloodlines of the first King can be laid here… Although Grandfather cheated a little with Grandmother, he took her ashes as part of his hoard and was buried with her. She'd died when Moma was a baby, you see…' Astra took a deep and thoughtful breath. 'If you die before Moma, she can take you with her as part of her treasure if you like…'

'I see.' Agnar tried to hide his amusement at the child's

easy discussion of his demise. 'She might want to take your father instead.'

Astra shook her head quickly. 'No, Pappa was buried at sea, Moma said he would have liked that. If you don't want to be buried at sea, you can have a burial mound down by Thrudheim.'

'It looks like I have a lot of choice.' Agnar said, slightly disgusted with himself for finding a twisted pleasure in the fact that Skadi had not wanted to keep Heimdall's ashes for her own afterlife.

Skadi had moved to stand in between the two stones. She spread out her arms, touching each rock at the same time as if she were greeting two loyal warriors, then after a silent moment of reflection she passed through.

Astra took his hand and tugged him forward, explaining solemnly, 'When you pass through the gate into the King's meadow, you are entering the land of the dead. You cannot see them, but they are there. Their spirits feast in Valhalla, but they are like Odin—able to return whenever you seek their guidance, or just want to wish them well.'

'But they're dead… How can you wish them well?' he teased and Astra's face wrinkled with momentary confusion.

'It's…polite. They are our elders after all. You need to be respectful.'

'Perhaps I shouldn't go in.' Agnar said, this time meaning it.

'But Moma will want to introduce you to Grandfather! She takes me every summer, so that he can see me. She says I grow so quickly that he might forget what I look like. Which is just stupid, because I have Moma's hair and eyes!'

'That is true, you look just like her.'

'Come on.' Astra tugged him forward impatiently and placed one hand on the stone closest to her and then glared at Agnar until he did the same. She closed her eyes and for some bizarre reason Agnar found himself doing the same. The cold of the stone beneath his hand was strangely calming. Perhaps, because it had been here long before him and would remain long after. In a world filled with chaos it was good to know some things would still remain.

In the centre of the meadow was a small mound, where the rocks encircling it were barely bigger than its peak. However, there was a much larger rock in front of it, like the dragon-head prow of a ship, as if the ship were in the dip of a wave and about to rear up on a crest.

As they passed it, Astra reverently whispered, 'The first King.' She bowed respectfully and Agnar did the same.

The runic inscriptions on the prow-stone were so weathered he couldn't make out what they said. The rock was a different colour to the rest, almost black. Imported from another land—presumably the motherland of the first King. A powerful reminder of Skadi's ancient bloodline and right to rule. The rest of the Kings were buried in a fan around the first King's ship, taking their place at his side like the spikes on Skadi's silver crown, or the petals of a flower.

For years, Agnar's entire focus had been on winning back this island. But standing here surrounded by the many Kings of Thrudheim that had come before him, he finally understood why Skadi had laughed at him for declaring that he wanted to reclaim his *birthright.*

He was a guest and a fleeting one at that.

Yes, to him and his mother, finally becoming the ruler of Thrudheim was the ultimate prize and a just reward for everything they had suffered. He had been born to be a king and his father and mother had both wanted that life for him.

But was Thrudheim's crown truly his birthright?

No.

It was an uncomfortable feeling to know that he'd been wrong. Very rarely did Agnar question his choices and reclaiming Skadi and Thrudheim had always been his north star and guiding light. To realise that Thrudheim wasn't his *birthright*, but Skadi's, was unnerving. But also…freeing, because he could let go of his resentment about the past.

Perhaps his mother had understood that better than him. Why else would she have instructed him as she had? Telling him, *'Become invincible and then take back what you were promised. Make Skadi your Queen.'* His mother had never once instructed him to overthrow Skadi, so she must have known what he'd only just realised.

It was Skadi's birthright, not his.

He was led by Astra to meet with Skadi a few feet away. She stood at the prow of her father's burial mound, her hands folded neatly in front of her.

He'd said nothing, but she must have seen him staring at the burial mounds, the weight of their history on his shoulders.

'Most of my ancestors are here.' Skadi explained, 'Although, a couple of them preferred to be closer to Thrudheim. My grandmother keeps watch over the ships in the harbour. She loved to sail and defeated Jarl Gunnar Bloodaxe at sea. Battling his fleet of ships and forcing him into the whirlpools and cliffs until nothing remained but driftwood. Nobody dared attack Thrudheim for another fifty years after her victory.' She smiled warmly, her face so much brighter when she was less guarded.

'She is the reason my father never worried about me ruling alone as a woman. I remember him saying that his mother was a fierce shieldmaiden and an even tougher negotiator. She took no husband and declared that my father was a gift from the ancestors. I imagine she just picked one of her warriors to be her stallion for the night.' Skadi chuckled with amusement. 'I think my father had hoped to do the same with you, Agnar. He believed he would live at least another ten or twenty years, and wanted me to be as independent and confident in my leadership as his mother had been. I imagine he thought I wouldn't have to take you officially as my husband until we were both fully grown.'

A sudden thought struck him like a hammer. 'I have never asked—how did your father die?'

Skadi raised a brow knowingly. 'You wish to know? No one else cared to, they heard the news of his death and descended on me like rats from a burning ship.'

Agnar nodded, his mother had done much the same, begging any merchant or Jarl to take her with them. It had been a moment of panic among the Kings, Jarls and Chieftains, each of them desperate to use the tragedy for their own benefit. 'I apologise for not asking sooner… I should have.'

Skadi's gaze shifted back to her father's mound. 'We'd been training with sword and shield. It was the first time I had defeated him and he was congratulating me and laughing about how he needed to train harder because he felt so tired. Moments later he was struggling for breath and then he died in my arms. It happened so quickly… I didn't even wish him farewell…'

Tears gathered in her eyes and she stopped speaking. He understood that feeling well, had battled it many times himself. He admired her for being able to talk about it as much as she had—he still struggled to even mention his mother, or those months traveling to Aldeigja. The sacrifices his poor mother had made, the starvation, the illness, struggle and ultimate loss.

It was why he had never given up on her dream—no matter how impossible it might have seemed. But if he were to move forward, he had to make a choice.

He knelt in front of the last King of Thrudheim's funeral ship, placed his hand over his heart and bowed his head respectfully. He hoped Astra was right and the dead visited from time to time. There was no place or woman more beautiful than Thrudheim and Skadi. He hoped his mother might also choose this moment to visit. To see her son make another vow, this time not to correct the past, but to look to the future.

'Greetings, Your Highness, I have married your beautiful daughter Skadi as you wished. Please forgive me for the delay and my rude arrival—I was determined to return to her and keep my oath. You trusted me without even truly knowing me, believing me worthy as her husband and King well before I became a man. In some ways, I have failed you. But I swear now to make amends. I will protect both your daughter and granddaughter with my life. I will honour Thrudheim and ensure your bloodline continues unbroken for the next generation.'

When he finished his oath, he stood and caught Skadi's shocked expression.

Slowly, she closed her open mouth and gave an appreciative nod. He followed her then as she walked around the burials, introducing him to her ancestors. Some of the names he could read from the funeral stones and some he could not, but Skadi knew all of them regardless, and when Astra repeated them as if committing the names to memory, he did the same.

They were his ancestors now.

Chapter Nineteen

The rest of her afternoon with Agnar was surprisingly pleasant, although Skadi still felt rattled from earlier. His vow to her ancestors had shattered the carefully built wall around her heart in a hundred ways.

If he was trying to manipulate her into lowering her guard…he'd succeeded. He had apologised to her father and sworn to protect Astra. But more than that, he'd taken the time to learn her family history, to listen to the stories of her ancestors… He'd *cared.*

Heimdall, even in the glory of his youth, with his charming smiles and flexing muscles, would have paled in comparison to Agnar on his knees. No man had stolen her breath like he'd done in that moment. His long dark hair fluttering in the breeze, those vivid green eyes filled with strength and promise, the scarred hand clenched above his heart and his vow—*Odin's teeth! His vow*—she'd almost felt faint staring at him.

Thankfully, she'd had a little time afterwards to compose herself. Astra pointed out all the farms and landmarks along the way. With endless patience he listened to Astra babble about *'Hilda's sheep farm'* or *'the ancient hanging tree'* where murderers were punished.

She'd tried to stop Astra from explaining the long tale of

Dagni's pig thief. 'I do not think Agnar needs to know that tale,' she said firmly, leaning forward in her saddle to try to catch her daughter's eye.

But Agnar didn't seem to mind, and even encouraged her. 'No, tell me, Astra. Who was the pig thief and how did they steal the prize sow from a locked barn? They must have had a lot of cunning.'

Astra was thrilled by his interest. 'Dagni couldn't understand it either! She'd locked the pig up before the midsummer feast and then it disappeared! She suspected her closest neighbour, because he'd always been jealous of her pig. But when she demanded to see his barn, no pig was to be seen! And, when she came home, the pig was back!'

'Had the thief returned it, fearing they would be discovered?' asked Agnar thoughtfully and Skadi almost ruined it by laughing.

'That's what Dagni thought! And she wanted her neighbour punished, claiming that its return was proof that they were the original thief! But the neighbour argued that the only thief was Dagni, because a bag of his apples were missing, and he claimed Dagni had made a fine mess of his stores while searching for her pig! Neighbour was ready to hang neighbour and the entire island was in chaos, about to wage war upon one another!'

Agnar looked at Skadi with wide, concerned eyes and she sighed. 'It wasn't that bad…'

'What did your mother do?' Agnar asked, ignoring Skadi's comment and seemingly enthralled by the tale.

'Well… *First*, she asked to see the store with the missing apples. *Then* she walked over to Dagni's hall to see the barn where the pig lived…' Astra began to giggle.

'And what did she find?' asked Agnar, leaning forward in his saddle to hear her better.

Astra snorted. 'The pig had dug out a hole beneath the back wall of her barn and had even covered its escape by moving its trough to cover it! Dagni hadn't thought to check if the pig had escaped by itself… Pigs are surprisingly clever!'

Agnar reeled back with a loud, 'Ahhh! And that is why the pig returned…after eating the neighbour's apples, I'd wager!'

'That's what Mother said!' laughed Astra merrily.

'Now tell me, how did your mother appease both neighbours? After all, Dagni had accused her neighbour falsely and her animal had stolen their apples.'

'Dagni had to give her neighbour the next batch of piglets from the sow as an apology and in payment for the stolen apples.'

'A harsh punishment,' said Agnar with mock horror, but there was a twinkle in his eyes when he looked at her.

Skadi interjected quickly, 'It was more that she had not checked all possibilities before accusing her neighbour. We are a close community; such behaviour is not acceptable.'

'A wise decision,' Agnar said with a smile that made her heart race.

'There's the crafters' village!' declared Astra excitedly.

Sure enough, the crafters' village came into view as they crested one of the gently rolling hills of the flatlands. The settlement was a series of barns and workshops encircling one large hall. No defences or walls, only farmland surrounded it. If it had been any other village, she would have been afraid for the inhabitants, but thankfully, Jörđ, the goddess of mother nature, had created the perfect defences of sea and cliff to protect them.

The warriors they'd sent on ahead were already pitching tents and helping prepare for their stay. As they approached, the crafters came out of their workshops to greet their Queen, with nervous glances towards Agnar. Skadi tried her best to smile broadly to reassure them all was well—her sudden marriage would be a shock to them.

'There are so many women and children,' said Agnar with a frown. 'Where are the men?'

Skadi nodded, 'The mines and raiding have taken many men from us over the years. Some of the women felt vulnerable in Thrudheim. We have many traders and merchants visiting our shores, not to mention warriors.'

Agnar appeared thoughtful for a moment, before saying, 'You gave the widows this land and the workshops so that they can support and feed themselves?'

Skadi chuckled. 'I think it works well. Have you not seen the beautiful things they make? I merely help them achieve their goals without interference. Of course, the silver mine is where the majority of our wealth comes from. But these crafters have an equal part to play in our prosperity. Thrudheim crafts are well respected and sought after along the northern trading routes, they do very well indeed.'

With surprising speed Agnar dropped down from his horse and then turned towards her with a raised hand, silently offering to help her dismount. She didn't need his assistance, but quite liked that he had offered. She hadn't even thought to wait for him to do so before, had always hopped down by herself as she normally did.

Heimdall hadn't done anything like that since before they were married. She had thought it was because they were equal. But Agnar's offer of help seemed somehow more respectful, as though he wanted to protect and care for her… because he valued her as his wife and as his Queen.

She rested her palms on the tops of his shoulders, the silk of his hair brushing against her fingers and making them curl into the wool of his tunic. He reached for her waist, and she dropped down into his embrace, trusting him with her weight.

He held her aloft for a moment, before letting her slide down the length of him, her breasts lightly brushing against his chest in an intimate touch that caused her heart to race. The rasp of their clothing was the only sound between them, and she bit her lip, hoping for more…a touch, a kiss…

She hadn't realised she was holding her breath until his head tilted and he asked, shrewdly, 'When did this begin? Was it your doing?'

Was he talking about the mutual lust growing between them? She couldn't be certain, wasn't sure if she could pin down the exact moment when she'd wanted him. It had come upon her like a quick flowing tide, swallowing her whole.

'What do you mean?' Her fingers flexed into the wool of his tunic, curving around his thick shoulders.

'The village…was it your idea?'

'Oh!' Belatedly, she remembered what they'd been talking about only moments before and she felt as if she'd been thrown into the sea. Her hands dropped to her sides, heavy with disappointment, and she took a step away from him.

There was a brief moment when his hands tightened around her waist as if unwilling to let her go and then with a flustered expression he released her. He rocked back on his heels with a deep and husky clearing of his throat, that softened the blow of her disappointment and she smiled, finally answering his question. 'Yes, it was my idea. Heimdall wasn't convinced the widows could work the land as well as the men. But he liked the idea of freeing up more men for his raiding parties, so he allowed it. Not only did the widows produce more food than the men, they also spent their free time creating crafts. Now they had a community of women to help with raising the children, it was possible to work on other things as well. Over the last ten to fifteen years, their crafts have meant they are not only the food basket of the island, but they are successful traders in their own right.'

'You are proud of them.'

'I am.'

Movement from the hall caught her eye and she smiled broadly, as Brenna's mother came running out to greet her, wiping her apron hastily as if she'd just come from preparing Nattmal—which Skadi imagined she would have been, knowing Gertrud as she did.

'Gertrud!' cried Astra with delight, already reaching down to Skadi, wishing to be helped down from the horse. To her surprise Agnar reached for her instead and without a moment's hesitation Astra leapt into his arms and was gently set down on her feet in front of him. She ran forward and was embraced by Gertrud.

'Greetings, Queen Skadi and King… Agnar,' said Gertrud, a little hesitant over saying his name, possibly because Gertrud had only just learned of Skadi's marriage. News was slow to reach the crafters—it was partly why Skadi had sent Oddmund on ahead. Although why Agnar was so reluctant to trust Oddmund was beyond her.

'Greetings, Gertrud!' said Skadi, hugging the woman before introducing her to Agnar. 'Gertrud, is the leader of the village, she looked after me when I was a child and she is also Brenna's mother.'

Was it her imagination, or did Agnar seem to take on a more respectful countenance after the introduction? It was as if he realised how important Gertrud was to her, which she was. She'd been like a mother to Skadi as a child—her father had been wonderful, but he'd also been a king with many duties to attend to.

It had been Gertrud who had nursed her through sickness and treated her grazed knees. She had been as loving to Brenna as she had been to Skadi and she now thought of Brenna as her sister because of it.

Agnar bowed to Gertrud and said, 'You have done well. This is a fine village. I have been impressed by the crafts and food produced here. Thrudheim thanks you.'

Gertrud smiled pleasantly, obviously surprised by his praise and relieved to see the fearsome *Wolf Slayer* and *Usurper* of Thrudheim wasn't as terrifying as she might have imagined. 'Nattmal isn't ready yet. We eat quite late at the village, so that we can use as much of the daylight as possible for our crafts and farming. Would you like to settle yourselves in the hall with some mead and cheese, or would you prefer to visit the workshops first?'

Astra was already running to play with the other children and she waited to see what Agnar wished to do. She wasn't surprised when he requested to see the workshops. It was reassuring to know that he cared so much about the running of her kingdom. Heimdall had never been interested in the daily grind of ensuring life ran smoothly. He had always been searching for glory and excitement. First by marrying her and then by leaving her at every opportunity he had to go raiding.

She suspected Agnar was the opposite to Heimdall, but only time would tell for certain.

You also trusted Heimdall once! she reminded herself, and she winced at the memories of her blushing and fawning over Heimdall. How was that any different from her recent behaviour? It seemed that age did not grant you wisdom after all.

Chapter Twenty

As the sun set, Agnar realised it was now officially winter by the colours of the sky, which were painted with frosty pinks and ghostly blues. The frigid chill in the air confirmed it.

They moved into the hall and the cheerful chaos of at least a hundred people gathered together under one roof soared around him. Gertrud and Brenna sat with Astra on the same bench as them, as well as Vali, Oddmund and a few of the village elders.

Agnar was used to the carnage of battle, but not this cauldron of excited voices. His body became tense at every unexpected laugh or sudden movement.

'Are you well?' asked Skadi beside him, leaning closer until her arm brushed lightly against his. He focused on the movement, of the heat of her arm against his. The quickness of his heart didn't change, but the reason for it was far more comfortable to accept.

'I am fine,' he lied and the little downturn of her mouth suggested she wasn't pleased with his answer.

He smiled, leaning closer towards her and inhaling her scent—it was strangely calming. 'Why would that not please you? It was only a few days ago that you wished me dead.'

She gave an imperious snort. 'I have already lost one

King. To lose another so quickly would seem clumsy, especially when it is not by my own hand.'

'So now you are happy to keep me?' he asked, unable to hide his grin, or the rush of pleasure through his body. He liked this playful teasing—after so much hostility it was a welcome change.

Skadi's increasing warmth towards him over the last couple of days had given him hope. Of course, she was far too beautiful to grant him anything more than that so soon, and for the moment he had to remain patient. Perhaps, once the new bed was made and the threat of Sven diminished, she might be comfortable enough to… He shifted nervously, ending that thought before it fuelled his lust and drove him mad.

More than once, he'd wondered at her feelings towards him. Imagined lingering looks and flirtatious touches… *Fool!* They were most likely innocent reactions, but they had still almost killed him. He hadn't realised how long he'd been starved of affection until Skadi's wicked fingers had brushed his neck, his hand, his shoulder…

Agnar clenched his fists beneath the table until his joints hurt, forcing a pleasant expression to hide the turmoil beneath as he waited for her answer.

'I wouldn't say I was happy…' she declared self-righteously, and then paused before saying more quietly, 'optimistic…perhaps.'

Skadi might as well have named him Emperor; he was so smugly pleased with himself. All of the discomfort he'd felt moments before disappeared under her praise. Might she one day want *him*, as much as she had wanted Heimdall?

If her attraction to Heimdall had been half of what he felt for Skadi now, then he pitied her, because there was nothing he would not do for her.

But dare he hope for more…for love?

Such a thing seemed ridiculous for a grown man and warrior to wish for. But each day, a secret part of him—a part of him he'd previously forgotten—grew louder and more insistent, until it felt like a great beast within him, wild and ferociously hungry, desperate for any morsel of touch or scrap of affection that Skadi might grant. He was losing control and the enemy was himself. But he couldn't seem to stop himself or find the strength to fight it.

Odin save him, he wanted her love!

A lyre and drum began to play and Astra pulled Brenna and Gertrud up to dance. To his surprise Vali joined them. He wondered if Skadi would like to dance, but the idea of making a fool of himself in front of her with his awkward dancing skills was less than appealing, so he asked her curiously, 'And, what have I done to warrant such a drastic change of heart?'

Bright blue eyes locked with his. 'You *want* to be King. I know that must seem obvious. After all, you want power just like any other man, but…to want to *be* a king, that is different…it's…special. To have the desire to learn and understand every aspect of the kingdom you rule, that is the true nature of a good leader. Heimdall never had much interest in that.'

For Skadi to take such a giant step with her confession and praise, humbled him and so he answered honestly, 'Why do you think I *want* power?'

Skadi sighed as if such a question was dull and obvious. She rolled her wrist as she spoke, the horn of mead in her hand tilting precariously. 'For glory, for control, for ambition and pride. For all the usual reasons that men do anything.'

He'd noticed she'd drunk far more tonight than he'd ever seen her drink before. She'd laughed more, too. The hall had been filled with easy conversation, reminiscing over past stories and telling light-hearted jokes. Skadi had visibly relaxed since arriving at the crafters' village, she loved these people and felt comfortable here. The divide between royalty, servant, friend and family blurred in this homely hall so far from the elegant formality of Thrudheim.

He drank deeply from his own horn of mead; it was rich and strong in flavour, leaving him a little light-headed—or was that just the effect Skadi's eyes had on him? 'I want power for the same reason a person with a starving family wants an axe.'

Skadi chuckled. 'A starving family would want food, not an axe.'

Agnar shook his head. 'No. Food once eaten is gone forever. But with an axe you can protect your family, hunt for food, cut wood for your fire and defeat anyone who tries to hurt you. Food delays death, a tool can give you a future.'

Her smile dropped as she listened to him, realising the truth of his words. 'I didn't know…about how you were treated after. But… I should have asked. I'm truly sorry for that.'

The bitter memories caused his teeth to clench, but he pushed forward regardless. 'I was angry. Sven took so much from me and I blamed you—at least, partly, for it—which was wrong of me. But I want you to know the truth…*all of it.* Not just what they told you.'

He took a deep breath. 'My mother and I were cast out by King Sven with nothing more than the clothes on our back and my father's ring on her finger. It was her punishment for arriving at Thrudheim without Sven's permission and disrupting his plans with you—not that it made any difference. She managed to get us passage on to a ship going to a trading town across the sea, still far from Aldeigja, but at least possible to reach on foot. It was with the same merchant who'd allowed us passage to Thrudheim.

'It wasn't until later that I realised she'd paid for our travel by selling her body to him. She sacrificed herself more than once to keep me safe—if we'd remained with Sven, he would have had me killed eventually. As a parting gift, the merchant gave me his axe. I almost threw it in the sea, I was so disgusted by him, but my mother stopped me.

'We walked through the wilderness for months in the middle of winter and I was grateful for my axe then… With power, *true power*, you and your family will always be safe. On her deathbed, I promised my mother that I would marry the Queen of Thrudheim and finally have true power—I would be invincible.' He looked her in the eyes. 'Skadi, I meant what I said before. I want power to protect the people I care about.'

Skadi stared at him wide eyed. 'But if your mother is dead…'

'You and Astra are my family now. I made a promise to your ancestors…and, once I give my word, I keep it.' He paused and took another deep breath, confessing the darkest secret of all. 'More than that… Before, I craved only power. But now all I want is you…and without you, I would be powerless.'

Skadi's eyes were wide with astonishment. She swallowed and took a deep breath, before taking a large gulp of her mead.

Had his words frightened her? Angered her? Embarrassed, he lowered his own horn, and stared at it in his scarred hand, unable to meet her gaze. She probably thought him a hopeless lovesick fool.

To his surprise a pale hand covered and then wrapped around his own. Skadi had taken his hand and was now rising from her seat, taking him with her. He followed, stumbling a little as he struggled to move his large body around the bench, 'If you wish to dance, I must warn you, I am not very good.'

She ignored him and they wove through the crowd, her hand not leaving his or loosening its tight grip. To his surprise they came out of the hall and walked a few feet away from the light of the open doors.

Skadi stopped suddenly, turning to face him. The wind whipped across them with a sudden chill and she pressed her palms against his shoulders and thrust him hard against the stone of the hall's wall.

There was a sharp and confusing moment when he wondered what he had done to enrage her so. *Yes, his declaration had been clumsy, but—*

Skadi pressed her lips against his and it was so unexpected he had to grab the wall behind him to steady himself. She pushed harder against his mouth and body, her breasts rubbed against his chest and a few of the stray hairs that had escaped from her braid tickled his cheek and neck. Before he could gather his wits enough to kiss her back, she pulled away and stared at him, the sounds of her breath heavy in the air.

Thunder rumbled across the sky, mingling with the distant hum of music and merriment from inside the hall. A nearby bucket was toppled over as another gust of wind rattled through the village, signalling the arrival of a winter storm.

When she pulled away, he thought she might head back into the hall, but she grabbed hold of his hand for the second time and dragged him with her. They darted into a nearby workshop as the first drops of rain splattered on the ground.

Squinting around in the darkness, he noticed it was a weaver's workshop by the loom in the doorway. Piles of fleeces and rolls of cloth filled the room, and Skadi turned to face him as lightning split the sky behind him, illuminating her face in a white light.

Her cheeks were flushed, her lips pink from the rough kiss she'd given him, and her eyes dark with determination and desire. Just as quickly the sky went dark and another roll of thunder rumbled even louder than the first. Her expression was now shadowed, but for once, he knew exactly what she wanted and it filled him with a raw and savage wave of lust.

He pulled her close, reclaiming the kiss. Their tongues sliding together in a wild and desperate dance. It was more than enough to ignite the mountain of kindling that had been slowly building between them for days… Desire he'd not realised until now had been returned.

Hot molten heat coursed through his body and his body hardened at the mere realisation that she *wanted* to kiss him. Eager fingers tugged wantonly at his tunic and his belt fell to the ground with the clatter of his sword and axe. He then helped her tug the cloth over his head. She pushed him against a stack of the fleeces and a few of them tumbled to the ground.

He broke away from her long enough to pull down a few more and drape his tunic over them. If she wanted him to take her, he would at least make it as comfortable as possible for her—there was no private chambers in the hall and they would have to sleep in front of people as with the hunting lodge. This was probably the only privacy they would have until they returned to Thrudheim.

He was about to try to help her out of her gown, when she pushed at his chest and commanded, 'Lie down.'

He did as she asked, still a little bewildered by the sudden change in Skadi. Gone was her measured and regal tone—in its place was a passionate and desperate woman.

It was like a dream…a dream he'd prayed for.

The tunic-covered fleeces weren't that large and he leaned his back against the wall as he lifted his hips and pulled down his trousers. He didn't have time to kick off his boots or pull off his clothing completely as Skadi was already lifting her skirts, and seating herself on his lower thighs. There was another flash of lightning from the open doorway and he saw Skadi desperately clawing at one of the silver-turtle brooches pinning her apron dress together.

The brooch finally released its hold on her gown in another flash of light and there was more scrabbling in the dark while she fumbled with her clothing. When the next lightning bolt lit up the sky, she'd managed to pull her shift and apron dress down to her waist, releasing her breasts and naked upper body.

She stared down at his engorged flesh with wide and eager eyes, rocking her pelvis against his thighs, as if in anticipation of him filling her.

He reached forward, cupping one breast before the light left them. He swept his thumb over the mound and when her nipple puckered, he covered it with his mouth and gently lapped and sucked on it until she began to pant and moan.

There was another rumble of thunder, but he no longer cared about anything more than making her moan drown it out. 'I want to hear you scream my name,' he growled. 'When I fill you, and when you come. I want to hear you shout my name.'

His hand slipped beneath her tangle of skirts and stroked up her inner thigh. Her legs tightened either side of him, as she groaned through clenched teeth, 'Make me!'

He chuckled at her stubborn pride, his length throbbing with anticipation. But he tried his best to ignore it, he wanted her pleasure first. 'Oh… I will.'

She gasped as he found her wet entrance and his finger

slid easily inside of her, as if he'd been preparing her for hours and not the handful of moments they'd spent kissing in the darkness.

He rolled the pad of his thumb against her most sensitive part and was rewarded by a wave of clenching wetness that had his body aching to thrust into her. Skadi rocked her hips against him and then pushed at his chest. 'Agnar, I want to ride you.'

He gritted his teeth against the desperate need and shook his head. 'Not yet.' He wanted her so much, but he didn't want to disappoint her, and he was afraid that if she climbed on top of him, he would fall apart in moments.

She jerked against his hand, her body riding his finger so greedily, that he added another. She moaned, her head rolling back as lightning lit up her body for him, in the most erotic image of his life.

Skadi, her head thrown back with pleasure, her breasts bare and bouncing beautifully at every grind of her hips. He only wished he could see her lower body, but a mountain of fabric was in the way.

'I want you, Agnar, now!' she demanded, grabbing him firmly around his shaft and pumping him tightly until he thought he would explode.

'Odin's teeth!' he hissed, removing his hand from between her legs, so that she could do as she pleased and she did with startling speed. Moving forward and lifting up, she continued to hold his shaft tightly before guiding it slowly into the soft, clenching heat of her.

He filled her body and was rewarded by the whimper of his name. She grabbed his head and tugged his hair as a spasm caused her body to tighten around him. His hips thrust upwards in eager response and she ground down with her hips, pressing his pelvis back into the fleeces and earth beneath him.

Primal desire took over and he clutched the wool beneath him in a desperate attempt to slow the release that was threatening to overwhelm him. Skadi was merciless, riding him with quick and confident thrusts of her hips. Her breasts bounced against his panting mouth. She pressed harder against his body, lowering herself into an angle that allowed for her loins to rub against him in a way that maximised her pleasure and deepened his penetration. She knew what she wanted and how to pleasure herself and it made him want to please her even more.

'Agnar!' she moaned in his ear, as the thrusts of her hips became faster and more desperate.

He reached around her pulling her close, thrusting his hips to match her pace. The lightning had faded into the distance and streams of rain were pouring down in front of the darkened doorway, muffling the sound of their climax, as they clung to one another, and rode the waves of pleasure that first flooded Skadi and was quickly followed by Agnar's desperate release.

Chapter Twenty-One

Skadi couldn't quite believe what she'd done. Not only had she lain with the man who had killed her husband, but she'd done so willingly…

No...worse than that—she had ravished him! Dragged him from the hall and made love to him as if they were young lovers sneaking away from the sight of their parents. Fast, desperate and passionate…but also so exciting and satisfying. The slow build of her interest in him had suddenly boiled over and she'd been unable to deny herself.

Which was why she was now sprawled half-naked on top of a man ten years her junior.

This was not the behaviour of an intelligent queen, or even a sensible woman. Two aspects of herself she'd tried for so long to perfect.

Her heart was still beating wildly from the after-effects of her shattering climax. She bit her bottom lip to stop herself from groaning at the delicious memory. Even on her better nights with Heimdall she'd never felt such all-consuming and blinding pleasure. The desire had overwhelmed her so quickly that she'd felt as if her body would burn away to ash if she didn't have him inside of her at that precise moment.

His words... Freyja save her, his words had lit up her heart like a beacon!

'Before, I craved only power... But now...all I want is you...and without you, I would be powerless.' Those words had been a soothing salve on an aching wound within her she hadn't realised was there. A desperate need to be desired and—dare she admit it—*loved*. He had not confessed to loving her, but it had felt close enough. Especially to a woman who'd been starved of affection for years.

Not only did he understand the true value of power—to protect and nurture those around you—but he viewed Skadi and, most importantly, Astra, as his family.

Astra! Would she be wondering where she was?

The dancing was always a joyous and chaotic time in the crafters' hall, it was why she had dived out with Agnar when she had. It was one of the few opportunities where she might not be missed. But...*she had to go back*.

Agnar's chest rose and fell beneath her head, the rain was still pouring in heavy sheets outside the doorway, which was wide open, and she winced that anyone could have seen what they were doing if they'd strayed far enough away from the hall and into the village.

The worst of the storm had passed and she sat up and fumbled with the shift and apron dress that had become a tangle of fabric around her hips. Without even the lightning to help her see it was difficult and she huffed bad temperedly when she caught herself on the pin of her turtle brooch, already regretting her hasty actions.

Would she always be a fool, desperately hoping for love?

Agnar's rough hand gently smoothed up the shoulder of her shift as she tried to retie the neckline. The skin of his calloused hand against the softness of her skin made her body tingle with excitement and she hurried to return her clothing back to normal before she was tempted to reach for him again.

Now that she knew the incredible pleasure she could experience with Agnar, she couldn't fathom how she was ever going to keep her hands off him.

Do I have to...keep my hands off him?

The answer was, no, they were married, but in the back of her mind she was still afraid of making the wrong choice. Her daughter's life depended on her. She couldn't risk her daughter's safety on a man she barely knew...who happened to say and do the right things to make her lusty.

She'd done that once before, with disastrous consequences.

Getting to her feet, she brushed down her skirts, conscious of his seed still wet between her thighs.

She was grateful that there was only light from a half-moon to see by when Agnar lifted his hips to pull up his trousers. *Odin's teeth!* She'd mounted the man before he'd even fully undressed, like some wanton beast! Hot flames danced up the sides of her face and neck and she swallowed nervously, looking around for something to cover her from the rain on the way back to the hall. She grabbed one of the fleeces from the floor and held it over her head. 'I will go back first.'

'No,' rumbled Agnar's voice from the darkness. 'We go together.'

Skadi rolled her eyes, but she didn't wish to argue any further. She ran out into the pouring rain, the fleece her only shield, and the heavy splashes of Agnar's boots following close behind.

The hall doors had been closed against the storm, but the smaller door used for winter access had been left open with a water barrel. She hurried towards the amber light and chaotic revelry of the hall within, as if it would somehow shed light on her own fears and burn them away.

As they entered the hall people barely noticed their return and she was quick to throw aside the damp fleece on a nearby bench. She breathed a sigh of relief, glad that no one seemed to have noticed their arrival, and glanced towards Agnar, who looked decidedly less pleased, his long hair messy and his tunic wet from the heavy rain.

'Why didn't you use a fleece to cover yourself?'

Agnar tilted his head, his green eyes piercing her soul. 'Are you ashamed of what we did?'

She almost choked on her outrage and quickly turned away from him, flexing her shoulders and neck absently, noting the sudden tension that had returned. But she was too embarrassed to answer him, because she had behaved wantonly and should be ashamed of herself. To her relief, Astra came bouncing up to her a short time later with Brenna at her side.

'Where were you, Moma?' Astra demanded, her braids a mess from all the dancing and half-unravelled. That child lost ribbons everywhere she went!

She laughed and plucked up the rat tail of a braid on her left side. 'What have you been doing? Crawling through a thorn bush?'

Astra's eyes narrowed and her lips pinched into a pout. 'It was my favourite dance and I couldn't find you!'

'I only went outside for a moment.' Skadi glanced at Brenna, who gave an awkward shrug, making it clear she'd known where Skadi had gone and with whom.

Astra was still not impressed and she scowled. 'You were gone for the entire dance and most of the following one!' Astra's eyes began to water and her daughter rubbed at them with a fist obviously worn out from all the travel and excitement. 'And… I didn't know where you were. You need to tell me when you leave! At least Pappa always said goodbye!'

Guilt and shame washed through her in an icy torrent and she leaned down to cup her daughter's face. 'I would never leave you without telling you. I only stepped out for a moment…to use the latrine.' She squirmed a little at the lie, she very rarely lied to Astra.

Brenna placed a hand on Astra's shoulder and said kindly, 'I think Astra is a little tired.'

Astra was quick to make a furious denial and Skadi grabbed her hand. 'Let us ask the musicians to play your song once more and then we will go to bed. How about that?'

Astra grumbled a little and was able to negotiate two extra songs of her choosing.

Later that night after everyone had gone to bed, Skadi lay next to a sleeping Astra and stared up at the rafters high above. Their bed was in a small partitioned area of the hall that was usually used by Gertrud as her personal chamber. After seeing Astra's obvious upset and exhaustion, Agnar had been quick to tell her to sleep with Astra there and that he would find a bench to sleep on with the rest of his men instead. It was a kind gesture and she began to think of everything that had transpired with Agnar.

Can I trust him?

Can I trust myself?

Did he really see Astra and herself as his family now? A girl that was not even his own by blood… Or, was he manipulating her, just like Heimdall and Sven had done? She'd been a fool so many times she sometimes wondered if she deserved her crown.

If he did want a family of his own…had she given him false hope by making love to him? How long would it take for him to be disappointed by the lack of his own child… his own son and heir?

Heimdall had more than once muttered about the bad luck of only having a daughter. That's what had turned Skadi further against him over the years, because her father had never treated her as such and she couldn't understand why Heimdall would… Had he not viewed her as a queen in her own right? Probably not.

Did Agnar? Probably not... Despite his promises and sweet words, could she ever trust anyone but herself?

No, because a queen couldn't afford to take the risk. It wasn't just Astra who depended on her, but hundreds of Thrudheim citizens—their families and children. Even her dead ancestors relied on her to make the right choices and continue the unbroken line of Kings.

And yet... How much easier would all of it be if she had someone reliable and powerful at her side?

His speech had affected her deeply, she understood him now and was hopeful for the future. If he truly viewed Astra as part of his family, then she would gladly accept him as her husband, because the truth was, she didn't have anyone else to support her.

But was she once again behaving like a lusty, stupid fool? Letting her desperate desire to be loved control her? Perhaps he was lying and trying to fool her into trusting him, but he'd also sounded more sincere than Heimdall ever had.

His hate for Sven, his need for revenge, the pain and suffering of his mother, it had all been heartfelt and genuine. He'd also not judged his own mother for what she had done to save him and that had said a lot about his character—considering she'd known many men cast aside women for lowering their morals, without once considering why. The tavern girls were a perfect example and she'd always done everything she could to support and help them without judgement.

But could she trust him with Astra's life?

No. It would take more than promises and sweet words to

trust him with her most precious possession, because without Astra she had nothing.

Her thoughts and arguments were constantly spiralling in her mind, never seeming to go anywhere, like a serpent eating its tail.

Eventually, exhausted and wrung out by her endless doubts, she decided that it had just been a long time since she'd found pleasure with a man…

Perhaps it was simply an itch she needed to scratch?

Chapter Twenty-Two

In the morning, they were ready to leave the village after a hearty dagmal of porridge, breads, fruits and cheeses with Gertrud and the other crafters.

Skadi was reassured that they had enough food to last the winter, but she was still worried about Thrudheim. She might need to request a pooling of resources if the stores became bare…but she would worry about such a possibility nearer the time. It wouldn't be until mid or late winter hopefully.

Gertrud's expression was firm, her wrinkled eyes squinting against the cold wind, as she wished Skadi goodbye. 'Do not delay at the hunting lodge. The snow and ice will blow in by the end of the week, I imagine. I can tell in my bones that winter is fast approaching and I suspect it will be a harsh one.'

'I wish we could stay longer,' said Skadi, 'It has been too long since I saw you last.'

Gertrud smiled and cupped her cheek in a motherly gesture that almost made Skadi sink into her like a warm bath. 'When there is peace and stability for Thrudheim, there will be time to visit us again. Do not worry. We have more than enough to keep us through the winter and come spring we can feast again.'

Skadi nodded and then embraced Gertrud in a fierce hug. Astra and Brenna did the same before mounting their ponies.

Skadi made a point of playing games with Astra on the way back up the mountain. It was quicker to get there directly from the village without stopping at any farms or the ancestral burial grounds along the way. So, despite the increased wind and damp chill in the air, they made it on to the steep path just after midday.

Grunting, they managed to lead their horses and ponies up the winding path, but it was a difficult climb and about halfway up Astra began to complain about the tiredness of her legs. They paused by a battered pine tree, its exposed roots making it look very precarious on the edge of the cliffside. Every year it teetered further over the edge, but somehow it still clung on—*not unlike Skadi's rule over the years,* she thought miserably.

'Should we stop?' asked Brenna, who was leading her own horse behind them.

Skadi shook her head. 'No, go on. We will need someone to go on ahead and prepare the lodge for tonight.'

Brenna nodded and continued onwards. Vali and Oddmund also asked if they were well, Oddmund even insisting he stay with them. But Agnar was now climbing the mountain path at the rear of their party and he yelled at the line of horses to continue.

Skadi had to admit she'd been glad when Agnar seemed happy to allow some distance between them. Perhaps he realised she needed time to accept what she had done.

'Is there a problem?' he asked as he came to stand beside them.

'Have you rested long enough?' Skadi asked Astra meaningfully, a firm edge to her tone that made Astra grumble.

'Fine…but my legs still hurt!' She stomped forward and Skadi couldn't help but smile at her child's antics.

'Would you like to ride on my shoulders, Princess?' asked Agnar casually and her daughter spun on her heels and stared back at him with wide excited eyes.

'Can I?'

Agnar nodded, handing the reins of his horse to Vali who with a smile continued up the mountain path with Oddmund, while a very excited Astra came running back down to meet with him, her sore legs apparently forgotten.

Skadi rolled her eyes. 'I doubt Agnar will be able to carry you for long, Astra.'

'Why not?' asked Agnar, looking slightly offended by her lack of confidence in his strength.

Skadi laughed. 'She's heavier than she looks…believe me.'

Agnar frowned, but still lowered himself to his knees and allowed Astra to climb across his shoulders. He gripped Astra's ankles and began to wheeze heavily as if the strain of the child on his neck was making it difficult for him to breathe. 'Hold on to my hair like they're reins,' he gasped. Astra gave her mother an uncertain look, but did as he asked.

With a speed and strength that shocked Skadi enough to make her stumble a few steps towards them, Agnar rose from the ground, easily picking up Astra, who squealed with delight as she bounced on his shoulders.

Skadi shook her head with a chuckle and fell into step beside him, her horse following on a loose lead behind them.

'It won't be so easy by the time we reach the top of the path,' she warned, calling up to Astra, 'When Agnar's had enough of being your horse, you'll have to come down and walk again.'

Astra grinned down at Skadi. 'Yes, Moma!' She was obviously delighted with her ride and with a twinge of sadness she realised that Heimdall had never carried their daughter like this. Skadi had loved being carried on her father's shoulders when she was younger and she was glad that Astra could now experience it.

Agnar turned towards her with an unexpectedly charismatic and sensual smile. 'One good thing about you having a younger husband is that I have the stamina to match… I imagine I could be ridden up and down this mountain with ease,' he teased.

Surely, he was talking about carrying her daughter…and not…

She tried to ignore the heated blush that crept up her face and neck, remembering how satisfying his *stamina* had been the previous night. She looked away and was sure his smile widened, but she couldn't be sure as her gaze was fixed resolutely on the path ahead.

The climb was pleasant, the weather holding off from another downpour like the one the night before.

As they arrived at the hunting lodge, Agnar finally allowed Astra to climb down from his shoulders. One of the servants hurried over and took the reins of her horse, leading it towards the stable. Astra, more than happy now that she was on flat ground, said, 'I'm hungry. Do you think Nattmal will be long?'

Skadi looked up at the sky with its ominous clouds. 'Hopefully not. Why don't you go in and find Brenna? I will follow in a short while. I wish to speak with Agnar for a moment.'

Astra, who seemed to have forgotten her upset from the previous night, nodded and eagerly ran into the lodge.

'What do you wish to speak with me about?' Agnar peeled his tunic from his body and flapped it a little to get some air to his skin. She imagined it had been harder work than he'd ever admit to carry her ten-year-old daughter up the side of the mountain. As he flicked the fabric, she caught glimpses of thick muscles and dark hair, her mouth dried immediately and wicked thoughts bubbled to the surface of her mind.

Odin's teeth! She wanted him again!

Something about his desire to care and look after her child did strange things to her body. Urges she thought she'd grown out of long ago came flooding to the surface, made somehow worse by the knowledge that she could easily find her release with Agnar.

Had he been merely boasting earlier? Or was it an invitation?

'There is a hot spring not far from here. It comes from the mountains and it's little more than a trickle, but you might find it refreshing after your climb,' she said.

Agnar could have rightly told her that the nearest source of water for him to drink and wash himself with was only a few feet away inside the cabin. But he seemed to realise her need to speak with him alone, so he nodded and gestured for her to lead the way.

They made their way through the bustle of people who were busy caring for the horses and unloading their packs, and entered the forest through a narrow path that wasn't obvious from the clearing until you stumbled upon it. She doubted anyone would follow them, though, even if they were noticed leaving camp. Agnar was the kind of man that did as he pleased and no one questioned it.

Skadi pushed through the forest, glad that most of the vegetation had died back for winter, leaving spindly branches and only a few fallen logs in their way. The path ahead was little more than a rocky climb uphill.

It didn't take long to reach the stream. It sprang from the cliff further up and trickled down through moss-covered rocks, until it reached a little pool and then ran towards the bigger stream further down the hillside by the lodge.

Even as she pushed through some bushes to reach the pool, she felt the heat of the spring immediately.

'Sorry to make you do more climbing, but the pool here is more refreshing than the main stream. It's always warm even in winter.'

'I see, I didn't realise you had hot springs here,' said Agnar, his deep voice causing a shiver to run down her spine, followed quickly by a wince as she realised how odd her dragging him here must seem.

'Only a couple of small ones.'

She perched herself on a boulder and folded her hands in her lap, afraid she would start wringing them otherwise.

He smiled, watching her with a tilt of his head, his messy long hair falling over his shoulder the only movement in the quiet rocky clearing. 'What did you want to speak to me about?' he asked, moving towards her and the stream. Pulling off his cloak and tunic, he threw them on to the boulder beside her, before bending forward to cup water from the pool with his hands, splashing it over his face, chest and arms.

She watched the water run down his back, suddenly feeling a little thirsty herself. 'I wanted to speak with you about last night…'

He straightened and the sight of him bare chested in front of her sent her pulse racing.

'Are you ashamed?' he asked sombrely.

Skadi swallowed and shook her head, even though she did feel a little embarrassed. 'Not…ashamed, as such…but…'

'Just say it,' he said darkly, washing himself thoroughly with the water, steam rising from his skin.

She pinched her fingers tighter together. 'Astra will always come first. I do not want you to hope for a child that will never come.'

He paused what he was doing and then said, 'I understand.'

She stared at him, momentarily distracted from his body to his face, unsure if he fully understood her. 'Do you think what happened last night will make a difference? There are ways for me to ensure against another babe.'

'If that is what you wish.' He reached for his tunic and she grabbed his arm.

'Surely that must bother you?'

His eyes fixed on hers and she realised similar shades of dark green surrounded them, but the colour of his eyes was the most intoxicating and vibrant shade the mother goddess had created.

'I have told you more than once that I will accept Astra as my heir…' His eyes widened, and he took another step closer. 'Was there another reason why you wanted to bring me here?' His hand cupped her face and then raised her chin with a brush of his thumb.

Skadi rose from the boulder, allowing her hands to do as they wished and touch his chest. She smoothed her palms up the ridges of his stomach and over the tattoos across his heart, her fingertips delighting in the strength and vigour beneath his scarred skin.

'I just needed you to know…that I do this because I want to,' she said quietly, before meeting his eyes. 'Not for the hopes of another child to secure my position as your wife, or for any other reason. I have made mistakes in the past and no longer blindly trust people. But… I also want…to feel pleasure…'

Agnar's hand slipped around her waist, pulling her close. 'You are my Queen. You can do whatever you want with me.'

He curved his body down towards her and eagerly she opened her mouth for him. 'I want you,' she gasped.

Accepting him even before their lips met, her cloak fell to the ground as their kiss deepened into panting, desperate strokes of tongues and licks. Both of them eager to feel the all-consuming fire that seemed to ignite so easily between them.

No one else had ever made her feel this way, filling her with hot lust. She tugged at his belt, desperate to have him inside her again, soothing the physical and emotional ache within her, as only he could.

Power and possession—she wanted to experience all of it and she dropped to her knees, staring up at him as his belt fell and she was able to lower his trousers enough to see him fully.

A thick and long shaft awaited her, rigid with desire. It made her want to whimper and moan as she remembered how it had felt riding something so large and powerful. But she wasn't a young maiden frightened by the sight of a naked man. She gripped him firmly with one hand and pumped him slowly, measuring the size of him, allowing herself time to enjoy the look of him and the pleasure she knew he would give her. She was ready to savour every moment of this private intimacy, in peaceful nature and away from all her responsibilities.

She had never made love in the open and last night during the storm had awakened a craving within her. She didn't want to be a guest in a king's chamber, she wanted it to be free and natural. To possess and be possessed.

She shifted slightly, widening her knees and then raising her skirts enough to be able to touch herself with her free hand. She leaned forward, sensually licking her lips and then moving forward to take his glistening head in her mouth.

Agnar groaned loudly, rolling his head back. 'You will be the death of me…'

She moaned, loving the combination of his lustful words, the stroke of her own touch and the thickness of Agnar in her mouth. He was completely at her mercy, his body bowing and groaning at every lick and suck she gave.

He didn't grab her head or thrust into her mouth. He allowed her to explore and taste the length of him in whatever way she desired. Each movement seemed agony for him as his hands clenched and unclenched beside his upper thighs.

'I need to take you,' he groaned, 'now.'

Skadi gave a throaty chuckle that had him hissing out another long breath. 'In a moment…' she said lightly, already more than ready for him by the slickness of her fingers, but she quickened her strokes until her body was almost at the precipice of release.

'Now,' she groaned, turning away from him and raising her skirts provocatively as she got on all fours. Looking over her shoulder at him, she commanded, 'You can take me now.'

Agnar slowly lowered himself to his knees, running a hand up the back of her thighs. 'Are you ordering me…my Queen?' he asked softly, the slight guttural inflection of his voice the only indicator of how deeply he was trying to restrain himself.

'Yes!' she hissed, as his palm smoothed around her hip.

A very light slap on her bottom made her rear up and glare at him over her shoulder. 'What are you doing? I want you to take me.'

He smiled and looked devastatingly carefree and handsome in that moment. 'Oh, I will…but I decide how and when I take you. You've been in charge for long enough.'

She rolled her eyes. 'I am losing the mood with this nonsense!'

One moment Skadi was glaring at him over her shoulder, the next moment she was tumbling on her back after being flipped over.

'What!' she gasped, not quite believing what he'd done.

Agnar grinned, then lifted her skirts, pushing them up her thighs to her hips. Skadi blushed as he took his time opening her legs, devouring the sight of her naked lower body.

'I want to taste you first,' he said and that was the only warning he gave before his head dropped between her thighs. No spot was left unkissed by his lips or tongue—she moaned and writhed against his mouth. The familiar build of her orgasm tightened with lightning speed and she dragged her nails into the mossy ground beneath her.

'Please,' she whimpered. 'I want to feel you inside me when I...'

Sitting upright, Agnar nodded, but she could tell his composure was frayed and that he needed her as much as she needed him. Eagerly she scrambled back on to all fours and lifted her skirts for a second time. This time he didn't, couldn't, deny her and they both gave relieved groans as he slipped slowly inside her. All restraint was gone after that first slow penetration. Skadi gritted her teeth against the wave of almost painful pleasure and gripped the grass beneath her, tightly panting into the rich earth, as his hips thrust into her with steadily more force and speed.

'Skadi,' he moaned her name over and over with each thrust, pressing her into the earth and muddying her clothes, but she didn't care. She wanted more, pushing back against his hips to ensure that each thrust filled her completely.

Her legs began to tremble and she couldn't hold on to herself a moment longer, she fumbled with her skirts, desperate to touch herself and find blissful release.

Agnar must have seen what she was doing because he

smoothed his hand over her naked bottom, along her hip, and then his fingers slipped beneath the bundle of fabric at her waist to her core.

'There?' he asked and within one stroke of her body she was screaming his name into the grass and dirt between her clenched fists.

Agnar held her hips up, while the rest of her body collapsed. He began to thrust wildly as she spasmed with the force of her pleasure, his own following quickly with a husky groan, *'Skadi!'*

Afterwards, they cleaned themselves up using the water from the stream, Skadi more than a little embarrassed by the grass and muddy stains on her dress, which even with a light scrub were obvious.

'Why didn't we spread out my cloak first?' she grumbled.

Agnar, who hadn't stopped smiling since he'd collapsed beside her, shrugged. 'They are not *too* noticeable…'

Skadi tutted, knowing that meant they were *very* noticeable.

'I shall say I fell,' she grumbled, pulling her cloak tighter around her. The wind was beginning to whip through the trees and their little tryst in the woods seemed more like madness considering the season.

'Is that snow?' gasped Skadi, reaching up to touch a falling speck. The ice landed softly on her palm before it began to melt.

Agnar looked at it thoughtfully, as he pulled on his tunic. 'Looks like it.'

'We need to head back soon. The mountain path is treacherous after the first snow fall.'

'It's almost dark, but we can go tomorrow morning.'

Skadi nodded, comforted by the thought. 'True, and at

least we did the treacherous side today.' She hurried down the path back towards the lodge, the confident stride of Agnar following close behind.

As they came into the clearing around the lodge, they saw Brenna speaking with Vali at the campfire. Brenna's eyes widened as first Skadi and then Agnar emerged from the forest. Skadi knew her sudden desire for Agnar was unexpected, but Brenna was usually open minded about most things…

Brenna's shocked gaze turned to Vali and she thumped him hard. 'You said they were together!'

Vali's brow furrowed. 'They were!'

Agnar moved to stand beside Skadi, equally confused by their strange argument.

Brenna's horrified gaze swept to Skadi and her stomach plummeted.

'Where is Astra?' she asked and could already tell by the blood draining from Brenna's face that she didn't have an answer for her.

Astra was missing…and it was Skadi's fault. She'd left her child to go and find Brenna alone, when the camp had been in chaos from their arrival. All so that she could have a tryst with Agnar.

She would never forgive herself.

Chapter Twenty-Three

Agnar put a reassuring hand on Skadi's shoulder, but she shrugged it off as though it was a fly, almost flinching from his touch as if she were ashamed to be seen with him.

Was that why all their encounters had been in hidden corners? Skadi dragging him away from the sight of her people. He'd suspected she'd been lying when she said she wasn't ashamed and that had hurt his pride more than he liked to admit.

Did she still love or feel guilty over Heimdall?

He couldn't deny that he was delighted about the new intimacy they shared, but in other ways he felt even more distant from her. It was as if she were still holding herself back from him while he fell deeper under her spell.

Would she ever trust him...love him?

Regardless, of her feelings—or lack of—towards him, Astra was currently missing and they needed to find her. Especially considering the snow was already beginning to sprinkle the ground with a fine layer of frost and the sun was low.

Skadi strode forward. 'We sent her into the hall when we first arrived. Did you not see her?'

Brenna shook her head, worry and fear clouding her expression. 'No, I was gathering some mushrooms and herbs for Nattmal and Vali said he'd seen the three of you climbing the last part of the path together. Perhaps she went to the latrine and I did not see her or she is hiding in the hall…'

'Vali, gather the men and women,' ordered Agnar. 'We need to know who last saw her and when. Is anyone else missing? Who last saw Oddmund?'

'Oddmund?' Skadi shook her head furiously. 'He wouldn't…he was Heimdall's friend.' But her eyes desperately searched the faces of the other people in the clearing, and by the increasing concern on her face, he knew she was growing more anxious and afraid. Picking up her skirts, Skadi ran inside the hall followed closely by Brenna, calling out Astra's name and grabbing servants to help them in their search.

Agnar turned to Vali. 'Gather the men. Find out who saw Oddmund and Astra last.'

It wasn't long until Vali returned with one of the men. 'Tell him what you know,' said Vali.

The man nodded quickly. 'The Princess was looking for Brenna. Oddmund told her she'd gone into the woods. He said he would help her find her.'

'Why didn't you say anything when Brenna returned without Astra?' snapped Agnar, already knowing that it wasn't the man's fault, but frustrated with himself that he'd allowed Astra to fall into such a trap.

'I didn't know. I have only just returned from felling one of the trees for firewood. Oddmund instructed me to do so.'

'I am sure he did!' snapped Agnar. 'Which direction did they head?'

'That way!' pointed the man and, with one nod from Agnar, the men began gathering their weapons. But Agnar didn't want to wait and he strode towards the forest. Skadi came running out of the hall, looking more terrified than before.

'She's not in the hall! We looked everywhere!'

'Oddmund has taken her.'

'No!' She shook her head, but at this point her denial was weak and full of torment. As if speaking to herself, she whispered, 'Why am I always such a trusting fool?'

'I will find her,' he declared, turning to the rest of the people gathered around. 'Split into five groups. One is to remain behind and keep the fire burning, prepare food and medicine just in case. The remaining four groups are to sweep out in a line. No path, tree or rock is to go unchecked. But move quickly, and take torches. The sun is beginning to set.'

He strode forward, snatching a torch that had been lit outside the lodge's doorway. 'If Oddmund went this way, then I will follow. Vali, I need you and two others to come with me.' Agnar took a sword and shield from Vali and his hand went to the old axe hanging off his belt, patting it for luck and reassurance as he moved out of the clearing.

The rest of his men were tripping over themselves to organise their parties. His parting comment was to shout, 'I want my heir safely returned. If Oddmund has taken her by force, then kill him. But Princess Astra *must* live!'

Skadi grabbed a sword and shield from a nearby warrior and ran to catch up with him. He didn't deny her, he couldn't deny her anything—besides, she was a good shieldmaiden and Astra's mother. The only thing that worried him was that she would put herself in danger to protect her child.

He was made aware of the other person to join their team when Vali hissed, 'Go back, Brenna! There's nothing you can do!'

'I'm coming!' she replied firmly.

Vali cursed, but managed to call over Leif to join them,

before they made their way through the trees a few feet away from each other in a fan. Winter meant there was little undergrowth and plenty of rotting leaves, so progress was quick, although the weather seemed to be against them. The snow fell heavier, darkening the sky and whipping through the trees with an icy chill. It felt like a bad omen and when he glanced towards Skadi, he could tell by her expression that she was broken with fear.

He gritted his teeth and pushed forward, swearing to himself and the gods that he would return Astra to her, or he would die trying.

Skadi's mind was racing with a flurry of a thousand fears, each one striking her like shattered glass. She couldn't stop imagining the very worst possibilities. Several times she had to breathe deeply to stop her mind spiralling into chaos.

We will find her.

She pledged the same words over and over, focusing on the ground and every step. Her eyes sweeping back and forth, not realising for a moment why she did so, then saying to the others, 'Astra is clever! She knows about animal tracks and hunting. She will also try to struggle, look for areas of disturbance...' But the snow was falling steadily and whatever tracks there might have been were being smothered with each moment that passed.

Nobody dared point that out to her, though, and diligently they also scanned the ground as they moved.

They arrived at the clearing around the mine and a chilling dread washed through Skadi. She'd sent the miners home for the winter, which meant three possibilities. Oddmund had taken her into the mine, or he'd used the dangerously steep miners' path down the mountain... He could even have taken her onwards into the forest—although that seemed unlikely, all that would await him there were the cliffs.

Agnar seemed to be wondering the same because he walked around the miners' camp, glancing into the hut and then walking back out again. 'Is there any way out of the mines—other than this entrance?'

Skadi shook her head. 'No, I don't think so...' She was beginning to doubt everything... Oddmund, Agnar...her own mind.

'And what lies beyond here?'

'More forest and then the cliffs. There's no way down that way, at least not until further down on the second ridge.'

Brenna gave a shout. 'Look! I think these are Astra's beads!'

They ran to Brenna, who stood by the pulley system that helped take the ore carts up and down the mountain. A bell was attached to the top and, when the rope was pulled, it would ring to tell the miners that an empty cart needed to be brought up. Draped across the top of the pulley was a broken string of beads, the kind Astra wore between her turtle brooches.

'It's hers,' said Skadi, grabbing the beads and clenching them tightly before tucking them into a pocket of her cloak. 'He must have taken her down this path.'

Grabbing hold of the rope, Skadi began to climb down the mountain with a speed that Agnar found terrifying. 'Slow down, Skadi!' he barked, running down behind her, the rope burning beneath his hand as he tried to keep up with her. 'We don't know for certain that she went this way!'

'Then go another way if you think it's better!' she hissed back, ignoring his warning.

'She probably did come down this way...but they won't

remain on the path. He wouldn't know how much of a head start he has, taking Astra was an opportunity. But he must have another plan…something prepared. He must be taking her somewhere. Where exactly does this lead—*Odin's teeth! Skadi, you almost fell!*'

Skadi had slipped on the path, but managed to right herself before she completely lost her footing. Her ankle ached from the sudden twist, but she ignored it. 'This path leads straight down to the smelting furnaces and workshops.'

'Exactly! Can you see her down the path ahead? No.'

'There's several ledges and twists along the way.'

'True, but what will he find at the bottom? It's not exactly a safe destination for a man stealing a princess!' huffed Agnar and thankfully Skadi slowed and took more care with her steps. 'The furnaces will be working on the latest batch of ore…people will see him! And the beads prove that Astra is no longer willingly with him. She left them for us to point the way. We need to keep our eyes out for another sign…and we can't do that if we're racing down a cliff face!'

Finally, Skadi slowed a little, her eyes searching the forest to their left. 'Then we need to keep an eye on that side. The other only brings him closer to Thrudheim—people would see him alone with Astra and question it. If he wants to escape with Astra, he'll need to have a boat. One at the old fishermen's harbour would most likely go unnoticed. The merchants and traders have to identify themselves and their cargo at the city harbour. But to reach the old fishermen's harbour, he needs to climb down the cliff edge at some point… Depending on how far he's willing to climb it might be at the next ridge or the one below.'

'Good,' replied Agnar soothingly. 'That must be his plan.'

Skadi turned fully away from him then, her head focused on the path below which was getting darker by the moment and slippery with the falling snow and previous rain. 'There is nothing good about any of this. I should never have left her alone, not even for a moment.'

Agnar sighed. He'd suspected she would blame herself, but his heart ached to hear it. His mother had done much the same after they'd been cast out. It had broken his heart. 'No one is to blame for this but Oddmund.'

At the first ridge they stopped and lit their torches because the sun was so low that the shadow of the forest was difficult to see through. They focused on the left-hand side of the ridge, but the bracken looked undisturbed and there were no other beads left behind. They had scrubbed at the snow around the treeline to see if anything had been dropped.

Skadi's bare hands looked red raw from the rope and cold, but he didn't have any gloves to offer her, so instead he insisted she carry the torch to light the way.

At the second ridge, Skadi was already running to the treeline before she made the plateau. He realised why a moment later when he saw the blue-and-white ribbon hanging from a branch. 'Clever girl!'

It was reassuring and filled him with pride to see it. Astra was still alive and conscious. From the height of the ribbon, he imagined she was being carried over Oddmund's shoulder and had draped the hair ribbon over the branch as they passed into the forest. She was obviously frightened, but had the wit to know when to leave signs and where.

Skadi snatched it off the branch and walked into the forest. The moon wasn't full, but the increasing snow reflected the light a little. Not enough to see into the shadows, but enough to ensure they didn't trip over a log or fallen branch. Skadi swept the torch in an arc.

'There!' said Vali, pointing at faint oblong marks and

scuffs in the snow. 'One set. He is carrying her, which is good. It means he's slower.'

Agnar nodded, but he'd carried Astra earlier and she was no heavier than a shield. But Oddmund was a little older—perhaps she would be enough of a burden to slow him down.

They ploughed on, sweeping out into a fan to cover as much ground as possible, trying to walk quickly, but not loudly. All of them painfully aware that they didn't want to put the Princess at any greater risk.

The rumble of distant waves increased as they approached the cliff edge, as did the whirl of snow that scattered through and from the trees. The weather had turned bitterly cold and their breath fogged as they each pushed forward.

The sun was little more than a slither of grey bleeding into the black sea beyond and barely visible through the cage of trees. But there was more light flickering in the distance…a campfire… Instinctively, he grabbed Skadi's arm.

She shrugged out of his hold as if it were a viper's bite and burst forward. But Agnar's reactions had been honed from years of battle and he managed to catch her again with an even tighter grip, tugging her close and whispering in her ear, 'Quiet! We need to surprise him! They're close to the cliff.' He then tapped his ear and Skadi took a moment to listen, her eyes widening when she heard a familiar voice in the distance, followed by several more.

It must have taken all of Skadi's willpower to hold back, but she reined in her instincts and gave a sharp nod, slowly removing her borrowed sword from its scabbard and the shield from around her back. Agnar lowered his torch to the ground and rolled it in the snow to extinguish it.

He signalled them to lower their bodies, then slowly they moved forward, their net tightening as they approached the men at the cliff edge.

There were at least twenty of them, far too many to fight off easily, and it looked as if they had been here for a few days by the scatter of tents, hunting equipment and felled trees.

It was clear they'd planned to kidnap Astra days ago and had been waiting for Oddmund to steal her away.

Agnar took no pleasure in knowing that he'd been rightly suspicious of Oddmund and the devastation on Skadi's face was enough to focus his mind and body. He would return Astra to her, or die trying.

Chapter Twenty-Four

Skadi's heart was racing, her toes and fingers numb. The pounding of her heart thrummed in her ears so loud that she was half-afraid the men gathered at the edge of the cliff might also hear it slamming against her ribs.

Each step closer filled her with more fear. They were only fifty feet away now, their steps slow and hunched within the shadows of the trees. She *needed* to see Astra, to know that she was still alive, and within reach. Every moment of uncertainty threw her further down into despair and panic.

'Stop whining like a whore, Oddmund!' growled one of the men. 'We've been up here for days freezing our balls off, wondering when you'd finally find the courage to do what I've been asking of you for weeks!'

It took Skadi a moment to recognise the voice. It was King Sven himself! Her hands clenched tighter around the handles of her sword and shield. She would gut every man who had taken part in the abduction of her daughter—including Sven!

Her stomach churned with bitter gall as she realised why Oddmund had come back alone. It wasn't solely to warn her of Agnar's attack, it was to take Astra from her. Then, with Astra under Sven's control, it wouldn't matter if Skadi lived or died against Agnar, he would have had a claim to her throne that even the petty Kings could not dispute.

Oddmund's reply only confirmed her fears. He grumbled bad-temperedly, with a bloody cloth pressed to his nose. 'I came as quickly as I could! I told you Agnar would be quick to take the island! Curse that little bitch, I think she broke my nose!'

Skadi vowed to do more than break Oddmund's nose when she got a hold of him.

Agnar had been right about Sven and Oddmund. The sickening realisation that she'd been fooled yet again by a man she trusted was enough to make her want to howl at the moon.

Was any man honourable?

Was Agnar?

Sven threw his horn at Oddmund, who was able to lean out of the way before it struck him. 'Insolence! Agnar is making greater defences and lookouts every day. Any longer and I would have been forced to leave empty handed. It shouldn't have taken you this long to grab a little girl! And I would not have had to come at all, if you and Heimdall had obeyed me from the start! Do you have any idea how difficult it was to get here? To find this damn beach for a start and then climb up this ridge in preparation to meet with you?'

Oddmund gave a scornful snarl. 'I could hardly leave Thrudheim with the struggling Princess over my shoulder! I had to wait for the right opportunity!'

'We make our own opportunities!' snapped Sven. 'I have been building towards this moment for nearly twenty years. I won't let Agnar snatch it away from me now!' He took a deep breath. 'But I suppose they'll be too busy searching the mountain to find us easily. The tide is coming in—soon our boats will be lifted and ready to set sail.'

Skadi would never understand the self-assurance and arrogance of some men. But at least it had worked to their advantage. Sven had no idea Oddmund had been followed and Oddmund was still unaware of Astra's guidance in helping them find her. Which was a good thing, because she was safer that way. As they approached, she noticed a small shadow that she'd presumed was a boulder shift slightly.

Leaning forward, she managed to see the bundle more clearly. Astra was wrapped in her cloak, with her hands and feet tied. Skadi couldn't see much of her face because of the hood of her cloak, but one of her braids was visible. The hair tie was missing and the white-blonde braid was beginning to unravel.

She's alive! She fought to stop herself from running to her. She glanced towards Agnar, who nodded with understanding when she pointed out Astra.

Agnar gestured to Vali and the other warrior to move around from the right. Skadi motioned to Brenna to join her on the left and Agnar headed a few feet forward, then stopped and waited for them to get into position.

Despite Sven having captured Astra, he still didn't seem pleased with the situation. He glanced over the cliff edge and gave a bad-tempered huff. 'Let's go.'

'Do you think this will work? Agnar might be grateful to lose the girl,' said Oddmund thoughtfully and Skadi flinched.

Sven gave a loud snort. 'It would not serve him to lose her, not yet at least. He has proclaimed to all that she is his heir. To deny it now will only show the petty Kings and Skadi that he cannot be trusted. This little Princess is the key to Thrudheim. With her in my possession I can claim I rescued her from Agnar—that he threatened her safety. Combined with a sea blockade and no delivery of grain, Thrudheim will fall quickly. Mark my words, this island will officially be under my command by spring. The Queen will be opening her gates, just as easily as she opened her legs for that *Usurper*, you'll see! Now let's move!'

Oddmund nodded. 'Someone strap the Princess to me. She wriggles and fights like a demon and I can't have her doing that while I climb… Or we really will be here until dawn!'

Panic quickened Skadi's steps and she hurried towards Astra, Brenna crawling close behind her.

There was a snap of a branch to their right, and the group of men stopped suddenly and stared into the trees opposite. 'What was that?' hissed Sven.

Skadi and Brenna had now made it within a few feet of Astra. They stilled and hunched low as Sven barrelled over to the campfire. He raised a lit torch from it and they huddled low in the undergrowth.

Thankfully, Sven didn't see them and he strode away to peer into the forest. Skadi wasn't sure if the snapped twig had been deliberate, but it had pulled the men away from them for a moment. She and Brenna pushed forward until they were just behind Astra, hidden behind a huge rock.

'Astra, it's Moma,' she whispered, but there was no reaction. Skadi reached out from behind the boulder with one hand. She was almost able to touch the cloth of Astra's cloak, but had to jump back when the light came sweeping back towards them.

'There's nothing there!' grumbled Oddmund. 'It's unlikely they will find us. The Queen and her servant were too busy behaving like eager lightskirts to notice the Princess was missing! They'll think I've fallen down some ravine somewhere. The Queen is too arrogant and stupid to imagine I would ever betray her.' Oddmund pulled Astra up and it was then Skadi noticed there was a gag around her mouth. 'Tie her securely.'

Rage filled her and she tasted iron in her mouth.

Meanwhile, half of Sven's men were beginning to climb down the cliff. The first one pulled on the rope tightly to check the tree it was wrapped around was secure. Skadi watched as slowly the group of warriors reduced to a more sizeable number and Astra was tied to Oddmund.

Her hand flexed around her sword and she prepared herself for battle. She glanced back at Brenna who gave her a pained look, but was ready with a small rock and knife in hand. Skadi absently realised that Brenna also felt guilty about Astra's kidnapping...had she been with Vali? The thought surprised her, but how had she been any better? Besides, Astra was *her* daughter, her responsibility.

She understood why they had to wait to narrow the odds in their favour. The more men that went down, the fewer men between them and Astra. But Astra was now securely tied to Oddmund's back and was approaching the cliff edge.

She had to act now, or risk losing her daughter for ever.

Just as she was about to stand, she heard the soft wet thud of an axe splitting flesh and bone. A warrior on the outskirts of the camp dropped backwards, Agnar's little axe protruding from his head. It was the only war cry they needed and each of them burst out of the darkness as Sven, Oddmund and their remaining men drew their weapons.

Skadi sprinted forward, her sole focus on reaching Oddmund, who had immediately placed himself in the centre of the group and was unfortunately the closest to the rope.

A warrior ran out to meet her and she engaged him with a ferocious scream, channelling all her anger and fear for Astra in each strike of her blade. The warrior was cut down in moments, the next was struck by a rock in the face and Skadi sliced his belly before he even realised what had happened.

Agnar and Vali were fighting men to the side of her. But she noticed the warrior who had joined them in searching for Astra had unfortunately been cut down by Sven in the initial attack. Agnar's throwing axe flew for a second time and she realised he was felling men, and retrieving it whenever he could.

It seemed that Sven's men were well trained and they were gathering to form a shield wall around the cliff edge. This allowed Oddmund to begin climbing down the rope with little Astra strapped to his back.

Skadi roared forward with all her strength and power, defeating one man and kicking another off the edge. His scream faded shortly after his body disappeared from view.

Sven, seeing the way of things, swung on to the rope like the coward he was, letting his last men battle it out with Vali, Skadi and Agnar.

Skadi slammed her shield into the man she was fighting, the impact shaking up her arm and reminding her that it had been too long since she'd trained with her sword and shield. She usually trained every day, but since Agnar's arrival it had been much less. Gritting her teeth, she took the returning strike to her shield, then lifted it in a sweeping block before thrusting forward with her sword.

The man dropped to her feet with a gargled yell. She felt no sympathy for him or any of the others whom she'd killed. They deserved their fate for betraying a queen and stealing her child. She channelled her mother's rage with each blow and strike of her sword and shield.

But it was not enough to stop Astra from disappearing over the side on Oddmund's back. The wave of agony almost broke her and she screamed with frustration as she cut down another man in her way. She pushed forward, grasping the rope, when a shout from behind drew her attention. Brenna was helplessly throwing rocks at a man who had

had enough of fighting and was eager to escape, charging straight towards Brenna.

Vali was fighting two men by the tree line and Agnar was at the rope. He grabbed it with both hands and nodded towards Brenna. A silent command, before he threw himself over the side with the rope in hand.

Cursing, Skadi ran towards the man who was a threat to Brenna and cut him down from behind. He fell on top of Brenna and she struggled to kick herself away from his dead weight.

'Are you well?' Skadi asked quickly and, after Brenna's shaken nod, Skadi sprinted back to the rope. Vali had just taken down the last man and now ran to meet her. They peered over the drop, Skadi using the torch that had been left on the ground by Sven to see better.

Agnar had made good speed down the rope, but he had Sven and Oddmund to face and they were halfway down. Skadi immediately dropped her shield and prepared to climb down after.

Vali looked worriedly behind him.

'Stay at the top! In case we need help,' she commanded.

Vali grabbed her arm, a sympathetic and pleading expression on his face. 'If the rope breaks, they *all* die!'

She glanced down the cliffs and the tide coming in. Soon the ship would be lifted from the beach and even with half their men gone they could still launch and sail out of the old harbour. The rope was thick, but it was also creaking loudly, the fibres stretched from carrying eight burly warriors and one child. She was no climber, but even she could see the fibres straining.

Agnar was now grappling with Oddmund. Skadi grabbed a nearby rock and was prepared to throw it, except the rope was swaying wildly and she was half-afraid of hitting Agnar or even Astra. Her daughter was helpless, strapped to Oddmund's back, tied and gagged, her pale face looking up at her with hope and fear.

Oddmund, aware of who followed him, was kicking down at the man below him, shouting at him to hurry.

Sven screamed up at them, 'Curse you, Agnar, I should have killed you years ago!' He jumped with his axe to a nearby ledge, slamming the blade into the rock to keep his balance. It was tiny, little more than something a goat might stand on, but Sven was obviously a practical man and would rather take his chances on the rockface than get between Agnar and his quarry.

Agnar glared at him as he climbed past and Sven laughed. 'You have to decide whether to kill me or save the girl, little brother!'

'You will never be my brother!' grunted Agnar, not slowing down his descent for even a moment.

Oddmund's kicks and shouts became more urgent and one man fell to his death on the rocks below. A painful reminder that there was still at least another hundred feet below them.

'Give me the Princess and I will let you go!' shouted Agnar.

'If I do that, you will cut the rope!' Oddmund shouted back, his eyes wild with panic. He struck out at Agnar with his knife, and it caught on the rope, causing a flurry of threads to break.

'As always, Oddmund! Wisdom tries to catch you, but you always manage to evade it!' This was said by a very disgruntled Sven, who was watching from his crow's perch on the cliff.

'You sliced the rope, you idiot!' screamed another man from below.

Oddmund cursed loudly, having lost patience with himself and his allies.

Agnar moved to grip the rope with one hand and dangled down to grab at Astra with the other. 'Hold on tight, Astra!' shouted Agnar and she immediately obeyed him by gripping on to Oddmund with her legs and arms.

He moved in a sweep, slicing at the rope binding Astra from side to side, managing to cut her mostly free. Her daughter seemed to find some courage from somewhere, because she tugged at the gag with her bound hands, then used her teeth to undo the ties at her wrists.

'What are you doing? Do you want her to die?' shouted Oddmund as he grappled with the rope that seemed to be bursting more threads with every moment. 'Move or die!' he screamed at the men below him. Not wanting to fall to their deaths, the men began sliding down the rope, many of them yelling with pain as it burned their hands.

Skadi dropped to her knees, feeling just as helpless as she had the last time her daughter's life had been in Agnar's hands.

'Be brave, Princess, reach for my hand!' shouted Agnar, dropping down a few feet more past the frayed section of rope. A few more stands sprung free and Skadi's heart scattered down the cliff with the rest of her courage.

The ties holding Astra to Oddmund's back fell away, and the only thing keeping her to him were her legs and arms wrapped around him. Astra looked up at her tearfully, her sapphire eyes more precious than any gem Skadi possessed.

'Moma?' she questioned and it was a fragile question wrapped in uncertainty and fear.

'Take his hand! Trust him, Astra, he's got you!' yelled Skadi and she prayed to all the gods that she had finally chosen the right man to trust.

Now that the men below Oddmund were moving down with speed, Oddmund did the same. Agnar leaned closer, dangerously close. She was afraid he would fall by mistake if he stretched much further.

Astra lunged for Agnar, letting go of Oddmund as he slid down the rope.

Skadi swallowed a scream, her fingers clawing into the earth, as her child dangled precariously from Agnar's arm. The image of him holding Astra up in her chamber that first night flashed through her mind.

This time she prayed he would not drop her. Thrudheim's future, her purpose and her heart depended on him.

Chapter Twenty-Five

Snow danced around them, snowflakes catching in his eyes and making it difficult to see. He wasn't sure if it was actually snowing still, or if the wind battering the cliffs was simply lifting it from the rockface.

He didn't care about the cold or discomfort. He had Astra and that's all that mattered.

Swinging her up and shifting his body awkwardly with a grunt, he managed to pull her on to his back, grateful that Oddmund had more sense than to try to fight for her. He was too terrified about the tattered rope to do anything more than scramble down as quickly as he could.

Astra clung to Agnar's neck so tightly, he had to gasp for air, her wretched sobs hot against his ear. She'd been so brave and he suspected her nerves were beginning to fray… not unlike the rope above their heads.

'I've got you, little one,' he reassured her, 'Wrap your legs around my waist, but…' He swallowed deeply as her grip tightened and he barely managed to croak out, 'Less tightly on my throat.'

Now that Agnar had Astra more securely, he began to climb the rope as quickly as he could. The frayed ball of fibres seemed so much further up than he'd imagined. With every moment that passed, every gust of wind that sent them swaying back and forth it seemed to lose more threads.

There wasn't enough time!

He grabbed the little axe at his belt and slammed it into the rock above his head, shoving his feet against cracks in the rock to find purchase. It was enough to keep him upright as the rope finally gave way and snapped.

It burned through his hand and whistled past him, slapping against his thigh like an angry cat's tail on its way down. Its rapid descent was met by the screams of men, followed quickly by wet thuds against rock, as well as splashes as a couple of lucky men fell into the sea and a horrible crack of wood as one hit the rigging of the ship below.

'Don't look down!' he shouted above the noise of the wind, obeying his own command and staring up at the end of the rope above his head. Now that Astra was his responsibility the knowledge filled him with fear and uncertainty. He could protect himself, had always been able to. Where he'd failed was in protecting others, protecting his mother and even Skadi.

The little axe that he'd relied on all those years ago was the only thing between them and a grisly fall and he could feel it straining under their weight, slowly slipping from the rock, like a creaky door. His feet were giving little support against the cracks in the rock. If the axe fell, so would he.

He reached up with one hand and could only feel the barest whisper of thread against his fingers. His other shifted on to the top of the axe, his hand slippery with his own blood, as he clawed up with his fingers a little further and was able to grip the bundle of frayed threads. Desperately he grabbed hold of it and forced his body up, fist over fist.

As if knowing its work was done, the little axe slipped free and clattered down the cliff. His heart ached at its loss. It had always been a reminder of his mother's sacrifice, of his own ability to never give up—even in the darkest of moments.

Perhaps it would find its way to the eastern sea, where his mother's ashes had been scattered, or it would help some other person in their time of need?

By letting go of the past, was he finally choosing to be happy?

Such strange thoughts filled his mind as he grunted and forced his body upwards. Afraid to drop Astra or the slippery rope, but climbing anyway in the hopes of a better future for all of them. He ignored the pain in his bloodied palms and the pull of Astra's arms as she wept against his neck. He would get her to safety, even—and most likely—if it killed him.

'Most impressive!' declared a voice to the side of him, and he was absently aware that it was Sven a few feet away, still on his ledge.

Agnar didn't acknowledge him. He was a little surprised that Sven hadn't tried to cut his rope with his axe. But the ledge was tiny, and he imagined Sven couldn't pull it free, let alone swing it without losing his footing. As always, Sven valued himself above all things.

'Any chance you can swing the rope my way? If you reach the top…'

Agnar continued to ignore him. But Astra was feeling brave and, through her tears, she snapped, 'I hope you're stuck there for a hundred years!'

Agnar chuckled, but then he spotted the terrified eyes of Skadi above. He gritted his teeth and pushed onwards. He couldn't relax until Astra was safely in her arms.

He knew he was close when Astra's weight was lifted from his shoulders and pulled over the top. To his surprise, more arms reached for him straight after, and not just Vali and Brenna's. Skadi yanked him up and over the precipice, falling on to her back with one arm tightly wrapped around Astra's cloak, pulling her weeping child close to her side, while her other hand clutched at his tunic, unwilling to let either of them go.

He flopped on to his back, so as not to crush her, and she dragged him to her. The three of them clung to each other with white-knuckled grips, still panting with relief and exhaustion.

The glow from the campfire was bright enough to see the relieved expressions of Brenna and Vali above them, Brenna curling into Vali's arms with obvious relief.

Agnar sighed, grateful that the gods had been kind and just. He would never have forgiven them if they'd taken Astra from them. There was a break in the snow-filled clouds and he was struck by how small they must appear to the gods, no bigger than one of the many stars scattered across the darkness.

One star fell, shooting through the sky in a sweeping arc and disappearing into the clouds and horizon.

'Did you see that?' gasped Astra.

'Yes,' whispered Skadi, her voice sounding raw from all the shouting she must have done.

'Agnar, did you?' Astra asked, her voice hesitant with hope.

'I saw it,' he said, unable to deny the smile that spread across his face, as he lay across Skadi's pounding chest. Astra reached across to hold his hand.

'The gods sent us good fortune,' whispered Astra and he couldn't agree more.

Chapter Twenty-Six

The royal family sat with their backs against the heat of the campfire, staring out into the darkness. Skadi didn't want Astra to see the bodies, she was already worried about what witnessing the skirmish and deaths would have done to her young mind. Not to mention the terror of her kidnapping. But they couldn't stay here, it was too cold and open, even with the campfire, and soon the smell of blood would attract beasts and vermin.

In a way, the snow had helped. It was falling so thickly now, that the bodies were covered in a white blanket.

'We should leave soon,' said Skadi. Then, with a little more curiosity, at the sounds of shouts below, she asked, 'What is happening down there?'

Vali walked over to the cliff edge and glanced down. 'Looks like Sven's crew are trying to save him. They are throwing up hooks and rope… They are making slow progress.'

Skadi didn't comment. Like Astra she did not care if the man spent the rest of his days on that ledge, fell to his death or even escaped. As long as he never saw Astra again, she would be content and at this moment she was more concerned about getting Astra home safely than seeking revenge. One day, hopefully soon, she would seek vengeance against Sven, but she would do so in an honourable way and with the support of her people.

On the other hand, she'd taken a dark satisfaction in watching Oddmund's body break against the rocks. She had trusted him and he had failed her more than once. But was he any better than Heimdall? Both men's sole purpose in Thrudheim had been to please and serve King Sven. They had never supported her, never believed in her and she had accepted their lies.

Agnar in contrast had been honest, proving himself with his actions. He'd even risked his life to save Astra. There were so many moments when she'd feared for both Agnar and Astra and watching them climb the rope had crushed her heart. She'd not been reassured until she'd pulled both of them over the edge.

Nausea churned her stomach like one of her whirlpools below and she knew she had allowed all this to happen. Agnar had not trusted Oddmund and she'd ignored his doubts. Refusing to trust him when he'd done nothing but prove himself to her. While all she'd done was doubt him at every step.

Brenna draped a couple of blankets from the men's camp around their shoulders and handed out food and drink from their supplies. Astra and Skadi refused and Agnar gave her a disapproving look. She couldn't help it, she was so sickened by what could have been, and Astra was swaying against her with exhaustion.

'Why don't you try to rest, Astra? You must be tired.'

With a nod Astra curled up in Skadi's lap.

The glow from the fire lit up the resolve in Agnar's expression. 'Tell me what you want me to do and I will arrange it.'

Skadi's heart ached at his devotion—she did not deserve

it—and she pulled Astra's body closer. 'Let her rest a little… But we should go home soon. The snow has stopped falling and it will take less time to get to Thrudheim if we go down rather than up. Then…' she paused '… Sven must answer for this. But winter will be soon upon us and I am still worried about the lack of grain.'

Agnar nodded, as if in silent agreement with her fears and worries. 'I will make arrangements.' It was oddly comforting to hear his reassurance, although she wasn't completely sure how he would manage it. Perhaps he just would…the idea of relying on someone else felt strange, but with Agnar she knew he meant every word.

'I am sorry, Agnar, about your axe. It was the one you used to protect your mother with, wasn't it?'

Agnar nodded, but his smile was gentle. 'She would be proud of how I lost it.'

'She would… Thank you, Agnar, for everything.' Tears filled Skadi's eyes and it didn't feel as if she'd said enough, but emotion threatened to engulf her and she knew she had to be strong for the journey back. She lowered her head and kissed Astra's hair, comforted by the scent of her.

The climb down to Thrudheim was difficult and time consuming. The snow had stopped, but it had carpeted the already wet ground with an icy sludge, which made the path treacherous. At least they could take their time now that Astra was safe.

They each took turns in helping to carry or guide Astra down the miners' path and a sigh of relief escaped all their mouths when the ground finally levelled and they saw the fires of the furnaces in the distance. It meant they were close to the workshops and ultimately Thrudheim.

The miners were woken from their beds and they immediately offered them shelter and hot mead. Messengers were sent out to notify the search parties that Astra had been found by the King and Queen. They were also offered a bed for the remainder of the night, but Skadi wanted the comfort of her own hall and it seemed foolish to stop when they were already so close to home. So, they were given ponies to take them the rest of the way, which wasn't far.

A short time later they entered Thrudheim's hall, with its wolf banners of blue and white draped from the beams, the central fire roaring cheerfully in welcome.

Agnar and Vali had stopped by the gate to deal with the messengers and presumably to prepare for whatever new challenge would fall upon them from Sven. They knew he'd made it down to his boat eventually, so they were prepared for another battle with him in the future.

They paused a moment to warm their hands and wave away the servants who hurried to offer them warmed wine and honey cakes. Skadi's body was so shattered and cold that she wanted nothing more than to curl up in her bed.

'Actually, Inga!' she called out, as she realised what she actually needed. 'Could you please put some hot stones in the King's bed, and bring a cup of restorative tonic for the Princess, honey and chamomile, perhaps?'

Inga nodded and there was a flurry of activity as all the servants hurried to do as she asked. Skadi wasn't surprised. Astra was well loved by the servants and her kidnap by a trusted member of the court had shaken everyone, not just Skadi.

She guided a sleepy Astra down the corridor.

'Am I not sleeping in my room tonight?' she murmured.

'No, tonight I thought you could sleep with me.'

Astra didn't argue, and seemed pleased by the suggestion. 'I wish I had Freydis. I left her at the lodge.'

Skadi paused outside her daughter's chamber. 'Would you like anything else instead?'

Astra shook her head and they continued on, Skadi quietly reassuring her that her doll would be brought down by the warriors when they left the cabin.

'Are you sure?' asked Astra nervously.

'I am certain they will see her and remember how special she is to you.'

A brazier had been lit in the King's chamber and Skadi smiled at Inga, who was fussing with extra blankets and furs on the bed. They began to undress, a half-barrel was filled with warm water and they each took it in turns to stand inside and wash themselves with a foamy cloth of soap and then be rinsed off with a jug. It wasn't as satisfying as a proper bath, but it was a welcome pleasure after the freezing cold and clammy sweat that had accumulated over the strain of their terrible day and night.

They had climbed up and down a mountain, had the fright of their lives and been exposed to the first heavy snowfall. This simple wash with hot water, followed by fresh linen shifts, felt like a luxury in comparison. She insisted on lamb's wool socks for Astra's feet and to brush and braid her hair in two plaits either side of her head, hating to see the ragged hair and knowing that Astra had been forced to tear at it to leave them signs of her kidnap.

Once she was done, Astra insisted she do the same. So dutifully she brushed and braided her hair in two girlish plaits and put thick socks on her feet, while Astra drank her tonic and even ate a small bowl of porridge that Inga had insisted on making.

Eventually, she could tuck Astra into bed and send the

servants back to theirs, before joining her daughter. As she did so, Skadi noticed for the first that the bed was the new one that Agnar had commissioned. It had a wolf's head roaring at the centre of the headboard, the fur inlaid with silver and a blue glass eye. Surrounding the wolf was intricately carved knotwork that looked like a swirling sea.

She smiled when she eased under the covers and noticed the ridged mountain range of Thrudheim carved into the footboard. It was also inlaid with silver to show the frost of its highest peak and the northern star above it was a matching blue to the wolf's eye. It was whimsical and filled with artistry and imagination, not how she would have imagined a bed ordered by the stoic and practical Agnar might have looked.

He made it for me. The realisation made fresh tears sting her eyes and she fought to control them.

Astra was already drifting off to sleep and she snuggled closer to the familiar warmth of her mother with a whimper. Skadi stroked her back and the whimper turned into steady even breaths.

A creak drew her attention and she noticed Agnar standing in the doorway. He took one look at Astra in bed with Skadi and turned to leave.

'Don't go!' Skadi whispered—as loud as she dared with Astra beside her. Thankfully, Agnar heard her, and he paused, turning back towards her with a curious expression.

Skadi slipped from the bed and padded towards him in her lamb's wool socks that matched her daughter's and the silly braids swinging at the sides of her head. She looked ridiculous, but she didn't care.

Agnar smiled as she approached him, lifting one of the white-blonde braids with his fingers and stroking the feathered tip lightly. 'This reminds me of when we first met. You had your hair like this.'

'Come,' she said, taking his hand and pulling him further into the room.

'I'm filthy,' he said.

'Would you like a bath?'

He scrubbed a hand down his face and she realised how weary and tired he was. He'd not stopped once all day and most of the night. Climbing, fighting, risking his life more than once. 'I'll just wash my face and hands… I was going to ask if you had any balms…'

'Your hands!' she hissed, grabbing hold of one and opening it out for inspection. She winced at the raw and ragged flesh. There were cuts and blisters from the rope all over his hands.

She tugged him by his arm to a stool and pushed at his shoulders until he sat down.

'Let me take care of you,' she insisted when he opened his mouth to protest.

His mouth snapped shut and he nodded. The half-barrel had been emptied and taken away by the servants. But she had a full jug of water on the table beside her for the morning so she poured some in a basin and lathered a small amount of soap in it, glad that it wasn't too cold. She then placed the basin on his lap.

'It will sting a little…but soak your hands. Oh, wait.'

Agnar blinked. He knew Skadi could be kind and nurturing, he'd just never seen her behave that way towards him. He'd been busy since they'd returned, was so tired he could fall asleep on this stool in a matter of moments, but if Skadi wanted to care for him, he would cut out his own tongue before denying her.

She moved the bowl aside and tugged at his tunic ties,

before pulling it off his head. The outer tunic came off, followed by the under tunic. She tossed the garments on the floor and kicked them out of the way without a care, showing that she really was royalty after all, despite the menial nature of the task she was performing.

The bowl was returned to his lap and he put his hands in the water. It stung, but he was more than happy to take the pain, letting himself admire Skadi as she began to use another cloth to quickly wipe his face and upper body.

Her hair reminded him of the first time he'd seen her when she'd been a lanky youth and had stared down at him with barely concealed horror. A tiny boy must have been an unwelcome betrothed. He couldn't help but flex his muscles as she cleaned him, proving to her how well he'd grown since their first encounter.

After a few swipes of his body with the cloth, she flushed and said, 'I will order a proper bath for you in the morning. Your hair needs a thorough wash.'

He sighed. 'I should cut it off. It's so tangled now; it might be for the best.'

'No!' Skadi gasped, wringing the cloth tightly with a horrified expression. 'I like your hair long… I will wash and brush it out tomorrow. It will be fine—Astra's has been far worse and I've managed to save it.'

Her confession that she liked his hair long and the insistence that she would detangle it herself made his chest glow with hot pride.

'Did you decide about the grain?' she asked tentatively and all of his pleasure disappeared.

'King Erik hasn't yet replied to my proposal.'

Skadi nodded. 'Then I will order rationing as of tomorrow.'

There was no blame in her words, no reprimand. 'I understand if you blame me for it,' he said.

But to his surprise she shook her head. 'No, I am the one at fault. I have trusted a man who could not be trusted more than once. Sven has been against me from the beginning.'

She gently lifted his hands from the bowl, cursing when some of the water dripped on his trousers. 'I should have put a cloth down first.'

'It does not matter.'

She patted his hands with a strip of linen, so gently it was as if she thought his hands were made of fragile glass. Then she reached for a chest and opened it to choose from an array of potions and lotions.

'If I'd known you carried so many herbs, I wouldn't have kept such a close eye on your perfumer.'

Skadi smiled. 'It is an interest of mine. In the summers I like to go to the forests and flatlands to pick herbs.'

She began to mix something in her palm that looked like runny wax.

'Should I ask what that is…or will I find out when I keel over?' he teased.

She rolled her eyes, trotting back to him with her fluffy white feet. 'It's not poison.'

Skadi looked adorable in her long fluffy socks and braids. It was distracting and encouraged feelings he'd thought himself too tired to be capable of. The soft sweep of her linen shift against his arm was intoxicating as she leaned over to get a pinch of another herb. Lusty thoughts filled his mind, but with Astra in the room such a path was inappropriate at best. So, when she slathered the balm on to his palms and it stung like a hot brand, he welcomed the pain with only a slight grimace.

'I'm sorry,' she said and he shrugged.

She bandaged his hands with strips of linen and, when she'd tied and tucked the ends, she cupped his face with both hands and gently tilted him up to look at her. The softness of her expression startled him.

'I am sorry,' she said sincerely and there were tears in her eyes. 'For everything. For how I treated you in the past and in the present.'

It was what he had wanted from her all along, a heartfelt and tearful apology.

He reached up and covered her hands with his, pulling them away gently. 'I no longer want you to be sorry. I only wish for you to be happy. This time of uncertainty will pass, I swear it.'

She smiled and his heart swelled in his chest. It wasn't until this moment that he realised he had always loved her, although in different ways. He'd been in awe of the young Princess, obsessed with the young Queen who had turned away from him… Over the years, bitterness, lust and ambition had combined into a storm of conflicting emotions, but she was the woman he'd dreamed of, wanted above all others—even when he'd hated her, he'd wanted nothing more than to go to her.

Over the last few days, however, he'd seen Skadi for who she truly was, a loving mother and devoted ruler. A woman who was trusting, kind, passionate and honourable. He'd helplessly fallen for her again, for the third time, but this time as a man and as an equal.

As a boy, youth, and man, she had always guided him, like the north star showing the way home.

Gently taking his forearm so as not to put pressure on his hands, she led him to the bed. She clambered in first and patted the feather mattress next to her. Little Astra slept soundly on the other side of her.

He knew it wasn't an invitation to join her sexually, but

a request for him to join her family and gratefully he took it, kicking off his boots and climbing into bed beside her.

As dawn broke, the hall was unusually tranquil, the servants and warriors moving quietly in respect for the sleeping family resting in their chamber.

Chapter Twenty-Seven

The following day, Astra and Skadi were the first to wake, although it was almost noon by the time they left the King's chamber. They hurried out of the room so as not to disturb the soundly sleeping Agnar.

Thankfully, Astra appeared to be recovering quickly and all her worries seemed forgotten when she was reunited with her doll.

Some of the children gathered around her asking questions about her ordeal and Skadi was about to silence them when Brenna shook her head. 'Let her talk—it may help her and I swear to keep an eye on her.'

Skadi gave her friend a grateful pat on the shoulder. 'Thank you, I really need to check our stores.'

After carefully checking and planning the meals with the cook, Skadi was confident there would be enough food to last them most of the winter. But she ordered that all traders pay for their taxes and harbour fees with any grain they had, over luxury items or silver—even if it meant a loss of income, it would help feed her people. It wasn't much, but it added a few more bags to her stores.

Visiting traders warned her of King Sven raging to anyone who would listen about the 'disrespect' of Agnar forcing himself on Queen Skadi. Not because he particularly cared what happened to her, but because it disrespected him and his 'dear friend' Heimdall. The news made Skadi's insides twist with rage. But she intended to fight back.

Determined to help Agnar in his deal with King Erik, Skadi loaded a ship of gifts for Queen Torvi, King Erik's wife. She didn't know the woman well, but remembered her speaking kindly about the elegance of her table when she'd last visited.

After she'd reassured herself about their supplies, she went to check on Agnar, who sat up in bed with a jerk as she entered. He sank back against the pillows with a sigh of relief when he realised where he was.

'Are you well?' she asked, bustling in and putting another log on the brazier as she passed it. The room was warm, but if Agnar had caught a chill it was best to keep it that way.

'I needed more sleep than I thought.' He rubbed at his face absently, frowned at the bandages and began to unravel them. 'Has something happened? Is Astra well?'

'She is fine.' Skadi opened the door and called to a nearby servant, 'Please heat water for the King's bath, and bring something substantial for him to eat.' Then she came to the bed and perched beside him, explaining about the gossip from the traders and the grain supplies. She went into great detail about her plans to increase the grain store at every opportunity—even if the cost was heavy on their purse. 'I thought it more important to ensure everyone is well fed. Do you agree?'

He nodded and she was frankly pleased by how intently he had listened to her, nodding and muttering words of encouragement regarding her plans, all while he unwrapped the mountain of linen and examined his hands. She thought they looked better than last night, but still looked very sore, and she winced with sympathy.

'Tell me your other plans, so that I can help,' she asked. 'Did you send messengers to my uncle?'

'Yes, I informed him of King Sven's attempt to kidnap Astra. I also sent messengers out to the petty Kings. I am hoping they will revolt against King Sven in the spring. But nothing can be done during the dead of winter, except to wait. King Erik promised me grain, but we may have to prepare for the worst. I am worried Sven will claim he was trying to rescue the Princess from me and that will cast doubt in their minds about our marriage and my right to rule. They will fear I forced you.'

Skadi tilted her head with a pout. 'Well, you did. It was not my choice to marry you.'

'Would you choose me now?' he asked casually and she realised that she had begun to understand him better. He asked because he hoped the answer had changed.

'I am glad we are married,' she said. 'But the past is still true. I would not have considered you before... You are too young.'

He chuckled, wincing as he stretched. 'I do not feel young.'

Skadi laughed, swatting the thick muscle of his arm playfully. 'You slept too long. Your body has become stiff from lack of use.'

'Is that so?' he asked playfully with a raised brow.

She rolled her eyes and was thankfully saved from further blushes by the arrival of several servants carrying buckets of hot water and a tray of food, which Skadi took and placed on Agnar's lap.

After the servants were done filling the wooden bath, which was shaped and carved much like a boat, they left. Skadi went to her little chest of herbs once again and chose some soothing oils and healing herbs to scatter in the water.

'You are pampering me,' Agnar observed with amusement as he ate his meal. She was pleased to see it was a hearty selection of cured meats and fish, as well as a variety of cheeses, pickles and bread followed by honey cakes and stewed plums. Enough to revive a man after the trials he'd faced.

'You are a king. You should look like one,' she answered, setting out the combs and pumice stones on the table beside his bath.

The clatter of his tray being put aside was enough to let her know he had left the bed and her heart raced in anticipation.

'Are you going to join me?' he asked huskily, the heat of his body bathing her back as she pretended to avoid him.

'I will tend to you.'

'You are not a servant, Skadi.' He stroked her hair gently. She'd only braided the top half today, letting the rest fall loosely around her shoulders. His fingers brushed against the nape of her neck and she bit her lip to stop the moan that threatened to escape. She could never have enough of him and the realisation frightened her.

She turned to face him, and saw the questioning look on his face. 'I want to care for you,' she explained.

'As an apology?' he asked, appearing displeased by the prospect.

She shook her head. 'Not just that… I…' She struggled to find the words. 'You saved Astra as if she were your own daughter.'

His jaw tightened and his green eyes were bright with emotion. 'It is my duty to protect you…and Astra is my heir.' He shook his head, as if in denial. 'No…more than that. She is *your* daughter. That makes her special to me.'

Skadi's heart filled almost to bursting. She did not deserve such devotion, had never received it from anyone but her father before. If he was deceiving her, then he was a greater liar than even Loki, the god of mischief himself.

'I believe you,' she said finally, not daring to say more, but willing to at least show her feelings for him in action if nothing else. 'That is why I want to care for you. Now, get in, before it gets cold.'

Agnar smiled at her censure and began to untie his trousers. Skadi quickly busied herself with choosing the right soap for him, not daring to watch him strip in case it made her climb in after him.

She rejected the soaps Heimdall used to use, tossing those aside and vowing to give those to Vali instead.

When she heard the soft splash of water she turned to face him with her chosen soap in hand, a little breathless when she took in the sight of him. He filled the large tub so much that the water threatened to spill over the side. His body glistened from the water and steam.

She swallowed, wondering how she would manage this task without succumbing to her own desires.

'You will get water all over your dress if you wash me yourself,' said Agnar, gesturing at the elaborate blue-and-white gown, which was trimmed in silk and fur. 'Give it to me.'

He held out his hand for the soap and she noticed once again the sore flesh of his palms. The sight strengthened her resolve. Shaking her head, she thumped the soap down on the table and began to shed her clothes. It was slightly easier as there were more laces and the clasps of her brooches held up the apron straps. She'd picked it for practical reasons, hoping Agnar might take it off her later.

It seemed she had beaten him to it.

Unfortunately.

'There!' she declared, picking up the soap again when she was down to nothing more than her shift.

She took her time wetting and soaping his long hair, and then worked the combs through it, apologising when the teeth snagged occasionally on a knot.

When it was smoothly combed through, she added some nettle-and-rosemary oil that she used on her own hair and smoothed it into the ends. Smiling with satisfaction when her work was done. It had taken a long time, but she thought the curtain of midnight hair was beautiful and she would have hated him to cut it off.

She moved around the bath to face Agnar, who cracked open his eyes to stare at her with a sultry look.

'Satisfied?'

She nodded, her body tightening with anticipation at his husky voice. 'Now I need to wash your body.'

She moved forward, taking a cloth from the table and soaping it up before wiping it across his chest and arms. He leaned forward and she obediently rubbed at his back. 'You are enjoying this a little too much!' she teased.

He sank into the water without warning, splashing her with a waterfall over the side of the bath. She didn't bother jumping out of the way, she was already soaking wet.

When he raised up again, she tapped him on the head with a comb. 'You just rinsed off the oil I put on your hair! It is expensive! What a waste!'

He turned his head and upper body to look at her, his eyes lowering slowly until they were staring at her chest. She followed his gaze, and gasped when she realised her breast and nipples were heavily outlined by the water.

Tugging at the shift, she then smacked him with the comb again, immediately regretting it when he winced. She was meant to be *caring for him!* 'Oh, sorry!'

'Don't apologise,' rumbled Agnar with a chuckle. 'The pain distracts me from your see-through shift.'

She gasped in outrage again, but then he pulled her towards the bath. She squealed and stopped him from dragging her in by grabbing the sides. 'No! I was meant to be caring for you. I had a plan to wash and dry you—'

Agnar laughed, but he released her, and she stepped aside, smoothing back her hair with a flustered sigh.

Her composure was short lived, however, because he rose from the water like a god and stared down at her, his raven hair falling forward over his broad shoulders. His body shimmered in the light from the brazier and torches like a bronze statue. Between his powerfully thick thighs his staff was erect and ready.

Skadi's throat bobbed with nerves and she watched with barely contained excitement as he stepped out of the bath.

'I should get a linen,' she said, although she made no move to reach for the several folded and waiting only a few feet away.

'I have never seen you fully naked,' he said with a tilt of his head, as if the thought had just occurred to him. He cupped one of her breasts with his hand, brushing a thumb over her nipple, and causing a river of need to rush through her. He smiled, 'Not even now…you are always only half-revealed to me.'

Her chest tightened with an unexpected longing. She had to admit that she had hidden her feelings for him. Showing her lust, only to shy away from him straight after. She had grown to love him, this man who had stormed into her life and forced her hand. But she still couldn't voice her feelings, because he didn't either.

Did he feel the same? Or was she just imagining it, wishing for a dream that was no more real than magic.

She untied the knot at her neck and slipped the shift from her shoulders, baring herself to him, physically at least. 'Is this better?' she asked, hoping he wouldn't notice the stretch marks on her skin, or the softening around her belly that had come after childbirth.

To her relief Agnar didn't seem to care, he wrapped her in his arms and kissed her like a man starving for touch. Their tongues danced and she ran her hands through his silky wet hair, desperate for the mindless pleasure he could give her. She didn't want to worry about the future disappointments or the threat of war. She wanted to feel alive, cherished and loved, all of the overwhelming emotions she felt in Agnar's embrace.

He lifted her and she wrapped her legs around his waist as he carried her to the bed, his manhood rubbing flat against her in ways that made her moan and pant against his lips as he kissed her thoroughly.

He lowered them to the bed, their wet bodies clinging to the sheets and each other as they slid against one another.

He trailed a hand down her body and she felt the callouses of his burns. She gripped his wrist to stop him, 'Not with your poor hands.'

He laughed. 'My *poor* hands are fine!'

She shrugged. 'I want you to use your mouth and tongue instead…would you deny me?'

His face sobered. 'I could never deny you.'

She arched her back, hoping it would tempt him, and it did. His mouth latched on to her nipple and gently sucked. She squirmed beneath him, hot pleasure coursing through her veins.

She clung to him, revelling in the heat and strength of his body. He shifted, trailing kisses down her body, and she opened her legs for him, her breath held tight with anticipation. The first touch of his lips and tongue made her moan with joyous relief. He kissed her between her legs until she couldn't bear it any longer, and her heels dug into the mattress as her spine arched.

'Agnar,' she groaned and she could tell he was also on the edge of shattering by the wild look in his eyes. She wrapped her legs around his waist as he raised up and positioned himself at her entrance.

But when he entered her, he did so slowly, easing into her with a sigh of satisfaction, as if he were revelling in the feel of her. Then he lowered his weight, being sure to slide in and out of her and let her feel every inch of his body moving against hers as he did so.

She clung to him, face to face, naked and exposed. Holding on to him with all her strength as they moved together as one.

When their climax came it was joyous and natural. They held one another tightly breathing the same air, satisfied and blissfully happy.

Chapter Twenty-Eight

The snow grew over the next few weeks and Thrudheim worked hard to keep the defences, training arena and pathways clear. Her men had been integrated into Agnar's warriors, as it was clear that Oddmund had been working with Sven alone.

They'd even found messages and bags of silver in his home—although they'd simply been temptations to keep his loyalty. The real prize was mentioned in a contracted alliance between Sven and Oddmund that clearly stated he would be rewarded with the role of Thrudheim's Chieftain, once Skadi was widowed and *removed* from power. The message had been sent well before Heimdall's death and it was the damning proof she needed to accuse Sven in front of the petty Kings of his conspiring to usurp her and kill Heimdall.

Unfortunately, gathering the petty Kings would be impossible at this time of year—they would be wintering in their halls and would not risk travelling. So, they had to make do with messengers sent out on the few trading ships leaving the harbour. Agnar didn't want to send out his own ships as it would reduce their warriors and Skadi agreed wholeheartedly.

They worked together well and she no longer feared his taking control of Thrudheim. He always discussed big decisions with her, their conversations thorough and interesting, usually agreeing on a solution quickly that suited them both. She'd quickly allowed him free rein to make their military decisions, as he was far more of an expert in that area, and he seemed pleased by her confidence in him.

The only decision that had displeased Skadi was minor and was due to her own doubts and insecurities, she couldn't even criticise Agnar for it. He'd commissioned the building of a new longship, which he'd named *Sea Queen.*

It had reminded her of Heimdall's obsession with raiding and she did not want Agnar to leave her. She viewed the ship as if it were a young second wife, a dangerous temptation that would eventually lead her husband's affections away from her.

However, she was too proud to tell him so. To be jealous of a longship seemed ridiculous even to her, so she remained silent whenever he spoke of it, or asked for her opinion on its plans.

For some reason she hadn't yet confessed her feelings for him. Still afraid that they wouldn't be returned.

Why spoil something that was working so well?

In the bedchamber they were confident of each other's affection. Their nights were full of passion and sensual exploration. But she still couldn't speak the words of her heart. After all, Agnar was younger…his desires could change with the direction of the wind. Heimdall's certainly had.

Perhaps, she was too old, and burnt by the past, to confess to such girlish dreams...

Life was easier and happier with Agnar in it, and she feared that if she did anything to rock their blossoming relationship, he would disappear as Heimdall had done and she would be even lonelier than she'd been before.

She couldn't go back to those miserable years. The pain

this time would be unbearable, for both herself and Astra, who grew fonder of her saviour and hero every day.

Agnar had lifted away some of the weight of her responsibilities and eased her burdens, allowing her more time to spend with Brenna and Astra, as she did now. The three of them were enjoying a cup of warm milk and honey cakes, while Astra practised writing her runes.

Skadi doubted she would have had time to do something like this when Heimdall had been alive. Even with the threat of Sven on the horizon, she had time to enjoy the peace before the storm. Almost losing Astra had made Skadi realise how precious time with her daughter was.

So, today she had spent the morning training with sword and shield, followed by listening to petitions from her people, and now she would spend the time before Nattmal with Astra.

Of course, after Nattmal she would enjoy her night with the King. How would he take her tonight? He certainly had the stamina of a young man…

Skadi had to smother a chuckle at her own wayward thoughts and she noticed Brenna seemed deep in thought, so she asked her friend gently, 'Is something worrying you?'

Brenna's eyes drifted up from the honey cake she'd been lightly picking at since they sat down. 'Vali wants to marry me. But I have…misgivings.'

Skadi tried to hide her smile by sipping her milk. 'I thought you liked Vali now?'

Brenna sighed, 'He's infuriating, but…yes, I love him.'

Skadi blinked. 'You love him? So soon?' Brenna's free and open admission shocked her, as Skadi couldn't imagine declaring herself so casually. *Was she wrong to hold back?* Brenna was so similar to her, opinionated and slow to trust, but if *she* could confess the truth of her heart, why couldn't Skadi?

Brenna smiled and nodded shyly. 'I have never felt this way about anyone else before. It is why I never considered marriage until… Well, Vali.'

Guilt curdled in Skadi's stomach. 'Because you saw how it was between Heimdall and me and you were too afraid to take the risk?'

Brenna's face dropped and she answered kindly, 'No, that wasn't why. It was because I had no reason to. I was protected by you. I had a home and a purpose at your side, I could afford the luxury of waiting for true love.'

Skadi frowned, not understanding the reason for Brenna's misgivings. 'I hope you are not having doubts because of me. I would never wish to hold you back, if you wish to go and be a wife—'

Brenna chuckled and waved a hand dismissively. 'I know that. I have loved working beside you for the good of Thrudheim and hope to continue doing so for the rest of my life. Vali understands that… In a way it's lucky he is Agnar's second. No, my misgivings are because I do not wish to marry without my mother witnessing it. But Vali is adamant that we marry before the spring. There is talk that Sven will attack during the spring thaw and that is only a couple of months away. He doesn't want to risk dying in battle without legitimising our union in the eyes of the gods…' Tears gathered in Brenna's eyes and Skadi leaned across to hug her, then gathered her hands in hers.

'You do not have to do anything you do not wish to do. I will ask Agnar to speak with him.'

Brenna nodded miserably. 'But… I do *want* to marry him. When I imagined my wedding, I always presumed it would be in the village, with my mother as Gothi.'

Skadi thought for a moment and then squeezed her hands. 'How about a small ceremony at Thrudheim's shrine, followed by a second ceremony at the village in the summer? Once the threat of Sven has passed?'

Brenna's face flushed and she couldn't meet her eyes. 'How could I demand two ceremonies when you barely had one proper wedding with Agnar?'

Skadi laughed, glad something so simple was the only thing holding Brenna back. 'Well then, I shall do the same! A big midsummer feast for both our marriages, and to celebrate the survival of Thrudheim.'

Brenna's face brightened. 'That would be wonderful.'

Skadi returned her smile, but it felt tight and hollow. She prayed they would make it to the summer. Nothing was certain and she felt as if the Norns of fate were weaving her future to the beat of every hammered nail in Agnar's new longship.

Another month passed.

No grain arrived from King Erik and the traders who visited became more infrequent as the winter smothered the land in snow and ice.

Until, one day, their greatest fear was spotted on the horizon, far earlier than they had expected. King Sven's fleet had arrived, and in greater number than before.

It was close to Yule, but they'd decided against a midwinter celebration, as they could not feast when Thrudheim's future and supplies were so uncertain.

A gloomy sense of foreboding had gathered around Thrudheim and it was almost with a sense of relief that their enemy revealed himself. The grain stores, despite rationing, would only last so long, especially without traders arriving regularly.

'I am grateful for Sven's impatience,' said Agnar lightly, reflecting her own grim thoughts.

Skadi frowned at the dots on the horizon, her fur cloak wrapped tightly around her head and ears to keep out the chill. They stood on one of the wooden jetties from which the fleet of Thrudheim was ready to set sail. They had fewer ships than Sven, but every warrior was ready to fight for their home, whether it was the land of their birth, or if they'd arrived recently with Agnar, it didn't matter. They would fight together.

'Why would he attack us now and in the middle of winter! Surely he must realise the danger of doing so?' she asked, worrying that they had missed some important detail in their preparations.

Agnar scowled at the distant ships, as they lowered their anchor stones into the mouth of their harbour. 'He thinks to frighten us, to block our trade and starve us into submission. He doesn't believe we will come out to fight him and, if we do, he believes he will win anyway.'

His words were confirmed when they received the first request to surrender and open their gates. Thrudheim responded by requesting a huge payment of taxes—as King Sven was squatting in their harbour without permission.

A sudden thought struck her and she smiled. 'He doesn't realise about the food from the flatlands or our other trade. He thinks we rely solely on selling him our ore. Heimdall was never interested in what trades and decisions I made for Thrudheim, only in raiding—and Oddmund went with him a lot of the time. Sven probably doesn't even realise about my other income as I never bothered to sell to him.'

Agnar nodded. 'That seems likely. Thinking back to Oddmund's dealings with Sven, he could only send messages between the ore and grain. His communications would have been limited…' He paused and caught her eye. 'Heimdall wasn't deliberately deceiving you with Sven… Yes, he married you under Sven's orders, but I believe he thought he was doing the best for Thrudheim, it was probably why he ignored Sven's requests to marry Astra. He couldn't face betraying you for a second time.'

Skadi looked out at the ships.

Would she lose Agnar to the sea as well?

She sighed, 'Heimdall wasn't all bad. I am as much to blame as he was. I was desperate and lonely, but I never admitted it… Stupid, really.'

Agnar took her hand in his. 'No, you did everything you could to protect your land and people. I never appreciated how daunting that must have been for you… I am truly sorry for that.'

A shout from a nearby guard drew their attention and they looked to the mountain. A beacon was lit, followed shortly after by another, and another. Until the entire ring of beacons that circled the island blazed to life. Skadi smiled. She had placed an effigy in every beacon, an offering to the gods in the hope that they would hear her prayers and protect Thrudheim's battle for independence. She'd even soaked Rán's effigy in oil to ensure it burned.

'It is time to go.' Agnar's green eyes sparkled with excitement and her heart flooded with pride and affection.

They embraced each other, one final hug before he faced battle and left her. Agnar cupped her face in his hands and pressed a kiss against her lips. 'I love you, my Queen,' he said and it was as if he had said it a hundred times before because it came so easily from him.

'What?' she asked, half-afraid she had misheard him.

'Has it not been obvious from the start?' He chuckled and glanced away for a moment, his traitorous eyes going to the *Sea Queen*, which was almost ready to set sail. When they returned to her, he brushed a thumb against her cheek, and continued, 'I have loved you for twenty years. I have loved you since I was a boy and first saw you put salt on bread and honey. I have loved you all through the years you were married to Heimdall—a man who never deserved you. I have loved you through loss and ambition. It is true that I always wanted power, but only so that I could be worthy of you, could *save* you from Sven. So that I could one day right the wrongs done to both of us and reclaim you as my—'

She frowned, interrupting him bad temperedly. 'I thought I was nothing more than a puppet queen, blinded by pride and lust?'

He stroked a finger down her cheek. 'You were and have always been *my Queen*. I had no right to judge you—this land is your birthright, not mine. My purpose is to love and serve you. Once I realised that, I fell in love with you all over again.' He straightened his spine and declared, 'I have decided to be happy. To let go of the past and love you.'

She knew she could not let him go now. Not without first telling him her true feelings.

'I love you, too,' she said, swallowing the nervousness of her confession and feeling as if her words were inadequate compared to his. 'But only since…' She paused, trying to think of the moment. 'Probably the night of the thunderstorm?'

He laughed loudly, and she grabbed his cloak to get his attention and pull him close. 'Please… Whatever you do… come back,' she begged, her heart breaking at the mere thought that he might not.

He pulled a little away from her, a confused look upon his face.

She rushed onwards, afraid that if she did not say it now, she never would. 'I was afraid that if I told you I loved you, it would only make you leave—just like Heimdall. Which is stupid…but I cannot help my fears. So, I want you to know that no matter what happens, I do love you.'

His hand covered hers. 'I won't leave you. You are coming with me. That is why I built you the *Sea Queen.* It's your longship.'

Skadi stared at the magnificent dragon ship with greater understanding. 'Mine?'

'Yes. I thought you knew that. You are wearing your armour, which I have to say is as enticing as I imagined it would be.'

She swatted at his chest. 'We are at war! I would wear my armour—even behind the gates.' Another thought worried her. 'What about Astra?'

'She has Vali and Brenna to protect her. If the worst happens—which it won't—she will be taken by them north to your uncle. I have arranged a ship to transport them from the old fishing harbour, if Thrudheim should fall, which it won't—I won't allow it. But you're sailing with me. It will give a clear sign to the petty Kings that you are the true ruler of Thrudheim, and you will be the one to choose your future, not Sven.'

She nodded, tears gathering in her eyes. Taking her hand, he helped her board her ship. They raised the blue-and-white-wolf sail of Thrudheim high, it caught the breeze and helped the rowers take them out into the harbour swiftly. The beats of their war drums proclaiming fiercely her right to rule.

Agnar took out a chest from the cargo hold. 'You forgot it this morning,' he said and with a smile he took out the helm and crown from within. At the head of the ship, with the roaring she-wolf carved on the prow before them, Agnar placed the symbol of her royalty ceremoniously on her head.

Crowning her in front of their enemy.

As he turned to face Sven's fleet, Skadi was surprised by

the change in her husband's expression. All earlier tenderness was gone, replaced by ruthless, Agnar Wolf Slayer as he prepared for war.

A startling transformation to watch, as Skadi had become accustomed to his smiles during their marriage. The man who fixed his gaze ahead now, raised his sword and shield to defend his Queen, was the same man who had charged into her bedchamber and threatened her without conscience.

It was thrilling to have such an incredible man fighting at her side. She unsheathed her own sword and gripped her shield tightly, preparing herself for boarding the first ship of their enemy.

The rest of Thrudheim's ships sailed either side of them in an arrow formation, the Queen's ship leading the charge. When she glanced behind her she saw the small figure of Astra at the end of the jetty. Brenna and Vali stood beside her. Her daughter held the ceremonial torch from the shrine high in the air and was dressed in a gown of blue and white, Agnar's wolfskin draped across her shoulders and billowing behind her in the wind.

Skadi raised her sword in acknowledgement and pride, then turned to face their enemy.

The battle was surprisingly short lived. The beacons had signalled the petty Kings' arrival to join against King Sven's tyranny.

They had answered Agnar and Skadi's call.

Later they would find out that King Erik had been so disgusted by Sven's burning of his grain ships—especially after his wife had been so pleased by the gifts sent by Skadi—that he had rallied the petty Kings to fill their ships with warriors and grain and sail out immediately in retribution for the sufferings of Thrudheim.

Which was why Sven had tried to attack Thrudheim early, before the petty Kings reached him. But he'd not been quick enough.

Neither had he appreciated what the sight of Skadi and Astra preparing for war would have on some of his men. Three of his ships were filled with old Thrudheim warriors, the same young men who had left with Heimdall. Seeing the Queen and Princess prepared to fight for their island had cast doubts in their minds about Sven's claims on their homeland.

In a matter of moments, they had torn down Sven's banners from their ships and turned on Sven.

Unable to retreat, Sven's ships were pushed during the battle towards the rocks and whirlpools of Thrudheim. As her grandmother had done before her, Skadi forced her enemy into the natural defences of her home. Several ships were sunk before their warriors could even raise their weapons or abandon their ships.

Sven flailed like a headless chicken, not realising his inevitable defeat until Skadi and Agnar boarded his ship.

His death was aptly quick and fitting, as his men cut him down and threw his body into the nearest whirlpool when he refused to surrender. Even in his last moments, he could not understand why they were so disloyal.

'I am your King!' he had screamed, 'You must obey me!'

He did not realise the truth about power and birthright, but Skadi and Agnar did, and they watched him fall without pity.

'He did not deserve his people,' Skadi said and Agnar nodded in agreement.

Epilogue

Thrudheim—Yule, eight years later

The Yule feast was as lively as always, with dancing, laughter, music and singing filling the hall and spilling out into the snow-covered city and harbour below. Braziers were placed along the paths to help guide them to the celebrations. The midwinter chill didn't bother the revellers walking to and from the hall, who still smiled despite their red noses and frost-covered lashes.

Thrudheim's winters were still brutal, but the prosperous trade, bountiful harvests and regular celebrations made life easy even on the darkest of days.

Astra was swaying to the music while bouncing Vali and Brenna's baby boy, Andor, on her hip. Her silver crown was slightly askew on her head, her braids unravelling at the ends, and her grandmother's arm ring wrapped around the sleeve of her fur-trimmed white-and-silver gown.

Andor was Vali and Brenna's second child. Their eldest daughter was running around the tables, chasing a hoop with a stick, her red hair flowing wildly behind her, as she darted between the throng of people with incredible speed. The other children screamed with excitement as they followed close behind her, causing more than one or two people to stumble or spill their mead and mutter bad-tempered curses.

Agnar chuckled and reached for Skadi's hand, which immediately slipped into his as familiar as a glove. 'How are these thrones still so uncomfortable?' he grumbled, shifting awkwardly in his seat.

Skadi laughed. *'No crown is comfortable to bear...'*

Agnar rolled his eyes. 'I know... *Especially on the bottom!* Your father was very wise.' He sighed at the bustling crowd. 'We haven't broken bread yet and it's already chaos.'

Skadi laughed. 'What did you expect?'

Agnar smiled, then raised her hand to his lips, kissing the palm softly. 'King Erik has asked to betroth one of his sons to Astra again.'

'Hmmm,' said Skadi, glancing over at her daughter, who was now laughing with her friends.

'She is eighteen and still not betrothed... Eventually it will cause worry and bickering among the Kings when she remains unwed.'

'I know,' said Skadi with a sigh. 'But she is still so young...'

Agnar nodded thoughtfully. 'Whatever your wish, I will support it.'

Skadi turned to face him; their hands still entwined. 'I would like to meet with them... King Erik and his sons. But I still want Astra to have a choice. I don't want her to feel compelled to accept someone just because it's convenient.'

'Perhaps we should have a celebration? Bring together all the petty Kings, and their families?' said Agnar thoughtfully.

'But they still may expect a betrothal and I do not want to see that pressure put upon Astra. I want her to be happy in her match, as we are.'

Agnar nodded in agreement. 'But if we are celebrating another occasion, there will be no expectation to arrange a match for her. Then, if we happen to agree on a man, it will be a natural choice that no one can argue against. Hmmm…we should pick an auspicious time for our family? Next summer, perhaps? We will have been married nine years by then… Nine is such a lucky number.'

Skadi laughed. 'You say you do not mind whatever decision I make and then you always delay it a little longer anyway. You are as bad as I am!'

'This time we shall both consider her choices carefully and help guide Astra into a match of her choosing—if she wishes it—which she may not,' Agnar said with a sombre expression that had her laughing all over again.

A platter was brought over to them by Inga. A silver tray, with a pot of honey, a dish of salt and a broken petal of bread. A hush descended over the crowd as they waited for the official start of the feast.

There was no formal serving of their meal in front of the thrones. Agnar had been glad when Skadi admitted she preferred to sit among her people at most feasts. But the Yule feast was an important occasion and some traditions still had to be maintained for the sake of the ancestors.

Agnar took the petal of bread, drizzled it with honey and a pinch of salt, then held it out to Skadi. 'My Queen,' he said formally and with a smile she leaned across the arm of the throne and bit into the bread.

'Mmm,' she said, with a knowingly wicked smile, brushing an errant drop of honey into her mouth with one elegant finger. Agnar's body stiffened in response and his pupils widened with obvious interest.

Skadi's own body filled with desire, anticipating the pleasure that was bound to come later that night. Despite their years together, she still felt as heated by his stares as she had that first night they'd spent together. The only difference was that she was now confident in their love.

As was their habit he popped the rest of the petal in his mouth and leaned forward to steal a honeyed kiss from his wife. 'Mmm…' he moaned, echoing the sound she'd made moments before.

Skadi blushed, and slapped his arm playfully, but had to compose herself when she saw Astra hurrying over to their thrones. Her daughter passed baby Andor back to Brenna along the way as he'd started grizzling and kept reaching for his mother.

'Pappa, did you ask Moma about the big midsummer festival next year? A big one with all the petty Kings and their families in attendance?' Astra asked excitedly, adding thoughtfully, 'We could invite Uncle Olaf, too. He loved our last midsummer feast!'

Agnar winced and Skadi raised a snowy brow at him in question. 'I was *just discussing* that with your Pappa. I didn't realise you were already aware of it as a possibility.'

It was Astra's turn to wince and she gave Agnar an apologetic smile. 'We thought you might allow it, if it was part of a bigger celebration… No expectation to choose a groom either way.'

Agnar grumbled quietly, 'Try to be subtle, Astra.'

Astra blushed, then clasped her hands tightly in front of her. 'Please, Moma! I have heard King Erik has many sons and they are all strong and honourable warriors.' Astra's eyes took on a dreamy expression and Skadi gave a beleaguered sigh.

'Let us dance, my Queen,' said Agnar, rising to his feet and offering her his hand. 'I am sure your mother will feel more excited about the midsummer feast once she's enjoyed the revelry of this one.'

'Thank you, Pappa!' Astra grinned and ran off to giggle her news to her friends.

Skadi rose from her seat and allowed Agnar to lead her

into one of the country dances. Soon she was laughing and singing with the rest of her people and her concerns for the future disappeared like smoke.

At the end of the dance everyone cheered and hurried to eat at the many tables now filled with platters of delicious food. Agnar started to walk her towards the nearest table, but she gave a little tug of her wrist and pulled him away, leading him through the rush of the crowds and out into the cold night air.

Agnar grinned, allowing his wife to do as she pleased. As they left, she took him around the side of the hall, just beyond the log store. Turning sharply, she pushed him up against the wall.

'And…why are we outside in the cold?' he asked mildly, already moving his hands to stroke down her waist and hips. She enjoyed making love wherever and whenever she pleased and he was always glad to oblige.

Nothing seemed to change the desire between them. Each day, they chose to love one another with passion, trust and respect. It seemed that Vali had been right for once. A happy wife did indeed make for a happy life.

She giggled, and brushed her lips against his in a teasing kiss. 'You know I love the fresh air.'

Agnar twisted his body, pushing hers against the wall and lifting her leg with one hand to press the hard length of him against her core. She moaned with anticipation and gripped his hair.

'I know you love this…' he whispered, trailing kisses down her neck.

'Oh, yes!' she gasped, 'I love this…and you.'

'As do I, my Queen.'

* * * * *

If you loved this story, check out Lucy Morris's previous captivating historical romances

A Viking Too Wild to Wed
Wedding Night with Her Viking Enemy
How the Wallflower Wins a Duke

And why not pick up the A Season to Wed miniseries, featuring Lucy Morris's charming romance

Only an Heiress Will Do *by Virginia Heath*
The Viscount's Forbidden Flirtation *by Sarah Rodi*
Their Second Chance Season *by Ella Matthews*
The Lord's Maddening Miss *by Lucy Morris*